# Prologue

*San Francisco*
*Late spring 1873*

"**M**aybe there was trouble."

"Don't look for it, Rose," Maggie Donnelly Cutter told her housekeeper and surrogate mother. "Lord knows, trouble finds the Donnellys easily enough without us going out to meet it halfway."

"Hmmph!" Rose held the coffee tray two inches above the polished surface of the dining-room table and dropped it. The heavy silver landed with a thud, and the china service it held clattered wildly. "A body would think there'd be a bit of concern in this room for a member of the family who's gone missin'!"

"Missing?" Cutter asked as he stepped into the room. "Who's missing?"

"No one," Maggie and her sister, Mary Frances Sullivan, answered together.

"Mary Alice," Rose said at the same time.

"Sean?" Cutter's gaze shot to the only other

1

man in the room. His brother-in-law.

Sean Sullivan shot a wary look at his wife, Mary Frances, before answering carefully, "I'm not sayin' she's missin', mind ya."

Rose Ryan frowned.

"But I will say she's a bit late now," he finished, shrugging his massive shoulders.

This time Mary Frances frowned at him.

He gave her a slow grin. "Now, Frannie girl," he said softly, "Al *is* late, and wasn't it she who called this special gatherin' in the first place?"

Maggie blinked. She still wasn't used to hearing Mary Frances called Frannie. But Sean insisted that Frankie, what the family called Mary Frances, wasn't dainty enough for his wife. Idly, Maggie wondered what the big man thought of the Donnellys calling Mary Alice Al.

"Why is everyone making so much of this?" Teresa Donnelly wanted to know. "Al is *always* late. And if not late, she manages to race into a meeting at the very last minute." Teresa reached for the coffee pot and poured herself a cup of the steaming black liquid, then helped herself to one of Rose's scones. "Today is no different."

Rose scurried around the end of the table and stopped beside the youngest Donnelly girl. Hands at her well-rounded hips, the housekeeper scowled at Teresa before saying hotly, "Of course it's different, missy! Hasn't your sister already said she's got trouble at the mine? Wasn't she in here just a couple of weeks ago askin' that we send a wire to your father? And isn't she ready and willin' to take on a partner just to help her out with the difficulties facin' her?"

Teresa's lips pursed defiantly, and for a moment it looked as though she might argue with the older woman. Cutter spoke up, though, and everyone's attention locked on him.

After marrying Maggie, the eldest Donnelly daughter, Cutter had slipped into the role of calling their family meetings to order. A role that Maggie allowed him to play until it suited her to usurp him.

Now the handsome gambler pulled a wrinkled, yellow piece of paper from his pocket and slowly unfolded it. "This wire was just delivered." He glanced at his wife. "It's from Al."

"Is she all right?" Maggie asked as she snatched the telegram from her husband's hand. Her gaze slipped over the printed words, and her shoulders slumped in relief.

"Maggie?" Frankie prompted.

"What is it?" Teresa asked.

"Ah, saints preserve us, she's dead." Rose lifted one corner of her apron to her eyes and blotted at the tears already beginning to roll down her apple red cheeks.

"Hush now," Sean comforted the older woman with a gentle pat on the wrist. "Hasn't Cutter already said the wire is from Al?" He turned his grin on Rose before adding, "She'd hardly be sendin' a wire from the heavenly gates now, would she?"

"She's all right," Maggie said, and handed the telegram to Teresa. Her gaze slipped from one member of her family to the next before coming to a stop on her husband. "But she wants Cutter and Sean to go to the mine. Says she needs help and can't wait for the new man to arrive."

Cutter covered Maggie's hand with his own, then flashed a quick look at Sean. "It'll take us a day or so to get to the mine. How soon can you be ready?"

"Does an hour suit ya?" Sean countered as he squeezed Frankie's hand.

The gambler nodded abruptly. "An hour it is. We'll meet here. Closer to the stables."

"Right." Sean stood up and gently tugged Frankie to her feet. "Come on then, love," he told her. "Help me gather me things."

Mary Frances moved into the circle of Sean's strong arms and wrapped her own around his middle. She held him as if she had no intention of ever letting go.

"Have you got a gun, Sean?" Teresa asked quietly as she set the telegram down on the tabletop.

"No, why?"

"I'll bring one for you," Cutter spoke up softly. "Shotgun, I think. They're good up close and don't take much aiming."

"Shotgun?" Frankie repeated, her head resting on Sean's barrel chest.

"The last line of Al's telegram," Teresa said, her soft voice echoing in the suddenly still room, "She says, 'Come armed'."

"Mother of God save us," Rose muttered.

# Chapter 1

*Regret, California*

"**O**ne more step and I will shoot you stone dead."

While sunlight splashed the ground at the mouth of the mine, a hundred feet into the body of the mountain darkness was held at bay by the feeble lights of a few candles.

Mary Alice Donnelly kept the muzzle of her shotgun trained on the three men standing opposite her. Ten feet of rocky ground separated them. In the flickering light, eerie shadows moved on their faces, and her mind worked furiously, trying to place them.

As far as she knew, she hadn't seen them before. But that didn't mean anything. Hell, there were more drifters riding through Regret every day than there were waves in the ocean.

Ordinarily, drifters wouldn't be of much concern to her. But ever since Rafe Bennet showed up in Regret, every stranger was a threat. Anyone could be posing as a harmless drifter, and in reality he could be hired muscle working for Bennet.

Even her own men weren't beyond being bought off by Bennet's money and power.

The smooth wood stock of her gun felt slick against her sweaty palms. Mary Alice swallowed past the knot of fear lodged in her throat and wished like hell she'd sent that telegram to the family a few days ago instead of just that morning.

She would give anything at that moment to see Cutter or Sean come striding up the entrance to the mine, even though it pained her to admit that a man could come in pretty handy from time to time.

And where in the hell, she wanted to know, was that damned partner her father was supposed to be sending her?

"Put the shotgun down, lady."

She stared at the man with cautious eyes.

"*Lady*?" the man beside him sneered. "That ain't no lady!"

Covered in dirt, her buckskin pants torn and stained and her auburn braid no doubt coming apart, Mary Alice was inclined to agree with the second man. She certainly didn't look like a lady. But then, he was in no position to be insulting her either, was he?

Deliberately, she lifted the barrel of the shotgun and pointed it menacingly at his middle.

"You think *now's* the time to go callin' me names, mister?"

Even in the dim light, she could see him pale. Mary Alice bit back her smile. This wasn't over yet.

"Shut up, Taylor," the third one, a fat, bearded man grumbled, and shoved his partner.

"Listen to him, Taylor," Mary Alice added.

"Look you"—the bearded one jerked her a nod—"we got orders to come in here and haul you out. Nobody said nothin' about what kinda shape you had to be in." His thick-fingered hands plopped down on what used to be his waist. "You can walk out on your own, or we can carry you out feet first."

Mary Alice's eyes narrowed, and the barrel of her gun lifted just a hair.

The man with cautious eyes and long hair spoke softly, his gaze never leaving the barrel of her shotgun. "No reason for you to get hurt here, ma'am."

"Me?" Mary Alice snorted a garbled laugh and waved her gun just a bit for emphasis. "*You're* the ones with the business end of a shotgun aimed at you."

The cautious one swallowed heavily.

Mary Alice heard the pounding of her heart. From somewhere in the belly of the mine, a steady drip of water plunked to the ground, sounding like a mantel clock. There wouldn't be anyone riding to her rescue. Every man on the night shift had gone home to sleep, and the day shift wasn't due to arrive for another half hour or so. And the new guards she'd hired only the day before hadn't shown up.

They'd either been bought off or "discouraged" from coming to work.

She was on her own.

Despite her nervousness, she kept talking.

"Don't know if you've noticed or not," she

said casually, "but this gun of mine's been altered some."

Carefully, she moved it from one man to the other, treating each of the three to a look down the short, black barrel.

"Yes sir," she went on, and gave silent thanks that her nerves weren't evident in the sound of her voice. "Had a gunsmith in San Francisco cut down the barrel."

The bearded man slowly reached up and scratched his cheek thoughtfully.

"It's easier to handle," Mary Alice continued softly, "lighter to carry, and when it goes off . . ."

The man called Taylor took one hesitant step back.

"Why, the spread of this gun at *this* range could cut a man in half."

"Lady," the cautious one urged, "this don't have to come to gunplay."

Only two of them were wearing hip pistols. Beard and Taylor. But a revolver was no match for a shotgun in close quarters, and everybody there knew it.

"I don't see any other way for this to end, boys." Mary Alice gestured with the gun. "Unless, of course, you want to change your minds about this whole thing and hightail it out of here. Now."

Cautious man looked as though that's just what he wanted to do. But the other two weren't convinced.

"Shotgun or not," the bearded one snorted, "she can't get all of us. She's only got the two barrels."

"Sawed-off barrels," Taylor reminded him.

"That's right. And at this distance, I might take all three of you out with one shot." She shrugged. "Who knows?"

"I say she's bluffin'," the bearded man muttered thickly and took a half-step toward Mary Alice.

She pulled the hammers back and the ominous clicks halted him abruptly.

"Maybe I can't get all three of you," she said quietly. "Maybe I'll only get two. Or maybe, if you're real lucky . . . only one of you will die."

The cautious one watched her carefully.

"The question is . . . *which* one of you?" Mary Alice swung that shotgun barrel back and forth slowly, covering them all with very little effort. "Which one of you heroes is willin' to die so his two partners here can run home to Bennet and collect their money?"

The three men looked at each other.

Mary Alice waited.

The steady drip of mine water pounded into the silence like the rhythm of a heartbeat.

Her shotgun felt heavy, and her arms ached with the desire to set it down. Hopefully they were thinking about just how much damage she could do with her shotgun and wondering if the money Bennet had offered them was worth the risk. The strained silence gnawed at her nerves, and the only consolation was that she could see it working on the three men, too.

Finally her patience was rewarded.

"It ain't worth gettin' killed over," Cautious man said.

"Dead men don't spend money," Taylor added and half turned away.

The bearded one looked as though he dearly wanted to stay. She could see it in his eyes. He wanted nothing more than to snatch that gun away from her and beat on her with his bare hands. But even he didn't want to buck a shotgun with a sawed-off barrel.

"All right. You win this one," he conceded grudgingly.

The other two men started walking slowly back down the tunnel to the entrance. Mary Alice listened to the quiet, reassuring sound of their retreating footsteps. Then the bearded man got her attention again with a promise.

"This ain't over, lady," he said softly. "Bennet ain't goin' anywhere, and you can't be ready for trouble *all* the time."

"Try me."

He shook his head and wild, knotted brown hair fell around his shoulders. "Not today." He pointed at her with his huge, dirty hand. "But someday real soon. Someday when you don't have that blasted widowmaker with you."

Mary Alice swallowed and tried not to pay attention to him. He was just talking. Just blowing off steam because he'd been bested by a woman.

"You wait and see, lady," he told her. "You and me are gonna meet again. Real soon. And things'll be different next time."

Deliberately, he turned his back on her as if challenging her to shoot him from behind. There was even a tiny voice in the back of her mind telling her that she should do exactly that.

But she couldn't.

Firing on three men bent on attacking her was one thing. She could have pulled the shotgun triggers then, without a qualm. If all three of them had been killed, she wouldn't have wasted a moment's thought on guilt or remorse. They would have gotten what they deserved.

But shooting a man in the back was something different.

Dammit.

Slowly, Mary Alice lowered the hammers again, then gripped the stock in her right hand, letting the gun hang down along her leg. It was too damn bad she couldn't simply shoot the big man down now and be done with it.

Because somewhere deep inside her, she believed him. They would meet again soon.

She only hoped that by that day, her partner would have arrived.

Mary Alice had a feeling that she was going to need all the help she could get.

"Lookit there, Al." The man on her right nudged her elbow. "Ain't he a pretty little thing?"

Mary Alice set her beer mug down on the scratched tabletop and hardly noticed when the table wobbled unsteadily. Hell, nearly every table and chair in the Hopeless Cause Saloon wobbled.

Cheap mail-order furniture to begin with, every stick of wood in the place had been gouged, kicked, thrown across the room, or tossed through a window at least once. The place looked like hell and smelled even worse. There probably wasn't a customer in the place who bathed more than once or twice a month. Added to the stench of unwashed bodies was the pervasive, sickly sweet scent of the whores' perfumes. The familiar odors always made Mary Alice think of flowers trying to bloom on a manure pile.

Dozens of men sat huddled over small round tables or were propped up along the length of the pine-plank bar. They neither cared nor noticed that the liquor they drank was just on the healthy side of poison. All they wanted was the momentary oblivion of whiskey-clouded dreams.

And Mary Alice knew what those dreams were. Heaven knew she'd shared them from time to time. Dreams of bonanza! Dreams of striking it rich and traveling back to wherever they'd come from in triumph. Prodded by cheap liquor, the shine of hope glimmered in their eyes again for as long as the drunk lasted. Then the men who staked their lives on a hole in the ground would stumble back out to their claims, push their dreams to the backs of their minds, and begin again.

But not everyone entrusted their plans and dreams to Fortune's cold hand.

Mary Alice glanced up from beneath lowered lashes to a table on the far side of the room. Six or seven men sat at a table watching the goings-on around them. They were at once a part of it all and separate from it.

Bennet's men.

Mary Alice's teeth clenched and she had to force herself to breathe slowly, in and out. Every day they were there. Not all of them, by any means. But Bennet saw to it that at least three or four of his men were always present. Always visible.

And like the bad smell that lingered in the saloon, Bennet's men had been accepted as just part of how things were in Regret.

Except by Mary Alice Donnelly.

She refused to give in. Refused to admit that Bennet and men like him could run folks into the ground just because they had more money than God.

"Al? Al, you're missin' the fun!"

Hank, the man on her left, prodded at her until Mary Alice gratefully pushed thoughts of Bennet out of her mind.

"What's goin' on?" she asked.

"Lookit, Al," the first one said and pointed to a small crowd of people standing near the front door. "Soon's them ya-hoos get outa the way, you'll see somethin' guaran-double-damn-teed to make you smile."

She looked at the familiar faces around her and sent up a silent prayer of thanks for her employees' loyalty. She still wasn't sure exactly what it was that kept her men from selling out to Bennet—but whatever the reason, she was grateful.

Drawing in a deep breath, she resolved to enjoy herself for a while. After all, the day shift was hard at work at the mine, the new guards were in place, and Cutter and Seán were on their way to Regret. For now, even if it was only for an hour or so, she would try to relax.

She reached for her none-too-clean glass and took a long drink of her warm, now flat, beer while staring at the center of attention across the room.

Then the small cluster of miners broke apart and Mary Alice grinned.

Hank hooted in delight and slapped his knee. A tiny cloud of dust rose up and settled again on his worn trousers.

"Ain't he a sight to make sore eyes?"

"Haven't seen nothin' that pretty since that actor fella come through town last year." George, the man on her right, leaned over the table and looked at Hank. "You recall how he bent over to take a big bow and them tights of his split so's his backside was hangin' out for all the world to see?"

"Oh my, yes!" Hank laughed until tears formed in his eyes. "But it was best when that seam ripped all the way 'round front!"

Mary Alice chuckled and ducked her head a bit. She remembered the incident clearly, too. That poor young actor, so tall and proud in his gray tights and flowing yellow shirt.

She recalled how the whores in town had studied the fella's *physique*, so blatantly outlined by his costume. And, Mary Alice remembered how they'd all groaned in disappointment when those tights had ripped right up the middle, and his manly build had been shown to be nothing more than a roll of socks, strategically placed. When those socks hit the floor, the young actor had run for cover, then slipped out of town in the middle of the night. Hell, she thought with a smile, he was probably still running.

George wiped his streaming eyes with the back of his hand and shook his head slowly.

"Never seen that many whores disappointed by the same man all at one time."

"Till now," Mary Alice interrupted as she stared unbelievingly at the man by the door.

Late-afternoon sunshine fell across the batwing doors and bathed the stranger in a peculiar orange glow. The color did nothing to help him.

Mary Alice set her elbows on the table and propped her chin in her hands. She'd never seen anything quite like him before.

Standing alone, surrounded by stunned miners, the man stood out like a preacher in a cat house.

His light brown hair was slicked back from his forehead and looked like it would stay that way even if a hurricane set down on top of the man's head. About average height, his narrow shoulders were slumped, and his bright yellow suit coat hung on his apparently too thin frame. The hem of a yellow and green flowered vest rested atop the waist of his light brown trousers, and the shine on his eastern shoes was splattered with fresh mud. In one hand he held a dirt brown bowler hat and, in the other, a carpetbag that was every bit as loud and garish as its owner's clothes.

Where on earth had *he* come from, Mary Alice asked herself. And why would someone like him come to Regret at all?

Her astonished gaze swept over him and came to rest on his features. From across the room, she couldn't tell much about his looks, but from what she could see, he wasn't homely. But Lord, someone should talk to him about the way he dressed.

Mary Alice quickly looked around the crowded room, noticing the men laughing, smiling, shaking their heads. For a lot of the miners in the Hopeless Cause, it was the first time they'd smiled in weeks.

Whatever his reasons for coming to Regret, Mary Alice was glad he had. At least the stranger had unknowingly brightened things up a bit.

Then a voice called out to the man.

"You a actor, mister?"

"No," the stranger answered, his voice deceptively soft.

"You mean to say you dress thataway cause you *like* it?" someone else yelled.

The man in the yellow coat flinched as if he'd been struck, then glanced down at his clothing uneasily.

"What in the *hell* are you doin' here, mister?" Sam, the bartender and proprietor, wanted to know. "You ain't a miner, are ya?"

The stranger cleared his throat, stretched his neck uncomfortably, then shook his head quickly. "Oh my, no. No indeed. I'm afraid I wouldn't know the first thing about mining."

"Then what brought you to Regret?"

"Business, sir." The stranger straightened up but somehow managed to keep his shoulders slouched. "Business is why I've come."

"But you just said—"

"I said I am not a miner."

Mumbled comments rumbled around the room as every man there watched the colorful stranger.

A terrible, sinking feeling began to seep through Mary Alice's bones and she suddenly felt like jumping up from her seat and running out of the saloon. Once outside, she would race all the way to the Four Roses Mine and lose herself in the tunnels.

But it wouldn't be enough, her mind chided.

Sam's voice cut into her reeling thoughts.

"You wouldn't be plannin' on openin' up a bar, now would ya?"

"A tavern?" the stranger asked, clearly horrified at the proposition. "Heavens, no."

Someone laughed.

Mary Alice closed her eyes and pretended that none of this was happening.

"Then what?"

"I prefer to discuss *that* with my business associate, if you don't mind," the stranger countered stiffly.

"Business what?" Sam asked.

"Associate. Peer. Partner."

Mary Alice groaned and felt the floor beneath her tilt ominously.

"You got you a partner?" Sam asked in astonishment. "Here? In Regret?"

"Here. In Regret. Actually, in this very establishment." The stranger's gaze swept the room. "*Somewhere.*"

Mary Alice opened her eyes reluctantly and watched as the stranger turned his head this way and that, inspecting the faces watching him.

"Your partner's here?" Sam chuckled as he shook his head. "What makes ya think so?"

"I was so informed by our employees at the mine."

"Which mine would that be, mister?"

"The Four Roses."

Every head in the place turned to look at Mary Alice. Her stomach pitched violently as she watched the stranger, her new partner, follow their lead.

When her eyes met his, Mary Alice sent a heartfelt curse into the heavens and only hoped it landed squarely where she'd wished it.

On her father's head.

# Chapter 2

*This* is the partner Da sent after I asked for help? Good God, what possible use could this man be?

Mary Alice stared at the man helplessly for a long minute. It looked like he had no more business in a mining town than she had at some fancy ball back east.

But at least, she told herself hotly, she had the good sense to stay where she belonged!

Shoving herself to her feet, she ignored the sympathetic murmurings from the two men at her table. Longtime friends of her father's, Hank and George no doubt meant well, but right now she didn't want to talk to anyone. Except her *partner*. And all she wanted to tell him was to climb back into that stage he'd ridden in on, before it left town.

After a brief, stunned silence, shouts of laughter filled the room. As she threaded her way through the crowd, Mary Alice tried to ignore the taunts and catcalls and kept her gaze locked on her new partner.

19

"Hey, Al," someone called out from across the saloon, "you finally have to go order yourself some fancy man from the catalogs?"

Mary Alice stopped dead in her tracks and scanned the mob of people, trying to find the owner of that voice.

"Sure she did," someone else hollered back. "Who the hell else would she get? She's got every other man for miles around scared to talk to her."

She turned in a quick circle, looking for the new voice, but immediately swung back when another man shouted, "Not Bennet. He ain't scared of no scrawny female who ain't even sure she's female."

A fresh wave of laughter lifted up and crashed down around her. Color rushed into her cheeks, and she felt the slow boil of anger begin to roll through her. Mary Alice's hands curled into fists, and she bit down hard on the inside of her cheek.

Whether her tormentor knew it or not, he'd touched on a sore point. She'd never been the feminine, flirty kind of female like her sisters. From her earliest memory, Mary Alice had preferred wearing pants to petticoats. The yards of fabric most women hog-tied themselves with were just a hindrance to anyone who had anything more to do than lounge on a settee and be waited on all day.

Besides, she'd always been of the opinion that fancy clothes and furbelows would be wasted on her. She simply wasn't as pretty as the other Donnelly girls. So she'd decided early in her life to go with her strengths. And Mary Alice Donnelly had plenty of strengths.

She wasn't afraid of hard work, for one. And her stubborn determination had always served her well. Just as it would in this new situation. As she glared at the miners surrounding her, Mary Alice felt an icy calm settle over her. She'd heard insults before. Long ago she'd learned how to handle them.

Being raised in a saloon had taught her how to deal with men at an early age. If she gave her tormentors the satisfaction of knowing that their barbs had hit home, they'd never stop. So she had two choices. Ignore them—or shoot back.

Not once had it ever occurred to Mary Alice to ignore an insult.

A slow smile curved one corner of her mouth as she let her gaze slip over the familiar faces turned toward her. Some of those faces were friendly, others disinterested. But it was to the few who looked at her with open enmity that she spoke. "You're right. Bennet isn't afraid of a female." Calmly she waited until the snorts of appreciation had died down before adding, "Why, from what *I* hear . . . he doesn't know *what* to do with a woman!"

Deep-throated laughter burst into the room, and she mentally patted herself on the back. Now most of the men in the room were laughing *with* her. Then Mary Alice let her gaze drift to the table in the far corner, where Bennet's men sat stonefaced, watching her.

Instinctively, her right hand slipped down to the holstered pistol on her hip. Maybe it wasn't very smart, baiting her enemy, but dammit. A woman could only put up with so much harassment before she either fought back or left town.

Mary Alice had been in Regret a hell of a lot longer than Rafe Bennet. If anybody was going to leave, it would be him.

Thoughtfully, she tapped her index finger against the black walnut stock of her handgun and stared into the strange gray eyes of Mike Thompson, Bennet's right-hand man. Mary Alice ignored her new partner, the other miners, the noise of her surroundings, everything. With her concentrated stare, she tried to tell the gunfighter that she wouldn't be scared off. That sending three men to her mine wouldn't be enough to run her out of town. That insulting her in public wouldn't make her run and hide.

After a long minute, Thompson gave her a nod that was so brief, she almost missed it. He'd barely moved his head and yet she knew that he understood. A cold chill touched her, and Mary Alice suddenly felt very alone.

"I should like to point out," a loud, deep voice spoke up, and Mary Alice whipped her head around to stare at her new partner, "that I am not a 'fancy' man as one of you said. I am a full partner in the Four Roses Mine."

His voice sounded a lot stronger than he looked, she had to admit. Still, she'd rather he didn't go making any more announcements until they'd had a chance to talk privately. He obviously didn't have any idea of the serious danger he could be putting himself in just by siding with her publicly.

"And quite frankly," he went on, his gaze sweeping over the surprised crowd, "I shall expect to be treated far better than you have treated my partner thus far."

"Thus?" someone whispered.

"What's that mean?"

"Hell if I know," the first voice said.

Enough, Mary Alice thought, and pushed past the last few chairs standing between her and the man in the bright yellow coat. Lord knew she'd have plenty of time to think about Bennet, Thompson, and the rest of her troubles. Right now, she had a more immediate problem to handle.

When she was at last by his side, she grabbed his forearm and tugged.

"How do you do? Miss Donnelly, I presume?" he started.

"Outside, mister," Mary Alice shot back, and tugged even harder.

He was surprisingly strong for someone who looked lost inside his own coat. Despite her best efforts, she couldn't budge him. Disgusted, she looked up at him, ready to fix him with a cold stare guaranteed to make a man move.

Instead Mary Alice found herself gazing into blue eyes so pale they almost looked the color of ice when it frosted over a lake in winter. And there was something else there as well. A flash of something that disappeared as quickly as it had come. In anyone else she would have thought it was anger. Shaking her head, she told herself she was imagining things.

As their eyes met and held, the sounds of the crowd around them seemed to fade into the background. His features were sharp, angular. His nose looked as if it had been broken once or twice, and idly, she wondered how on earth such an injury had happened to someone like *him*.

A shadow of stubble lay along his jawline, testifying to the fact that he must have been traveling for some time. His flesh was golden brown from the sun, and Mary Alice asked herself how a man who looked as though he did nothing more strenuous than comb his hair had come to be so tanned.

But she pushed the silent questions aside. No doubt he stood in the sun so he could see into his mirror more clearly.

Whatever the reason for his sun-bronzed skin, though, it didn't matter now. The only thing she was interested in at the moment was getting him back on that stage before it left without him. Regret wasn't exactly a big enough town to merit a daily coach run. There wouldn't be another stage for a week.

"C'mon mister," she muttered thickly. "We got some quick talking to do."

"Very well," he said, and finally began to move. "If you're sure you wouldn't rather have our conversation inside, where it's more comfortable."

"Comfortable?" she repeated with a shake of her head. She wouldn't be comfortable until she was far enough away from Thompson and his boys to draw an easy breath. "Mister, you've got a real strange idea of what's comfortable."

The miners were still watching them. She could feel their eyes on her as surely as she felt her partner's surprisingly strong forearm beneath her fingers. If they stayed inside, it was a sure bet they wouldn't be able to get any talking done.

She'd be too busy watching for trouble.

"Come on," she urged, and turned for the door.

"Hey Al," a voice called out from the shadows. "You go easy on him, huh? He don't look any too strong, y'know?"

Good Lord, she thought disgustedly.

More raucous laughter rose up and shook the rickety walls of the saloon. She cringed and told herself that when her father eventually turned up back in San Francisco, she was going to tear into him like the Rafferty brothers on a pot roast.

Laughter followed them outside, and the man following Mary Alice gritted his teeth against the taunting sound. He allowed her to pull him out of the saloon and across the ramshackle boardwalk. He didn't say anything when she stepped down into the muddy street, though he *did* wish he'd been wearing his boots.

Thick, warm mud oozed over the tops of his city shoes and soaked into the legs of his trousers. With every step, the mud sucked and pulled at him, trying to trap him forever in its grip. He groaned quietly and tightened his hold on the carpetbag in his left hand.

He'd hardly been in town more than a half hour, and already he was beginning to rethink his decision to arrive disguised.

Briefly, he swiveled his head first one way, then the other, glancing over the huddled shacks that made up the downtown business district of Regret.

Hardly more than a hundred yards long, Main street was a sea of mud. The buildings on both sides of the street looked as though they'd sprouted up overnight, built by a blind man. The raw, unpainted wooden structures leaned against each other for support, and Travis told himself that a good stiff wind could probably carry the whole damn town to Arizona territory.

Miners, drunk and sober, lined the boardwalks that ran the length of the street on both sides of the muddy road. The boardwalks themselves rose and fell like waves on the ocean, and here and there, a plank or two was missing, which probably added to the adventure of strolling through Regret on a dark night.

Late-afternoon sun shone down on them, and he squinted into the dying light as he turned his gaze on his new partner.

Still tromping through the mud to the other side of the street, and stubbornly dragging him along behind her, Mary Alice Donnelly was nothing like the woman he'd been led to expect.

Nor was she like any other woman he'd ever seen.

Shaking his head slightly, Travis's gaze dropped to the curve of her backside. Her tight, worn buckskin pants hugged her form and left little to the imagination. And they thought *he* was dressed oddly. If he wasn't seeing it for himself, he never would have believed that a female would wear such an outfit—let alone in the middle of a mostly male town. Although . . . His brows lifted as he admired her long, shapely legs and the swing of her hips as she fought the nearly knee-deep mud. At least she had the figure for it. Her rich, auburn hair was confined in a single braid that ended and swung lazily just above her waist.

One corner of his mouth lifted in a half-smile as his tired brain dredged up the memory of staring into her eyes. Cool, deep green, they were the color of a forest on a spring night. Travis stopped himself abruptly. Hell, this was not the time to be getting fanciful.

But, he thought in disgust, Kevin might have warned him about this daughter of his. Instead, all the old devil had said was "Al's a fine girl. Strong, capable. She's the son I never had".

*Son*? Travis snorted. Was the old fool blind? Jesus, Travis had arrived in Regret expecting to be met by some huge, tobacco-chewing, cussing, Amazon of a woman! Instead, he finds . . . Never mind, the voice inside his head warned.

"Hurry up, mister," she said, and splintered his thoughts. "That stage isn't going to wait all day."

"Stage?"

"Yeah."

Confused, Travis stopped abruptly and Mary Alice staggered, caught off balance. Clearly disgusted, she frowned and looked up and down the street before turning her gaze on him.

"This is no place to stop and chat, mister," she said. "You'll get us run over by a freight wagon or trampled by some drunk miner's horse."

"Miss Donnelly."

"Al."

Travis frowned. He refused to call a woman Al—even if she was dressed like one. "Miss Donnelly, I have no intention of getting back on that stage. I've only just arrived."

She impatiently pushed a long, loose strand of

hair behind her ear. "That's right. You arrived—now you're leaving."

Travis reached up and plopped the ill-fitting bowler on his head. The tone in her voice was one he hadn't heard since the last time he'd visited his sister and observed her using it on her youngest child. Grinding his teeth together in a futile attempt to control his frustration, he grabbed Mary Alice's elbow and guided her forcefully to the boardwalk opposite the saloon.

They stepped up on the precarious walkway and stood just outside the Mercantile. Travis spared a brief glance through the open door of the store before turning his gaze back on the woman beside him.

Sunlight made the red in her hair look like a fire in the dark. She squinted up at him, and he noticed for the first time the faintest sprinkle of freckles across her nose and cheeks. His gaze dropped to the swell of her bosom, hidden beneath a tattered blue cotton men's work shirt. Not that he was interested in her, of course. But hell, he was only human. The rise and fall of her chest quickened, and he realized that she was watching him watch her.

Slowly and deliberately he lifted his gaze. "I believe," he began in a quiet tone, "that we should talk about our partnership, Miss Donnelly."

"Look mister . . ." She cocked her head to one side, folded her arms across her chest, and asked, "What the hell is your name, anyway?"

"D-*Deal*." He cursed mentally at his near slip. "Travis Deal."

She frowned a bit at his hesitation over his

own name, but thankfully, she went on again quickly.

"Well, Mister Deal, I think there's been a mistake."

"Really? A mistake?"

"You see, I was expecting someone . . ."

"Yes?" he prodded, suddenly enjoying watching her squirm. He knew exactly what she'd been expecting. Hell, Kevin had told him about the trouble at the mine. He'd insisted on being completely honest about the situation before accepting Travis's offer.

The older man had even shown Travis the telegram he'd received from Mary Alice asking for help. And judging from the expression on her face, she was sorely disappointed in the man her father had sent her.

So they were both surprised. She wasn't what he'd been expecting, either.

Mary Alice waved her hand in front of her face as if trying to wipe away what she'd just said. "Never mind," she went on. "The thing is, Mister Deal . . . I simply don't think that it's a good idea for you to be here."

"Why is that?"

"Well," she backed up a step and staggered a bit as her boot landed in a dip in the boardwalk. Travis reached for her, but she shook her head. "I'm fine." Looking him up and down thoroughly, she finally said, "You clearly don't belong in a mining town, Mister Deal."

Though he knew it was ridiculous, Travis was offended. He'd *wanted* her to think him a useless man. Actually, he'd wanted her enemies to think him useless. But somehow, now that he'd succeeded in making himself look the fool, it irritated the hell out of him.

"I assure you," he finally said, "I'm not a stranger to hard work." Lord, it was galling having to sound like such a damned idiot.

"Mister Deal—*Travis*," she amended, and offered him a strained smile that never reached her worried eyes. "I'm not trying to cheat you out of your share in the mine." Mary Alice's shoulders lifted in a shrug. "Tell me where you'll be and I'll see to it that your money is sent on to you."

He swallowed past the knot of frustration in his throat and managed to mutter, "I'll be right here."

"Dammit!" she shouted, and stomped one booted foot against the boardwalk.

Travis felt the whole structure shudder with the impact, and for one brief moment thought they would both tumble into the mud.

A tall fat man with greasy-black hair and small blue eyes stepped out of the Mercantile and stopped in the doorway. The apron tied around his vast middle was filthy, and there was a tiny, interested smile hovering around his lips.

Mary Alice flicked a quick, disgusted glance at the man. "Afternoon, G. W."

"Al," the fat man nodded, and turned a speculative gaze on Travis. His marble-sized eyes widened as he took in the stranger's clothing, but he didn't say anything.

Mary Alice moved off a few feet, and Travis nodded a greeting to the other man before following her.

She looked past Travis to the storekeeper, then

lowered her voice deliberately. "Don't you understand? You can't stay."

"No, I don't understand," Travis said politely. "Why not?"

"Because I have enough to worry about already." She leaned in close and tilted her head back to look directly into his eyes. She inhaled sharply and exhaled on a rush, then said outright, "I don't have the extra time needed to baby-sit a . . . *dandy!*"

Torn between embarrassment, anger, and laughter, Travis swallowed down the chuckles building inside him. It looked as though he'd played his part well. Too well, perhaps.

His act was so convincing that his own partner wanted to send him out of harm's way.

As he stared down at her, all thoughts of amusement faded away and were replaced by a warm smile. Kevin Donnelly hadn't told him nearly enough about this daughter of his.

Not only hadn't he mentioned her beauty, the old goat hadn't said a word about her generous nature. Despite the fact that she was in trouble and needed all the help she could get, Mary Alice Donnelly was bound and determined to save a man she thought incapable of defending himself.

Altogether, this new partner of his was turning out to be quite a surprise.

He suddenly wished that he could tell her the truth about himself. It would make everything a lot easier. On the other hand, if she knew the truth, she'd treat him differently. Her enemies would wonder about him, and Travis would never be able to get this trouble of hers all straightened out.

No. It was best for *everyone* in town to think that he was just as he appeared. Useless. If the men she was up against didn't think him a threat, they'd be more apt to lower their guard around him. And when a man's guard was lowered, anything was possible.

So, though it irritated the hell out of him to have the woman he'd come to help think so little of him, Travis was stuck.

Choking back the words he desperately wanted to say, he told her instead, "To assume that a man is a *dandy*, as you put it, simply because he prefers elegant attire . . ."

Her eyebrows lifted and her lips quirked. Apparently, he realized Mary Alice's opinion of his clothing had nothing to do with the word elegant.

"Is a mistake," he continued. "I'm sure you've heard the old expression—'Never judge a book by its cover.' "

"Yes," she nodded. "And I've also heard the one, 'Don't suffer fools gladly.' "

Travis's jaw clenched tight, but he still managed to say, "Perhaps we should both wait for a while before making any hasty judgments about each other."

A shout came from a distance and Mary Alice's head snapped up. She stared past Travis with a disappointed, beaten expression.

Travis turned around and watched as the stage pulled away from the boardwalk and slowly made its way through the mud of Main Street toward the countryside beyond. A slow smile curved his lips as he looked back at her.

"It appears, Miss Donnelly, that a decision has been reached. At least for today, I will be staying in Regret."

She drew in a long, deep breath and threw her hands wide, as if to shrug off all responsibility for him. "All right then, partner. Get your gear and I'll walk you to the mine."

"The mine?" Travis looked around quickly, studying the signboards over the different businesses, pretending distress. "I had thought perhaps a hotel?"

"In Regret?" Mary Alice snorted a laugh and started walking. "Around here we pitch tents or build shacks. In case you hadn't noticed, this isn't exactly San Francisco."

"Yes," he agreed wryly, "as a matter of fact, I *had* noticed that very thing."

Shaking her head, Mary Alice didn't even look back at him as she said, "I sure hope you don't come to feel just like the name of this place."

"Oh," Travis countered quickly, and hurried his stride to catch up with her, "I assure you—"

A gunshot cut off the rest of his speech. In seconds, two more blasts from a gun echoed after the first.

When her new partner didn't start talking again right away, Mary Alice turned around to check on him.

"Saints and angels of mercy, protect us," she whispered, and stared down at Travis Deal.

Curled into a protective ball on the boardwalk, he had his hands clapped over his ears and his face buried in the crook of his arms.

"My hero," she muttered.

# Chapter 3

**"I**t's safe," Mary Alice said wryly. "You can get up now."

Travis's arms uncurled from around his head, and he looked up at the woman. Impatience was etched into her features and disgust shone in her eyes. He swallowed back the sharp taste of bitterness that rose up in his throat. No woman had *ever* looked at Travis Delacort like that.

He caught himself suddenly and narrowed his gaze on her, half expecting her to have heard his thoughts. As he pushed himself to his feet, Travis reminded himself that his name was Deal now. Not Delacort. Deal.

"You gonna drop like a stone every time you hear a gunshot, Travis?" she asked, arms folded over her chest.

"Certainly not," he said, and brushed at the dirt covering the hideous jacket he was forced to wear. "I was caught ... unawares."

"Huh!" Shaking her head, Mary Alice let her arms drop to her sides as she turned and started walking again. "Unawares. Well Travis, I think it's safe to say most everything in Regret is going to catch you 'unawares.' "

Travis hurried his steps to catch up with her long, quick strides.

"If you're lookin' for a nice safe place to live, you sure as hell came to the wrong town."

No truer words were ever spoken, he told himself, and he deliberately shifted his gaze from her curved backside.

"I tell ya, he's nothin'."

Rafe Bennet leaned back in his chair, propped his elbows on the wooden arms, and steepled his fingertips as he looked at the man opposite him. "You seem to have dismissed the man rather quickly."

Mike Thompson laughed. "You didn't see this fella."

"Tell me again."

Frowning now, Thompson took a long drink of whiskey, leaned forward, and set his glass on the desk's polished surface.

Bennet glanced at the offending glass briefly, then turned his attention back to the man speaking.

"One of the boys inside the saloon shot a round into the ceiling, and that fancy man of Donnelly's dropped like he'd been hit." Shaking his head, he added, "Funniest thing I've seen in a coon's age."

"Hmmm." Bennet pushed himself up from the chair, turned his back on Thompson, and walked to the window overlooking Main Street. At first he saw only his own reflection. A tall, well-set man in his middle forties, with just a touch of gray streaking the blond hair at his temples. His suit was impeccable, made for him by the finest tailor in Denver. His brown eyes looked black in the window glass, and they narrowed slightly as he glanced at the small scar above his right eye. An imperfection that he could do nothing about now, at least Rafe had the satisfaction of knowing that the man who had marked him so long ago had been rotting in his grave for more than twenty years.

Bennet blinked and looked past his own reflection. Staring down at the afternoon crowd, he allowed his mind to wander briefly over the past that had brought him to this disreputable spot. Which decision was it, he wondered, that had led him here? Which choice too hastily made? Which road that he had left untraveled? Or was it closer to the truth to say that they had all conspired to land him here? In Regret.

A trickle of amusement wandered through him. Regret. How singularly appropriate.

Then his sharp brown gaze narrowed and concentrated on a fight brewing in the street. Two miners, in threadbare clothing, were just a harsh word or two away from coming to blows. A crowd had gathered around the men, and Rafe could almost feel the tension building. Bennet's breath quickened. His fingers moved to curl around the windowsill tightly. His heartbeat skittered in anticipation.

He watched the two men circling each other warily. The ever-present mud sucked at their feet as they moved unsteadily in their ageless dance of aggression. A small smile curved Rafe Bennet's mouth. Wars had started from less. As old as time itself was this clash of men. This he understood. This he believed in. The survival of the best.

Not necessarily the fittest, he amended silently.

The best.

And how a man came to be the best, ensuring his survival, didn't matter. Cheating? What was cheating? An intelligent man looking for the shortest possible answer to a too-long question.

No, there were no rules in survival. No niceties to be observed in a battle between men.

There was only winning.

His mouth dry, Bennet watched, waiting for that first blow to land.

When another man stumbled up to the combatants and dragged one of them away, Rafe almost groaned aloud at the physical ache of disappointment stabbing at him. Below, the remaining man now stood like a lone warrior in the mud, shaking an empty, useless fist and screaming his outrage at being denied a battle.

Rafe Bennet slowly turned away from the window and walked back to his desk. He would not be left alone, shouting into the silence. He would not be denied his victory. And by God, he would not be denied his war.

Glancing sourly at Thompson, Rafe said, "Find out everything you can about Miss Donnelly's new partner. I want to know all there is to know."

"Yes sir," Mike said and stood up. He lifted his whiskey glass, drained it, and set it back down on the desk. Then he quickly and quietly left the room.

When the door closed behind the other man, Rafe frowned and reached for the empty glass. He pulled a pristine, white handkerchief from his inner pocket and delicately blotted the desk top until the water mark was gone. Then he tossed Thompson's glass into the trash basket and went back to work.

The Four Roses Mine was nothing more than an open slash on the mountain's face. Men trickled from the wound, walking slowly, burdened by the heavy picks, axes and single jack hammers slung over their shoulders.

Here and there a tall, straggly pine lurched toward the sky, the bottom half of its trunk stripped bare of branches by miners looking for fuel or softer beds. Cool green grass dotted the drab brown earth in sparse patches, the rest of the meadow grass having long since been trampled to dust beneath hundreds of boots. Even sunlight seemed to shine sparingly over the mine and its workers, the golden spears of light poking through a thick layer of clouds overhead.

Travis's gaze slipped quickly but thoroughly over the entire scene. In an instant he took in the dozen or so canvas tents pitched near the mine's entrance. There was a hastily built door of warped planks leaning against the mountainside, ready to be moved to cover the mouth of the mine.

In front of the miners' tents stood a makeshift outdoor kitchen. Just four poles and a roof, the wobbly structure sheltered a cooking fire and a battered stove over which a man of about seventy hovered. The cook dropped a long-handled wooden spoon into a huge pot and gave the contents a quick stir. Immediately, the rich, spicy aroma of seasoned Mexican beans lifted on the wind and drifted to Travis. His stomach rumbled in appreciation.

He ignored it.

Muffled sounds of tools crashing into stone echoed out from the mine's belly, telling Travis that trouble or not, Mary Alice Donnelly wasn't about to close her mine. He had to admire her for it, even knowing that it would have been a hell of a lot safer to close down her operation until things were settled.

He tossed a quick look at her and hid a smile. Travis doubted very much if she would be interested in his opinions. After the scene he'd made in town when those gunshots rang out, she'd most likely prefer to forget he existed.

Jesus, the look in her eyes when he'd crawled up off that boardwalk! This little idea of his was already beginning to wear almighty thin, and he hadn't been in town a full day yet!

"You can bunk in with a couple of the men," Mary Alice said, pointing toward the tents.

Travis hardly spared the sagging canvas structures another glance. He wanted, *needed* his own tent. If he didn't have a place where he could go and get rid of these ridiculous clothes and step out of his character as a useless dandy, he'd lose his mind. He could hardly tell her that, though, so all he said was, "I prefer to have private quarters, if it's all the same to you."

"Private quarters," she repeated. Shaking her head, she said, "Well, no, Mr. Travis Deal, it ain't all the same to me. I already told you, this ain't

San Francisco. There's no hotel, there's no privacy, there's no nothin' here that will be to your liking."

It wouldn't be the first time, Travis thought. Though it was the first time he'd had a dressing down from a woman who was dressed more like a man than he was.

She might not have been able to read his mind, he told himself, but she could certainly judge his expression. Balling her fists and setting them on the swell of her hips, Mary Alice Donnelly widened her stance and planted her feet. With her chin high, she shrugged her long braid back over one shoulder and challenged, "Look your fill, *partner*. Look long and hard and get it over with now."

Travis blinked, shrugged deeper into his oversized coat, and tried to hide his admiration for her guts and honesty behind a bland mask of confusion.

"I beg your pardon?"

Mary Alice smiled tightly. "Beg all you want, mister. But you'll not get another chance to slide your eyes over me in disgust without getting a fist in your teeth."

"Miss Donnelly," Travis said, hating the sound of his voice, pitched much higher than its normal range. "You misunderstand me."

"No, Travis. I don't think I do." Shifting her right hand from her hip to the walnut stock of her holstered pistol, she went on. "I've seen looks like that before. Looks that a man wouldn't dare aim at a 'good' woman. Well mister, I may not dress like a lady, but you'll notice I ain't dressed like a whore, either."

"True enough." All right, Travis had never seen a woman dressed in pants before. But the way he was staring had more in common with shock than desire. Although he was willing to admit that seeing a woman's legs defined by tight trousers might appeal to a man with less on his mind.

"I'm willin' to make allowances this once," Mary Alice said softly. "But not again. You may be my partner, Travis Deal, but that don't mean I have to put up with you lookin' down your nose at me."

"I assure you," he started to say, but she cut him off.

"I will admit to bein' a bit surprised." She looked him up and down dismissively. "A man like you, I wouldn't have thought—"

Travis stiffened. "Thought what?"

"Never mind."

Oh yes, he thought disgustedly, this disguise is going to be a real test of endurance. Once again he shot a silent black curse back to the head of Kevin Donnelly. The man might have warned him.

"I've got some things to see to," Mary Alice said, and half turned. "Go on over to the kitchen. Chucker, he's the camp cook, he'll set you up in a tent."

She'd only gone a step or two when his quiet voice stopped her.

"As I said, I prefer privacy." Travis held his bag out to her and waited until she took it. "If it's all the same to you, I'll just hurry back to the Mercantile and procure myself a tent. Besides, I have to arrange for my trunk to be delivered."

"Trunk?"

"Yes. The trunk containing the rest of my clothes."

"Good Lord. There's more?"

Travis refrained from pointing out that any woman dressed as she was, was in no position to throw stones at someone else's attire.

She stared at him for several long moments, then finally shrugged. "I don't have the time to walk back with you, and none of the men are free right now."

"I assure you, Mary Alice," Travis said through gritted teeth, "I do not require a guide."

"The name's Al," she said. Then she added, "Maybe not a guide, Travis, but wearin' those clothes and talkin' like you do, you surely need a bodyguard."

"I can take care of myself."

"Yeah, you did a helluva job back there on the boardwalk."

Travis winced inwardly. It appeared that his ruse was working even better than he would have wished.

"Nevertheless," he countered, "I am a grown man accustomed to seeing to my own needs."

"Now that I can believe," she muttered, shaking her head.

He ignored her comment and said, "If you'll excuse me, Mary Alice, I shall return forthwith."

"Forthwith?"

"Expediently. Quickly."

"Oh."

He turned and this time, her voice stopped him. "I told you, Travis. My name is Al."

Giving her one long look over his shoulder, he

said, "As you say." Though it galled him to address a woman as he would a man, it would be better if he didn't make her any angrier than she already was. "I shall return directly . . . *Al*."

Mary Alice felt his gaze as surely as she did the kiss of wind caressing her neck. Those eyes of his shone with something that looked like a banked fire. Her stomach suddenly churned unsteadily, and she felt a weakness in her knees.

Then Travis turned and began to walk away and the odd sensations stopped. She stood on the rocky path watching him go until he'd rounded the bend and was lost to sight.

Alone again, Mary Alice looked down at the carpetbag in her hand. Garishly bright, the case was heavy with God knew what. For just a moment, she considered opening that case and finding out what was inside. She had a feeling the carpetbag was concealing something altogether different from what she might expect. Much like the bag's owner and his outlandish clothing.

An instant later, though, she dismissed the thought. Travis Deal and his bag were no more than they appeared to be. Ridiculously out of place and most definitely in her way.

"How far away is this place, then?" Sean asked as he stepped down from the saddle, dropped the reins, and stretched his aching muscles. They'd already been riding for hours, and every bone in Sean's body ached with the constant motion of the horse's canter.

Enjoying the countryside had long since lost its appeal. A man could only stare at so many pine trees, rocks, and scrub bushes, after all. He winced at a sharp twinge of pain in his backside and reached around to rub the ache out.

Cutter grinned as he led his horse to the narrow, clear running creek. "What's wrong, Sean?" he asked. "These weeks of marriage and staying in one place making you soft?"

Sean's gaze snapped up at the implied challenge, but he relaxed as soon as he saw his brother-in-law's knowing smile. "Aye, I guess it has at that. Why, there was a time not so long ago when I could sit on a horse all day and stand at a gaming table all the night without so much as gettin' tired."

"Missing the bachelor life already?"

"Not on your bloody life, man!" Sean reached for his horse's reins and led the big animal to the stream. "I'll take Frannie and blisters on me hands from fixin' up that hotel to wanderin' about on me own any damned day."

Cutter pulled two cigars from his inside coat pocket and handed one to Sean. "I know just what you mean, Sean," he said. "Though I'll wager my Maggie keeps me a helluvalot busier than Frankie does you. Maggie's got energy enough for three healthy men! Why these last few hours in the saddle is the most rest I've had in a couple of weeks."

"Energy is it?" Sean struck a match on the sole of his boot and held it to the tip of his cigar. When it was glowing nicely, he countered, "I wouldn't know about Maggie, mind ya. But I'd be willin' to bet that Frannie kills me with work long before Maggie wears you down."

"I'll take that bet."

Sean smiled to himself. They were both liars and they both damned well knew it. Sean had seen the same look of happiness on Cutter's face as the one he knew was carved into his own face these days. Why, if the man was half as contented with Maggie as Sean was with Frannie, then there were no two more fortunate souls walking the earth.

Shifting his gaze out to the open country, Sean stared at the trees and meadow grass without really seeing them. He'd worried so about leaving the circus. The only family he'd ever known. What a fool he'd been not to realize that he wasn't losing a family at all. He was gaining one. Now he had not only the Calhoun circus folk but the Donnelly clan as well to claim as his own.

And with family comes problems. Although, he told himself, he'd never been called on to bring a gun in defense of Calhoun or the rest. A fist, certainly. But not a gun.

Frowning suddenly, he slanted Cutter a long look and asked, "What d'ya think's goin' on with Mary Alice?"

"Hmmm . . ." Cutter inhaled and released a long stream of thick blue smoke. The fragile streamer twisted in the soft breeze, then dissolved completely. "With Al, it's hard to say."

"How d'ya mean?" Sean hadn't known any of Frannie's sisters long enough to know them well. Mary Alice and Teresa, he knew even less about than he did Maggie. With Mary Alice always at her mine and Teresa spending most of her days on the family ranch, there simply hadn't been time enough to get acquainted.

But Cutter, Sean knew, had known the Donnelly sisters since they were girls. Who better to tell him what he wanted to know?

The gambler turned his back on Sean and strolled over to a nearby tumble of rocks. Perching comfortably on a sun-warmed boulder, he rested his right ankle on his left knee and took another long drag at his cigar. Then, flicking the ash from the tip, he glanced up at Sean.

"Even when she was small, Mary Alice was the wild card in the Donnelly family deck."

Sean chuckled, tipped his hat back further on his head and waited.

Staring at the glowing tip of his cigar, Cutter spoke again, his voice thick with the memories rising up in him. "Maggie would singlehandedly fight an army if she had to, to protect her sisters, or anyone else she felt couldn't defend themselves." He sighed, took another puff, then blew the smoke out again. "Frankie—" He broke off and grinned at Sean. "I know you prefer to call her Frannie, but she'll always be Frankie to the rest of us."

Sean nodded knowingly.

"Frankie liked things to be just so," Cutter continued. "She likes rules. Order." He laughed gently, shaking his head. "How Frankie ever got her start from Kevin, I'll never understand."

Sean smiled. He admitted silently that his Frannie did indeed admire order. Discipline. Propriety. Then again, Sean thought, as he remembered that morning in their bedroom at the hotel and Frannie's ardent good-bye, she wasn't a woman afraid to try something new. Sean frowned at a sudden, all-too-familiar discomfort and shifted his stance.

"Terry Ann," Cutter broke off quickly and grinned. "Lord she hates that name. *Teresa* was always trying to find her own way."

"Huh?"

"Well, it was as if she wanted to be like her sisters, but at the same time, she wanted to be different." Cutter sighed, leaned back against the rocks, and shook his head. "Hell, I don't think even Teresa knows for sure who she is. Or what she wants."

"And Alice?"

"Al." Cutter squinted up at the sky, "Crazily enough, I think Al is the most mysterious of the bunch. Kevin raised her like a son and she loved it. Hell, she thrived on it. She's good with a gun, knows her way around a bull whip—though not as well as Teresa—and she's damn near amazing with a knife."

Sean shook his head and rubbed his jaw thoughtfully. He'd have to remember never to make Mary Alice Donnelly mad at him, he told himself solemnly. Or Teresa, for that matter.

"And yet," Cutter went on, "every once in a while, I'd see a look in her eye when she didn't think anyone was watching."

"Like what?"

"It's probably nothing," Cutter said, and pointed his cigar at Sean. "But sometimes, when she'd look at Maggie or Frankie, all fixed up in nice dresses with their hair all curled and such . . ."

"Yeah?"

"Sometimes, I'd get the feeling that Al would have dearly loved to get all fancied up, but she just didn't have any idea how to go about it."

A mental image of Mary Alice leaped up in Sean's mind. He tried to imagine the tall, capable woman in a dress rather than her worn buckskins, but he couldn't do it. What's more, Sean had a feeling that Cutter was wrong about this Donnelly sister. He hadn't noticed a thing about Mary Alice that a body could call "ladylike." Oh, she was a fine woman, no doubt. And apparently, a veritable tigress with weapons. Definitely, she was someone to have on your side in a fight.

But in a dress?

At a dance?

No, Sean thought. On this score at least, Cutter was wrong. He'd bet on it.

"But none of that matters," Cutter spoke up, and Sean pushed his meandering thoughts aside. "All that matters now, is that she's family. And she needs our help."

"True an' all," Sean muttered.

Sticking his cigar into the corner of his mouth, Cutter stood up and walked to his horse. Snatching up the reins, he stuck his left foot in the stirrup and swung aboard. He glanced down at Sean briefly. "We've a long ride still, before we reach Regret."

"Then we'd best get goin'," Sean answered, and mounted his horse.

"Ready, brother?" The gambler asked as he watched Sean lower himself gently onto the saddle.

"Aye, brother. You lead off. I'm right behind ya."

# Chapter 4

⌒◯◯⌒

The inside of the Mercantile smelled like something had crawled in there and died.

For the first time since beginning this ridiculous charade, Travis was glad of his disguise. Quickly, he pulled a silk hankie from his inside coat pocket and used it to cover his mouth and nose.

A snort of derision shot from the darkened corner of the store, and he turned slowly toward the sound.

"What's wrong, mister?" the owner of the store asked as he pushed himself to his feet, "Yer nose too *delicate* for western air?"

Air? Travis thought. What air? The atmosphere in the store was thick enough to slice with a bayonet. As he watched, the proprietor of the store stepped into a slash of afternoon sunlight. The pale, golden light lay across the big man like a silk coverlet tossed on top of a pig wallow.

A dirty apron, spattered with God knew what, strained to cover his formidable belly, and the faded blue shirt he wore was in no better shape.

Greasy black hair was combed straight back from his forehead, and his small blue eyes shone like two pebbles dropped into day-old dough.

Travis's eyes watered as the big man moved closer. Here, then, he told himself, was the source of the odor choking off the air in the room. Aloud, though, he only said, "I've come to purchase supplies, if you please."

Instantly a flash of greed streaked across the other man's features. Those blue eyes took on a glittering shine, and Travis mentally grabbed hold of his wallet.

Obviously the proprietor was hoping to make a week's worth of sales to the "city boy." And despite his reluctance to do the man any favors, Travis knew he would oblige him. After all, he stood a better chance of getting information out of the smelly son-of-a-bitch, if the man was so busy counting coins, he didn't notice anything else.

"Why didn't ya say so when ya come in?" the big man asked, and held out one grubby hand.

Reluctantly, Travis grabbed it in a brief handshake.

"The name's G. W. Truesdale," the man told him, and puffed up considerably as he hooked his thumbs under the bib of his apron. Rocking back and forth on his heels, he added, "The G. W. stands for George Washington, o' course."

"Of course."

"Yes sir, my folks was real taken with ol' George. Figured I'd do big things if'n I took his name." He paused to glance with pride around his establishment. "And if I do say so myself, I think ol' George would be real pleased with what I done with myself."

Travis forced a smile. If *ol' George* ever found out about his namesake, he didn't have a doubt that the former president would rise up from his grave and send Truesdale directly to hell.

G. W. slapped his palms together and rubbed them briskly. "So what is it you'll be needin'?"

Travis's gaze slipped over the jumble of shelves and the piles of merchandise stacked haphazardly on the floor. Hell, he'd been in worse places.

Besides, as far as he knew, this was the only general store in Regret. For now, anyway. Of course, if the little town grew as fast as most mining towns did, old G. W. would be having plenty of competition. But for now it was buy here, or do without. And to have the privacy of his own tent, Travis was willing to put up with a lot. Including G. W. Truesdale.

Lifting his gaze to meet the other man's, Travis said, "To start, I shall need a tent." He grimaced inwardly at the whiny tone of his voice, then swallowed back his own humiliation and went on. "I simply refuse to share habitation with perfect strangers."

"Habi . . ." G. W. scratched his greasy head.

"Habitation. A place of rest. A home . . . or, in this case"—Travis sighed—"a tent."

"Ah . . ." G. W. grinned and hotfooted it to the end of the plank counter. Turning sideways, he managed to squeeze his considerable bulk through the opening in the counter, then he hurried to the back of the store.

From under a pile of Levi's and red woolen

underwear, G. W. pulled out a heavy roll of dirty white canvas. Standing up, he tossed it to Travis, who just barely remembered to stagger slightly under the weight.

"There ya go. Got some tent poles over yonder." He pointed at the opposite corner. "What else?"

The man's greed was like a living presence in the room. He'd seen this before, of course. There were always people willing to take advantage of a newcomer to the area. Although, he told himself with disgust, he'd never been the poor fool getting fleeced before.

Jesus, it was humiliating.

And it was about to get worse.

"I should be grateful for your help in this, Mr. Truesdale," he said from behind the safety of his handkerchief, "I'm sure you are more knowledgable than I as to what I shall need."

A short, sharp intake of breath was the only visible sign of G. W.'s delight. Apparently the storekeeper was bright enough to at least *try* to disguise his larcenous heart.

"Proud to help ya, stranger," G. W. said softly. "Though what you'll need is gonna cost dear."

No doubt of that, Travis thought. "I understand, sir."

Quickly then, obviously terrified that his customer might change his mind at any moment, G. W. began scurrying about the room. Muttering to himself, he burrowed through the sliding stacks of merchandise, ignoring whatever fell to the floor in his haste.

In seconds it seemed that a veritable tower of supplies had simply appeared on the counter.

Travis's eyes widened as he counted five blankets, four lamps, three cans of kerosene, two cots, pots, pans, dishes enough for a family of four, shovels, pick axes, and a threadbare oriental rug.

His gaze slid knowingly to G. W., who was still busy burrowing through his stock. "Are you quite sure I'll be needing *all* of this?"

"Huh?" The other man tossed him a quick look. "Oh, every little bit of it," he assured him. "You got no idea at all what to expect."

"Two cots?"

"Well, sure," G. W. told him. "You might get comp'ny sometime. Don't want 'em sleepin' on the ground, do ya?"

"I suppose not."

"No sir, Mister Deal. Knew ya wouldn't. I had you pegged as a real gent."

"You know my name?" Travis asked, though he wasn't really surprised. He was willing to bet that he'd been the talk of the town since he stepped into the Last Chance Saloon.

"Word travels fast in a place the size of Regret."

"Then you know I'm a partner in the Four Roses Mine?"

"Surely do," G. W. admitted, and reached into a nearby glass jar for a licorice whip. Stuffing the candy into a corner of his mouth, he talked around it. "And if ya don't mind my sayin' so, you really stuck your head into a hornet's nest, mister."

"What makes you say that?"

G. W. took a deep breath, swelling his already huge body to monstrous proportions. "Well, sir, ol' Al, she's a right fine girl. But she's in

somebody's way. And that somebody don't care
if she's female or not. They're fixin' to move
her."

A cold, hard knot tightened in his gut, and
Travis held his breath, waiting for the man to go
on.

The front door swung open and a blast of pine-
freshened wind swept through the store. Travis
inhaled deeply, filling his lungs gratefully.

G. W. glanced at the man standing in the doorway and his features tightened. Fear began to
glaze over the greedy shine in his small eyes.
Intrigued, Travis turned his head slightly toward
the newcomer. He met a hard, gray stare.

Recognition stirred in his soul. He knew that
stranger. Knew him as well as he knew himself.
Oh, he didn't know the man's name. In fact, he'd
never seen him before. This knowledge was
more basic than that. More complete. More in-
stinctual. As one predator recognizes another,
Travis knew that *this* man was part of the trouble
surrounding Mary Alice Donnelly.

"Afternoon, Mr. Thompson," G. W. said, and
for the first time, his voice sounded thready, uneasy.

Thompson never shifted his gaze. Instead, his
threatening stare narrowed perceptibly.

"Who're you?" he finally asked.

"This here's Al's new partner," G. W. offered.

"Travis Deal," he said, interrupting the storekeeper to introduce himself. The sound of his
own voice offended him. In fact, everything inside him howled at the injustice of having to play
the pompous fool before this man. They should
be meeting as equals. Enemies, surely.

But equals.

Thompson's right hand moved to caress the walnut stock of the pistol holstered to his hip.

How many times, Travis wondered, had he done the very same thing? Adopted the same, seemingly careless stance that disguised his readiness for battle.

"Mister," Thompson said softly, "you ain't wanted here."

Absently, Travis noted that G. W. had stepped far to one side, obviously convinced there was going to be gunplay. But he could have reassured the man. Nothing was going to happen. Not yet, anyway.

"Wanted or not, here I am," he replied, and deliberately tugged at the cuffs of his too-large jacket.

"You ain't listening, mister. I said, we don't want you here."

"Just *who*, might I ask, is *we*?" Travis shot the other man a quick, covert look. Here was another chance at information gathering. If he could get Thompson talking.

"None of your concern."

"I beg to differ."

"Huh?"

"Differ. Argue. Disagree." Travis was beginning to enjoy himself despite his disguise. Obviously, Thompson didn't know what to make of him. That gray stare of his looked more confused than intimidating now, and Travis had to fight down a smile. After all, if he couldn't have the pleasure of facing his opponent squarely, he could at least enjoy harassing him. "If there is someone who doesn't want me in town," he continued archly, "I assure you, it is most definitely my concern."

Thompson reached up and pushed his hat back a bit farther on his head. Narrowing his gaze even further, he cocked his head before asking, "Mister, don't you get it? I'm tellin' you to leave town."

"But I only just arrived."

"And now you're goin'."

"Oh, not quite yet, I think."

Travis glanced at G. W., just to assure himself of the man's position. He needn't have worried. The owner of the Mercantile was half-crouched behind a cracker barrel, the licorice whip dangling limply from his clenched lips, his interested gaze flicking back and forth between the two men facing each other.

"You been warned, mister."

"I certainly have," Travis nodded, looking back at his opponent. "And thank you."

Frowning, Thompson looked as though he wanted to say something else but wasn't quite sure what. Then he turned suddenly and disappeared through the doorway.

Travis stared after him for a long moment before pivoting to watch G. W. rise slowly from his hiding place. He snatched the licorice from his mouth and wiped his lips with his sleeve. The storekeeper swallowed audibly before turning a new, more interested eye on his customer.

Clearly, G. W. was beginning to wonder if the new man in town was as much of a dandy as he was pretending to be.

To dispel any such dangerous notions, Travis waved his handkerchief in the air, coughed, and said, "That man was positively barbaric! If I hadn't known better, I would have sworn he was trying to injure me in some way."

G. W.'s small, piggy eyes widened as much as it was possible for them. "Mister Deal," he said, reaching up to wipe the sweat streaming from his brow, "he wasn't kiddin' you any. That there was Mike Thompson. A meaner son-of-a-bitch don't exist."

"Do you mean to say . . ." Travis let his jaw drop and his voice take on a hushed, horrified tone. ". . . the man was *serious*?"

"You damn right he was, Mister Deal." Then the storekeeper seemed to remember that he might very well be canceling the big sale he'd been about to make, by scaring his customer off. Halfheartedly he asked, "Suppose you don't want none of this stuff no more, huh?"

"What's that?" Travis smiled inwardly. Obviously, G. W. was now convinced that the easterner's "bravery" was no more than ignorance. "Oh. My supplies. Well, Miss Donnelly *did* tell me that the next stage coach through Regret won't be for another week. So I suppose I shall need these things anyway. Don't you think?"

G. W. perked right up. "Yes sir, you surely will. I'll just tally this up for ya, all right?"

"You do that," Travis said, and wandered over to the dirty storefront window. "Also, would you have my trunk delivered to the mine? I left it at the stage office."

"It'll cost extra."

"Of course."

As he stared out at the bustling little mining town, his brain began to race with hundreds of different possibilities. Was Thompson in charge? Was it he who was behind Mary Alice's trouble? Or was he simply the gun hand for the man who held the whip? What would their next move be? And when?

A small, satisfied smile flashed briefly across Travis's features.

The game had begun.

Torchlight flickered over the rocky ground, and Mary Alice squinted into the growing dusk.

From her position near the mouth of the mine, she could keep a wary eye on both the men in camp and the bend in the road leading from town. Though she hated to admit it even to herself, she'd been watching that road for what seemed like hours.

It was none of her business what that damn fool partner of hers was up to. He'd been in town. He'd seen for himself that he didn't belong. Hell, he'd even dropped like a rock the first time he'd heard gunfire. The man was an adult. Was it up to her to see that nobody shot him just for sport? Didn't she have enough to worry about already without having to concern herself with yet one more person's safety?

Deliberately, Al looked away from that section of road toward the miners in camp. Shadowy figures threaded their way through the maze of tents. Small fires littered the ground, and the soft, metallic *chink* of forks smacking against tin plates sounded almost like a tune being played in time with the deep rumble of male voices. Snatches of conversation drifted to her on the evening wind, but Al didn't feel the soothing wash of comradeship those voices used to bring her.

She hadn't felt that sense of rightness, of belonging, in months. Ever since Rafe Bennet arrived in town.

Bennet, with his money and promises. And when the lure of easy money didn't work to sway a man's loyalties, she reminded herself, Bennet turned his thugs loose.

Instantly she recalled the scene in the mine earlier that day. Facing down those three men alone. If she hadn't been there, what might they have done? Set off some dynamite? Sawn through some support beams? Al's jaw clenched tight. There was just no telling how far Bennet would be willing to go. She was just grateful that she happened to be inside the mine when those men showed up. More than that, she was eternally grateful she'd had her shotgun with her.

Without that gun, she would have been at the tender mercies of those three. And she was willing to bet that their version of mercy wouldn't have stretched far. A shudder rippled down Al's spine as the memory of that short, tense moment rose up in her mind. She remembered everything about those men. From the fat one's hard, dead eyes to the quiet one's hesitation. She remembered their voices. She remembered that heartstopping moment when she'd waited for them to decide whether or not to charge her, shotgun or no.

Mostly, though, Mary Alice remembered the feeling of aloneness that had swamped her as she had faced her enemies across a few feet of ground.

No stranger to a fight, Al was still used to having people in her corner. Or at the very least, she'd always had the knowledge that, should she need it, help was there. First, of course, there had been her father. Then, her sisters. Now, she told herself wryly, there were her sisters' husbands. The only problem was that they were so damned far away.

Al shifted uncomfortably on the rock she was perched on and laid her shotgun across her lap. Husbands. Hell, two of her sisters were *married*.

Immediately, images of Maggie and Frankie filled Al's mind. They'd been lucky, both of them. They'd managed to find husbands who appreciated them. Even though Al had never been real fond of Cutter, she was willing to admit that he was a good match for Maggie. As for Sean, well, she didn't even know him yet. But any man who could bring Frankie out of that quiet, too-proper shell of hers was all right with Mary Alice.

Two out of four sisters married, and all because their father had taken it upon himself to sell out his shares of the businesses and find "partners" for his girls. At the thought of the word partner, Mary Alice scowled. Sure, she told herself, Kevin Donnelly goes out and finds Cutter and Sean on his own. Then, when Al actually wires her father, *asking* for help . . . he sends Travis Deal.

What had Da been thinking? she asked herself. Why in God's name would Kevin send her a cowardly dandy when she was in desperate need of a strong man to stand beside her in this fight? A hideous thought suddenly occurred to Al and she stiffened in response. Surely her father didn't expect her to actually *marry* the pompous fool he'd sent her?

"Hah!" Her short, harsh laughter sounded explosively loud. Al frowned again and stared down at the rocky ground. If that was her father's plan, she told herself, he would be sorely disappointed. She had no plans to marry at all. *Least* of all to a man more ladylike than herself!

She didn't need a husband for God's sake. She needed help. Soon.

Silently, thoughtfully, Al let her gaze drift over the men who worked the Four Roses Mine. Of the fifty or so miners, she figured that she could trust maybe a handful of them. And they were the older men. Men like Hank and George, and Chucker, the cook. Men who clawed a living out of the bowels of the earth and asked nothing more than to be paid honest wages. Good men, but long past the age of wanting to find themselves hip deep in a fight.

The young men, Al had found out recently, were too eager, too hungry for their dreams. When the riches they'd planned on didn't appear, they were all too willing to turn to Bennet. How much easier it was to be paid *not* to work in a mine than to actually have to slide down into the belly of a mountain and be swallowed by darkness.

"Bennet," she muttered, and reached down to flick a clod of mud from the toe of her worn boot. "It always comes back to Bennet."

"Talkin' to yourself, huh?"

Al jumped and grabbed at the shotgun lying across her knees. A deep-throated chuckle stopped her even as her fingers curled around the stock.

"Take it easy, girl."

"Goddammit, Chucker," Al snapped, and dragged in a shaky breath. "You ought to know better than to sneak up on a body."

"Hmmph!" The older man stepped into a patch of torchlight and frowned at her. "I'm too damned old to be *sneakin'* anywheres! You wasn't payin' attention is all."

He was right and she knew it. Dammit, she couldn't afford to sit around wool-gathering. There was a man in town who at that very minute was willing to pay hard money to put Al's mine out of commission. And she damn well better be ready for him.

"So, you want your supper or not?"

Al looked up and nodded. As the camp cook walked toward her, she took a moment to study his familiar features. Sparse gray hair stood up at odd angles all over his egg-shaped head. A beard that had more promise than bristles covered his narrow chin, and his deeply tanned face had more lines and creases than a mine had rocks.

Chucker handed her a plate of beans and tortillas, then set a cup of inky black coffee down on a nearby rock.

"So," he asked as she picked up her fork and started eating, "where's that new partner of yours?"

"Prob'ly gettin' himself shot by now," she answered, and tore off a corner of the still-warm corn tortilla. Popping it into her mouth, Al talked around it. "I told him not to go, but he didn't want to listen."

"And that's it, huh?"

She swallowed and tilted her head up to look at the old man. The wavering torchlight behind him threw Chucker's features into darkness. Al squinted, trying to read his expression. "What's that supposed to mean?"

"You know durn well what I mean, girl." He shrugged deeper into his sheepskin-lined coat. "The man's your partner, Al. Whether you want him or not. You shouldn't let him wander around gettin' hisself killed."

"I don't have time to ride herd on him *and* keep an eye on Bennet."

He grumbled something unintelligible as Al scooped up the last of her beans and reached for the coffee cup.

"When are your sisters' husbands gonna get here, you figure?"

She flicked him a quick glance, set her empty plate down, then shifted her gaze to the road leading from town. It was nearly impossible to see anything now. Twilight was fast fading into night. Despite what she'd said to Chucker, Mary Alice couldn't quite prevent a spiral of worry from coiling in the pit of her stomach. That fancy man should've been back by now. Dammit, what had her da been thinking, sending a man like Deal to her? And where the hell was the fool? Had he gotten himself lost? Was he wandering around the mountainside, looking for camp? Or was he lying face down in a muddy street, his foolish looking clothing stained with blood?

"You gonna answer me sometime tonight?"

"Huh?"

"Your new brothers-in-law. When're they gonna get here, you figure?"

"Hell, how should I know?" Mary Alice stood up abruptly, cradling the shotgun in the crook of her arm. "I sent the wire this morning. If they left right away, they'll get here prob'ly early tomorrow. Maybe."

"Well now, that's real helpful."

"Chucker . . ."

He lifted one hand for silence, bent down and snatched up her empty dinner plate, then straightened again, groaning slightly with the movement.

Instantly Mary Alice's anger disappeared. Chucker had looked exactly the same all the years she'd known him, so sometimes she forgot just how old he was. Too damned old, she thought now, to be spending his nights on a cold mountain with nothing more than a tent and a campfire to keep him warm.

"Why don't you go on to bed?" she said softly.

"Why don't you mind your business?"

Suitably chastened, she reminded herself that Chucker was no better than she was at taking advice.

"You gonna sit up here all night again?" he asked quietly.

Mary Alice's shoulders lifted in a tired shrug. "There's nobody else."

"I could get George. Or Hank."

"No." She shook her head. "I need them on the shift during the day to keep an eye on everybody else."

Chucker nodded, and Al was relieved that he

wasn't going to fight her on this. Maybe when Sean and Cutter arrived, she could get some sleep. Until then, she had to be on guard.

"What about the new man?"

She slanted her old friend a long look and sighed. He was right. She couldn't just leave her partner on his own. Not in Regret, anyway. Whether she liked it or not, she was going to have to watch out for him—at least until she could get him on a stage headed out of town.

"Ask George to go look for him."

"All right." Chucker half turned to start back down the path toward camp, then caught himself and stopped. "Ya know," he said slowly, "I got a real strange feelin' about this Deal fella."

"Me too." Mary Alice laughed shortly.

"No," he reached up and scratched the top of his head slowly, "I mean I got a itchy feelin' when I saw him."

"When did you see him?"

"When you two was talkin'. Just before he went back to town."

"Hell, you were fifty feet away!"

"I'm old, girl. My back ain't strong anymore and most of my hair's gone, but there ain't a damn thing wrong with my eyes."

Mary Alice nodded and waited. She'd known Chucker too well and too long not to listen when he had something to say.

"There's somethin' about him that just don't set right."

"Huh! There's *plenty* about him that don't set right."

"No, that ain't it. And you're not listenin' to me, girl." Chucker took a half-step toward her and lowered his voice, as if afraid someone was listening. "I seen that man somewhere's before."

"Where the hell would you be seeing a man like him?"

"That's just it," Chucker interrupted. "I seen him. But not like he is now. Him, but different."

"Different how?"

He shook his head and straightened up. Grimacing slightly, he admitted, "I ain't remembered that yet." The old man waved his index finger at her. "But I will. Sure as mornin' comes too damned early, I will. But till I do, you keep a sharp eye on that fella. If not for his sake . . . then for yours."

Without another word, Chucker turned and started back down the rocky path. Mary Alice watched him go, hearing his words echoing over and over in her mind. Just what she needed, she told herself wryly. One more thing to have to think about.

If Chucker said that he'd seen Travis Deal before, then he had. The old man was rarely wrong. Deal had been *different*, huh? Different how? As new worries and doubts began to flood her brain, Mary Alice asked herself once again just why her father would send such a man when she needed help.

For the first time, though, she considered something new. Maybe her father *hadn't* sent Travis Deal. Maybe he'd sent someone else and Deal had taken his place.

But why would he?

Why would a dandy show up in Regret, California, in the middle of a war?

And why wasn't he afraid?

Could it be because Travis Deal was already working with Bennet?

She stiffened and narrowed her gaze thoughtfully. The darkness lying just outside the circle of torchlight suddenly seemed blacker.

Deeper.

More treacherous.

# Chapter 5

**T**ravis stopped just outside the circle of light. Hidden within the shadows of the pines, he watched Mary Alice Donnelly. Now that he was actually taking the time to study her, he could see beyond the mannish clothing to the raw, untouched beauty that she successfully managed to hide. He also noted the strain that her troubles had brought her.

For the first time, he noticed the pale blue shadows lying beneath her quite lovely green eyes. He saw lines of worry etched into her tightly vigilant expression. Travis's gaze slipped lower, and he took note of the grip she had on her shotgun. It would be best, he told himself firmly, if he remembered *not* to come up on her unawares.

She shouldn't be out here, alone. What the hell had Kevin been thinking of, leaving his *daughter* to look after a mine?

Travis recalled everything Kevin Donnelly had had to say over the years about his third daughter. He'd called her dependable. Trustworthy.

69

He'd praised her cool head in time of trouble and the fierce Irish temper and pride that gave her the courage to fight for what was hers.

But, Travis thought with disgust, it seemed that the older man had never taken the time to see what that pride and courage was costing Mary Alice. She looked as though what she needed most right then was a good night's sleep, far from the mine and its worries. Unfortunately Travis was in no position to insist on that. She would never hand over the mine to him. Not yet, anyway. Hell, she was already convinced that her new partner was pretty much useless.

Otherwise, he told himself wryly, she never would have sent George into town after him.

"Come in slow, mister," Mary Alice spoke up suddenly, and her quiet voice seemed to echo out around him. "I've got a shotgun here, and I don't mind usin' it."

"It's me, Mary Alice," he said softly. "Travis."

"Step into the light."

A slow smile lifted a corner of his mouth before disappearing. He'd noticed that she hadn't promised not to shoot. Grimacing slightly, Travis reached up, plucked his hated bowler hat off, and ran one hand through his hair. Then he ducked a bit and stepped clear of the trees.

"Closer."

He'd feel a lot better if she'd put that damned shotgun down, he told himself. After all, what better way to rid herself of a partner she didn't want, than by shooting him—"accidentally," of course.

Another two steps brought him up to within an arm's reach of the flaring torch. He deliberately kept his gaze to one side of the brightness. Staring into a night fire was the surest way he knew to momentarily blind a man to whatever dangers might be lurking in the darkness. And Travis had a feeling he was going to be needing *all* of his senses when he was around Mary Alice.

"Will you lower your weapon, now?" he asked.

The suspicious glint in her eye told him she really didn't want to. In fact, Travis had the distinct feeling that Mary Alice would like nothing better than to pull both triggers on that gun of hers. He held his breath and glanced to either side of him, mentally debating which way he should jump for cover. But after a long, thoughtful moment, she reluctantly took her fingers from the double triggers and laid the shotgun barrel along her knees again.

Travis felt each coiled nerve in his body slowly relax. Then he met her gaze. "Do you greet all of your visitors so warmly?" he asked. "Or have I offended you in some way?"

Mary Alice's gaze swept over him quickly, thoroughly. In the flashes of expression that crossed her features in a lighting-like progression, he read suspicion, disgust, wariness and, finally—as much as it pained him to admit—Travis saw dismissal.

She sighed, pushed her long, thick auburn braid over her right shoulder and shook her head. "No, you didn't offend me any, Mr. Deal."

"Travis."

She nodded slowly. "Travis."

"Then may I ask why you were holding a gun on me?"

"I told you, there's been trouble." Cocking her head to one side, she asked, "Didn't Da tell you any of this before he sold you his half of the mine?"

Of course he had. Travis Delacort—*Deal*, he reminded himself—wasn't a man to take on a pig in a poke. He'd wanted every scrap of information that Kevin had possessed. It hadn't been much. Which, he thought wryly, accounted for the ridiculous disguise he'd had to adopt.

But he couldn't very well admit to that now, could he? Instead, he strolled across the patch of ground separating them and took a seat beside her in the dirt.

"I seem to recall your father saying something about a man who was running, 'rough-shod' I believe he called it, over the townsfolk."

"And that's all he said?" She looked stunned.

"I believe so," Travis lied. "Why? Is there something more?"

She laughed, but there was no amusement in it. Rather, the laugh sounded pained, forced. "That would be fair to say, I guess."

"Is it because of this trouble you sent George after me?"

She cocked her head at him. "Where is George?"

Travis waved one hand in the direction of town. "He's riding the wagon, bringing my things to camp."

"Your *things*?"

He hid a smile and ignored her question to ask one of his own. "Do you know a Mr. Thompson?"

Her features tightened and her cool green eyes narrowed. "Where'd you see him?"

"He dropped by the Mercantile to offer me a piece of advice."

"What was that?"

Travis tugged at the sleeves of his jacket and let his gaze slip away from hers. "He seemed to think I should leave town. Immediately."

Al laughed again and rubbed her eyes. "And here I thought me and Thompson would never agree on anything."

Quietly, Travis asked, "Is Thompson the source of your trouble?"

"No," she sighed, "but he's part of it."

"Would you mind telling me what this is all about?"

Mary Alice shifted her gaze away from him to study the towering pines lancing toward the night sky. "Suppose you got a right to know," she allowed softly. "But if it's all the same to you, it'll wait till tomorrow."

Travis heard the exhaustion in her voice. He saw it in the slump of her shoulders and the tired droop of her eyelids. Yes, he told himself. He could wait until morning. Right now, all he wanted to do was make sure she got some rest. Ridiculous as it seemed, even to himself, Travis hated seeing her look so . . . beaten.

"Certainly," he said. "As for now, why don't you go on down to your tent and get some sleep? I shall stand watch for you."

She snorted, then quickly began to cough in a futile, if well-meant attempt to hide her amusement at his suggestion. "'Scuse me," she said after a moment or two. "But I don't think you're exactly—"

"Yes?" Travis interrupted, astounded at the depth of his irritation.

"... *ready*," she qualified, "to stand guard on your own. Hell, you only got into town this morning."

At least she hadn't laughed in his face, Travis thought. He supposed that was *some* consolation.

"Very well," he said as he reached up to undo the top button of his too-high collar.

"What're you doin'?" Mary Alice asked, while at the same time scooting a few inches away from him.

"If you won't go to your rest," Travis told her determinedly, "I shall stay right here and see that you at the very least close your eyes for a while."

She smirked at him, eyed his open collar, and asked, "For that you need your shirt buttons undone?"

"I thought I might as well be comfortable." Or, as comfortable as he could be, dressed in the clothing he was beginning to hate more every minute.

"I see." She deliberately put another few inches between them. "Thanks for the offer, but I'm fine."

"Mary Alice . . ." He caught himself and started again. "Al."

She nodded.

He shook his head, amazed that a woman, *any* woman would prefer to be called by a man's name. "I'm going to stay right here. Surely even you must admit that I am capable of waking you immediately if a problem presents itself."

"I suppose . . ."

At last, he thought wryly. She actually thought him qualified for something. Granted, it was a job any halfway decent dog could do, but it was a start. Immediately, he pressed his case. "Good. That's settled. Now, if you will hand me your weapon, you may feel free to use my shoulder as a pillow."

A slow smile curved her mouth and Travis frowned. On any other woman, he might have thought it . . . attractive.

"I'll hold my own gun, mister. And I don't need a pillow."

Travis sighed his disgust. Obviously, Mary Alice Donnelly was every bit as hardheaded as her father had claimed.

She rested her head against the rocky incline behind them and let her eyelids slide shut. Her left hand was curled around the sawed-off barrel of the shotgun and her right rested on the worn stock, her fingertips just inches from the trigger guard.

"You hear anything . . . anything at all, you wake me, understand?"

"Of course."

Jesus, this was humiliating for a man who'd been riding guard on stagecoaches when he was just sixteen. Travis had been in and out of more scrapes than Mary Alice could even dream about. He'd ridden with the Texas Rangers for a time, been a head scout for wagon trains, done a hitch in the army, and he'd even sneaked across the Rio Bravo into Mexico a time or two after some fugitive or other.

Now he wasn't trusted to wake her if there was trouble.

"Don't you go fallin' asleep, Travis." She opened one eye and glared at him. "You feel yourself driftin' off, you give me a shove, all right?"

"Yes, yes . . ." Travis snapped. "Go to sleep, Alice."

"Al."

He glanced at her and watched as the lines of stubborn determination slowly faded from her features. In seconds her deep, even breathing told him she was asleep. A well of admiration rose up in him for her. Obviously she was used to making do on a moment's notice. He was willing to bet that when she woke up, she would wake up ready and alert, too.

Frowning, Travis allowed his gaze to move over her unobserved. The worn, faded work shirt strained across her generous bosom. He watched the rise and fall of her breasts and felt his mouth go dry. The fabric, soft from dozens of washings, smoothed over her curves like a lover's touch.

He shook his head, determined to rid himself of any such notions. His gaze slipped down to where the tails of her shirt were tucked into buckskin pants that hugged her hips and legs like a second skin.

And nice, long, shapely legs they were, too. One eyebrow lifted. Bizarre clothing or not, he was willing to bet that not many women could wear trousers with such amazing results. He'd learned early on that long skirts hid a multitude of sins.

She shifted in her sleep and Travis looked

away. It was damned disconcerting to find himself actually enjoying the sight of a woman in pants.

She half turned her head, looking for a more comfortable position. Travis glanced at her and watched her hair fall across her shoulder. He lifted the heavy braid in one hand and smoothed his thumb and forefinger over the deep auburn strands. Soft, he told himself. And the color seemed to catch the torchlight, making the dark red mass gleam like old, polished mahogany.

A confusing woman, he thought. Her one obvious claim to beauty and she kept it locked down into a tight braid so no one could notice it.

Deliberately, he released her hair and let the braid fall back to rest atop her breasts. He had no bloody damned business idling away his time thinking about pretty hair. Or why Mary Alice Donnelly chose to ignore the fact that she was a woman.

He was in Regret for one reason and one reason only.

He was being paid to be there.

A rattle of small stones chased each other down the mountainside, and the fat man turned to glare at his clumsy partner. "Damn you, Taylor," he snapped, his voice nothing more than a strained, tight whisper. "Why don't ya just fire off a gun, let 'er know we're comin'?"

"My foot slipped, Jim," the other man said just as softly.

A stupid, lumbering fool, Fat Jim Sikes told himself. How was a man supposed to do his job when he had to work with bungling idiots? His gaze, locked on Taylor, narrowed thoughtfully. Maybe it would be best if he just rid himself of the man right here. A knock on the head and a quick slide down the back face of the mountain to the gully below, and it would be over. No one would think anything of one more miner taking a fall.

Sikes's thick fingers curled around a nearby rock, clenched momentarily, then released it. No. Not now. It would be just like Taylor to get off a good, loud scream before he died, and then Sikes's plan to sneak up on Al Donnelly would be shot to hell.

Soon, though, he promised himself. Soon he would get rid of Taylor and maybe, he thought, he'd get shut of his other partner, too.

"This whole idea is crazy," the third man, Bill Moore, pointed out.

"We wouldn't be doin' none of this," Sikes reminded him, "if we'd taken care of that woman earlier, like I wanted."

"She had a shotgun," Moore fired back.

"She was bluffin'."

"I don't know 'bout that, Jim." Taylor shook his head, and Sikes swore he could hear the rocks rattling inside.

"She wasn't bluffin'," Bill Moore said quietly, and tilted his head back to look at the fat man in front of him. "And you know it, Jim."

"Don't know nothin' of the kind," he said grimly. "All I know is, Thompson's payin' us to get her the hell outa that mine. How we do it is our business."

"How come, ya figure he wants her out today, all of a sudden-like?"

"Don't know," Sikes shrugged, "And don't care. He ain't payin' us to ask questions. 'Sides, it ain't sudden. Thompson and Bennet's been after her for a while now."

"Al Donnelly's not a woman to take on lightly," Moore whispered.

"You always was too damned gutless for your own good," Jim snapped.

"I'm alive, ain't I?"

"It ain't what I call livin'."

Maybe not, Bill thought. But it was life, just the same. He looked past Sikes at the trail snaking upward behind him. At the end of that trail was the Four Roses Mine. And a whole lot of grief for whoever tried to face down that Donnelly woman. Unlike Sikes, Bill Moore knew in his bones that she wouldn't scare. He'd known it that morning, when he'd looked down the double barrels of the shotgun she'd held on them.

There was no bluff in that female.

And there was something else, too.

Sikes might put it down to him being gutless, but Bill didn't much care for the idea of fighting women. True, he didn't much care for fighting at all and avoided it when given half a chance. But a man shouldn't cross some lines, he told himself, else he wouldn't be able to look at his own face while he was shaving. And this here line was one that Bill Moore was going to walk away from.

He glanced at the two men he'd partnered up with only a couple of months before. Fat Jim

Sikes was a mean bastard by anybody's book. –
Hard and cold, the man enjoyed dishing out pain
. . . and he was good at it. Taylor, he wasn't
much on his own, so he tried like hell to be whoever Fat Jim, his hero, wanted him to be.

Moore shook his head and half turned around,
his decision made. Maybe he'd head for Montana. He'd heard there was plenty of color being
found at Fort Benton. He could get him a job
there, easy. And he wouldn't have to sleep with
one eye open anymore, either. Not with a few
hundred miles between him and Jim Sikes.

"Where ya think *you're* goin'?" the fat man
hissed.

"Montana."

"You can't leave now."

Bill kept moving. Sikes wouldn't shoot him, he
knew. The man didn't want any more noise
messing up his plans. But if he was close enough,
Sikes wouldn't mind strangling a man to death
with his huge, bare hands, either. Bill deliberately hurried his steps.

In seconds, he was out of sight. Low-hanging
pine branches sheltered him, and the darkness
closed in behind him, leaving only two men on
the lonely mountainside.

"What now, Jim?"

"What d'ya think, ya fool?" Sikes started up
the path again. He didn't need Bill Moore. Hell,
he didn't need anybody. He'd get the woman,
stash her where Thompson had told him to, and
at the same time, prove his worth to Bennet.
Maybe then, Sikes told himself, he'd start getting
the kind of respect a man like himself deserved.
Grimly determined, he moved slowly, the only

sounds, his own labored breath and the occasional skitter of stones underfoot.

Al woke up immediately when a hand clamped across her mouth.

"Shhh . . ."

She realized then that it was her new partner's hand forcing her to be silent. Instinct kept her perfectly still while she gathered her wits and tried to figure out what was going on. Seconds ticked by as she realized that it was nearly dawn. Darkness was slipping away into the soft hush of morning twilight.

Instead of catching a quick nap as she'd intended, she'd slept all night. And worse, she'd slept the night away with her head on Travis's shoulder. Her eyes squeezed shut as she concentrated on the feel of the heavily padded fabric under her left cheek. A faint scent of tobacco and soap drifted to her, and his very nearness sent unexpected shimmers of heat rattling through her body. She ignored it. Obviously she hadn't had enough sleep.

Sleep!

That's a helluva good impression to make on a new partner, she told herself. Not only hadn't she awakened to take her turn at standing guard, she'd cuddled right into a perfect stranger and made herself at home. And this, despite the fact that she was harboring more than a few doubts about him.

"You awake?" he whispered, and she felt his breath brush across her ear.

Al nodded and raised her head to look up at

him. When he took his hand from her mouth, she asked quietly, "What is it?"

"Not sure. Noises coming from over there."

She frowned and glanced past him at the low line of scrub brush and the tangle of pines that swept along the far side of the mountain. She didn't see anything. And even as she strained to listen, Al admitted she didn't hear anything, either.

Maybe he was just jumpy. After all, a city man probably wasn't used to the night sounds heard out in the wide open. Hell, there was probably some critter in the trees, stalking breakfast. She opened her mouth to say as much, but stopped before speaking when a rustle of sound reached her.

Frowning, she glanced at Travis. His mouth was tight, grim. He looked at her and nodded, letting her know that *this* was the sound he'd heard.

That was no animal, she told herself. That rustling noise was the unmistakable scrape of fabric against brush. Someone was out there. Someone intent on being quiet.

And whoever it was, she thought, it was a sure bet they'd been sent by Bennet. Her heartbeat quickened and her senses sharpened instinctively.

Travis patted her hand gently, and when she looked up at him, he poked himself in the chest with one finger, then gestured at the mouth of the mine. Then he held up one hand, palm facing her, telling her silently to stay put.

Warily, she nodded. Maybe it would be best if he was in the mine and out of her way. If she didn't have to worry about looking out for him, she could get rid of whoever was trespassing on her property. A sinking feeling settled in the pit of her stomach. Even though she agreed with his idea, it surprised her just how much his cowardice bothered her.

Hell, it only brought home what she'd already suspected. That Travis didn't belong in Regret. Now, that momentary flash of warmth she'd felt at his touch seemed even more ridiculous. But she couldn't help wishing that he'd been just a bit braver about standing his ground with her.

Although, as her Da used to say, "If wishes were horses, beggars would ride."

She looked up into Travis's icy blue eyes and told herself she was imagining things when she thought she saw a brief flash of excitement. Fear was probably closer to the truth.

And who could blame him? He'd been in town hardly a day, and already he'd stood guard duty all night and was now trying to hide from what could be real danger.

At least for her. Chucker's words came rushing back, despite the fact that Al did her best to silence them. What if Travis *wasn't* in danger? What if he was working for Bennet? What if he knew exactly who was out in the trees and had already worked up a plan with them? After all, he'd been in town, alone, a long time the evening before. He could have met with anyone.

Made plans.

Made deals.

Travis frowned a silent question at her and Al shook her head, then waved one hand at him, telling him without words to go on into the mine.

He moved quietly for a city man, she thought absently. If she hadn't been watching him go, she wouldn't have been aware of any movement at all.

When he was safely out of sight, hidden in the shadows of the mine, Al shifted, pulled her shotgun into a more comfortable position in her lap, and settled down to wait.

Seconds crawled by.

She heard her own heartbeat and wondered how Travis was holding up. Was he cowering in a corner? Or, she asked herself, was he waiting impatiently for his friends to arrive?

Staring into the brush opposite her, Al held her breath and listened for the telltale sounds of movement. But there was nothing.

Minutes stretched out, and she thought about calling to the camp below. She could have some of her men up here in an instant. There was no reason why she should wait this out alone. But she wouldn't call for help, and she knew it even as the thought presented itself.

Most of the men who had stayed with her were probably loyal. But a few of them were no doubt ready and willing to sell out to Bennet— if they hadn't already. And she didn't dare run the risk of asking for help only to have her enemies answer the call.

No, she thought, she would face this alone. Just like she always did.

From directly behind her came the sound of a boot sliding across rock. Before she could so much as turn around, a thick, muscled forearm snaked around her neck and tightened.

"Surprise," a deep throated whisper rasped into her ear.

Al tried futilely to bring the shotgun up, but the big man holding her used his free arm to knock her weapon to the ground. Panic rocketed through her momentarily. Unarmed and grossly outweighed by her attacker, her chance at escape now rested solely with her new partner.

A sobering thought.

"I figured maybe you might've heard us earlier," Sikes whispered. "That's why we circled around and come in the other way."

Al's fingers curled around the man's arm and tugged ineffectually. It was like trying to lift a fallen tree off a road. For the first time in years, she wished that her fingernails were as long and sharp as her sister Maggie's. At least then she could gouge her captor up a bit. Instead, she twisted viciously in his grasp and tried to smack his face with the back of her head.

In response, his forearm tightened around her throat. Then he leaned backward, forcing her to her toes as she fought for breath. Eyes wide, she stared blankly at the tops of the pines and gasped futilely for air.

"You gonna behave now?" he grumbled.

Al's eyes closed as she felt darkness swirling in around her. Her head began to pound. Her lungs were going to burst. She needed air. Stiffly, she nodded.

The pressure loosened slightly, and Al dragged great gulps of air into her chest. She'd never realized before that clean, fresh air had a taste and a scent all its own. Now she inhaled it, gratefully, hungrily.

"You shouldn't have pointed that gun at me yesterday," the voice said.

Al hadn't needed the reminder. She'd known almost immediately who it was holding her. Not only by his size and the straggly beard scraping against her face, but by the rolling thunder of his voice ... even in a whisper.

"Bet you're sorry now, though, huh?" he asked.

She nodded. Al was sorry all right. Sorry she hadn't shot him when she'd had the chance. And if she got the opportunity again, she'd take it. The hell with worrying about back shooting.

"Too late for sorry," he said, and briefly closed off her air again, just to remind her who was in charge now.

After only an eternity-filled moment or two, he allowed her to breathe again. Rage bubbled in Al's chest, but there was nothing she could do to ease it. All she could hope for was that the big man might let his guard down for a second. She wouldn't have much of a chance against a man his size without a gun ... but any chance was better than none.

"Taylor," the fat man's whispered shout splintered Al's hopes. Against two men, her slim chance dissolved to none.

From the corner of her eye, she watched as a slighter man scurried into view. She remembered this man, too, from the confrontation in the mine, and wondered if the third man was also out there in the pines, waiting.

At the same time, despite the situation, Al felt a small curl of relief unwind in her belly. If

Travis was working for Bennet, surely the fat man would have called out to him for help, too.

But then something else occurred to her. If Travis wasn't in league with these men . . . where the hell was he?

Hiding?

Was he really going to stand by and watch these two manhandle her? All to save his own miserable, dandified hide?

"Grab her feet," the fat man ordered, and Taylor ducked his head in a short nod.

Instantly, Al stopped thinking about Travis. If she wanted to get out of this in one piece, she told herself, obviously, she'd have to save herself. So she'd damned well better pay attention to what was happening and wait for her chance.

It wasn't a long wait.

The smaller of the men hurried in front of her and bent to grab her legs. Just before he could, though, Mary Alice brought her right leg back and up, kicking him, hard. The toe of her boot caught the little man right under his chin and sent him tumbling, ass over end. He landed with a solid *thump* and lay sprawled out, unmoving, on the rocky ground.

"Bitch!" The fat man tightened his forearm again, and this time, when the darkness quickly narrowed her vision, Mary Alice saw stars dancing before her eyes. As if from a great distance, she heard the big man's rough voice again. "I'll show you who the hell's in charge here, you Irish whore!"

A hollow sounding, sickening thud cut the big man's words short. His grip on her throat loosened, and when she felt him release her, Mary Alice stumbled away from him. Her hands at her bruised throat, she turned and watched her captor drop limply to the dirt.

# Chapter 6

**"W**hat took you so damned long?"
He knew she'd meant to shout at him, but her voice hadn't been able to manage more than a derisive croak.

Travis stared at her for a long minute, allowing his rage to subside as he reassured himself that she was all right. His fingers tightened briefly around the rock he'd used as a weapon, before letting it drop to the ground. He flicked a glance at the huge, still form at his feet and only barely managed to keep from kicking the unconscious man.

Though it had been his own idea, hiding in that damned mine while Mary Alice met those two alone had almost killed him. Logically, he knew it had been the right thing to do. If they'd stayed together, the two men would have held all the cards in this little game. There would have been no way for Travis to help her.

And yet, hiding was something completely foreign to his nature. He wasn't a man to be found cowering in a corner in times of trouble.

Hell, it was more like him to go hunt it down and bring it home on his own terms.

Until now.

Briefly, he remembered the helpless rage he'd felt while watching that son-of-a-bitch slowly strangle Alice. Travis recalled the instinctive grab he'd made for the pistol, normally strapped to his hip, and the momentary panic he'd felt when he'd found nothing there.

Travis Delacort carried a gun.

Travis *Deal* carried a goddamned Derby.

Except for the practically useless derringer he had tucked into his waistband at the small of his back, he was unarmed. The small-caliber two-shot weapon wouldn't do him a damn bit of good unless he was up close—and then, he'd better not miss.

Any gun smaller than a shotgun probably wouldn't bring the bigger of the two men down.

His brain racing, searching for a plan—*any* plan, Travis had wanted to shout when he saw Alice's well-placed kick take care of the smaller of the two men. Then, it had taken him only another moment or two to find a good-sized rock and bring it crashing down on the fat man's empty head.

And as satisfying as it had been to watch the man slump over and fall to the ground, the rage still simmering inside Travis would have been better fed by a bullet. Instead, he stepped over the unconscious man's still form and went to Mary Alice's side. Her fingers clutching around her throat, she continued to draw long, deep breaths.

She glanced at each of the fallen men before

lifting her gaze to Travis. To his credit, he didn't even flinch at the fury he saw in her meadow green eyes.

"What the hell's wrong with you, anyway?" she said, and winced at the pain. "Were you waitin' for him to finish chokin' me to death before you stepped in?"

"I had to wait for the right time," he shot back.

"*Any* time would've been all right for me!" She swallowed heavily, stretched her neck, and glared at him again. "He damn near killed me!"

"But he didn't." Travis's hands curled into helpless fists. Goddammit. Couldn't she see what it had cost him to wait? No, his mind answered, she couldn't. And why should she? She didn't know him from Adam.

Hell, this whole situation was crazy, he told himself. He was nothing more than a paid bodyguard for a woman who looked as though she could pretty much take care of herself. Why the hell he'd been so damned worried about her in those few, frantic moments was beyond him.

All he knew for sure was that the idea of those men putting their hands on her had driven him into a blinding fury.

For her sake ... hell, for *his* sake, he had to stop the wild ideas riding him. With that thought in mind, he kept his voice steady. "If I hadn't waited for the proper time, we would both have been captured."

"Yeah." She nodded grudgingly, but couldn't quite hide the disgust in her tone. "I guess *when* you did it doesn't really matter much now, anyway."

Oh, Travis thought, it mattered, all right. In

fact, everything about this mattered a hell of a lot. *Somebody* had paid those two to come in and carry Mary Alice off. Why? Why kidnap her? Why not just kill her outright?—Not that he wasn't grateful, mind you. But it was curious. He scowled and glanced over at the smaller of the two men, when a deep throated groan erupted from him. Travis had a feeling that Thompson's boss was behind all this. And he would be damned if he didn't find out exactly why.

"Do you know them?" he asked abruptly.

"No." She shrugged and glanced from one fallen man to the other. The man she'd kicked moaned again and curled up into a tight ball in the dirt. Alice smiled. "Not their names, anyway."

"What do you mean?"

"Oh, you might say we 'met' yesterday."

"Tell me," he ordered, and ignored the flash of curiosity he saw in her eyes.

As she talked, telling him about her encounter in the mine, he felt the knot inside him get tighter and tighter. He heard what she wasn't saying, too, though he doubted very much that she would appreciate the fact that he *knew* she'd been frightened by those three men.

Three.

His sharp, quick gaze swept the edges of the clearing, looking for any sign that the third man might even now be hiding, biding his time.

Mary Alice followed his line of vision, and when she'd finished her story, added, "I know what you're thinkin'. But I don't think he's out there."

"We don't know that, though, do we?"

She stiffened slightly at his tone. "Not for sure. But of the three of them, he was the one most ready to walk away." She shrugged halfheartedly. "My guess is, he's halfway to hell and gone by now."

Travis told himself that she was probably right. That missing man wouldn't be hanging around now that their plan was ruined. Of course, they couldn't be sure of that unless someone went out and searched for the man. But Travis wasn't about to leave her alone. She'd already been near strangled. That was more than enough for one day, he figured.

As a bodyguard, he'd been pretty much worthless so far, Travis silently acknowledged. But, by damn, he was going to find out what the devil was going on in Regret. Or he was going to die trying.

Either way, he wasn't going to sit back and let Mary Alice Donnelly be a target again.

"I need a doctor."

Both of them turned as one to stare at the man Alice had kicked. His features twisted into a mask of pain, he glanced at them, then moaned again, louder this time.

"You're all right," Alice said.

"The hell I am," the man called Taylor answered. "I think you broke it."

Alice frowned. "Broke what?"

"What you kicked," he answered on another groan of misery.

Alice's eyes widened and her mouth fell open. A small smile curved Travis's lips as he watched her. In the uncertain, early morning light, he couldn't be sure. But he would be willing to swear that Mary Alice Donnelly was *blushing*!

She recovered quickly, though.

"Serves you right!" she said, and avoided looking at Travis. "Maybe you'll think twice about attackin' a woman again!"

The groaning man tipped his head back to look at her. "You ain't no woman! No woman would do somethin' like that to a man. You're some kind of she-cat straight outa Hell!"

Alice sucked in a quick breath as if she'd been slapped.

Travis looked at her and saw that the man's words had hit her hard. Why should she care what that fool thought of her?

There were shadows in her eyes and a tightness around her mouth that hadn't been there before. She stood stiffly, as if a pole had been rammed down the back of her shirt, and as he watched, she lifted her chin defensively.

"It's not broken," Travis said quietly.

"It feels broke!" the man wailed.

"If you don't quit your whining now," Travis went on, his gaze locked on Alice, "I can certainly guarantee that it *will* be broken. Soon."

Taylor quieted down instantly.

Al's stance relaxed a bit, and she glanced at Travis briefly. He thought he saw gratitude shining in her eyes, but he didn't remark on it. All he said was, "Do you have any rope?"

"Rope?"

The look in her eyes told him that she was still shaken from her brief ordeal. Not to mention Taylor's baiting. He couldn't really blame her, either. Hell, even *his* insides were still stormy. It wasn't fear or shame haunting him, though.

It was pure, raw, pounding anger.

"We'll need rope to tie these men up before we take them to your town sheriff."

She snorted a choked laugh, then winced at the accompanying pain. "There *is* no sheriff."

"What?" Dammit, what next?

"This is still a mining camp, Travis," she said. "A little older than most, but no more settled. The only law here is a miner's court."

Shit! Travis's temper boiled, but he managed to keep it from showing in his voice. "Then where do we take them?"

She shrugged. "Haul 'em into town, I guess."

"I'll take them."

"You're new here," she said quickly. "I'll go."

"You stay in camp," Travis argued quietly. "These two here were after you, remember. Why give whoever's behind this another chance?"

She inhaled sharply and chewed at her bottom lip for a moment or two before nodding. "All right. You take 'em. But Hank and George go with ya."

"Fine." Hardheaded she might be, he told himself, but at least she could see reason. "Once in town, then what?"

"Talk to G. W. Tell him to call a meeting for tonight. We'll let the judges decide what happens to these two."

Judges.

Travis shook his head in disgust. The judges here wouldn't be men of law. They would simply be other miners, elected by the citizens of Regret to do a job that none of them wanted. He'd seen it so many times before, it was a wonder he hadn't figured on encountering miner's law here. But somehow he'd thought that a mining town as settled as Regret would have finally decided to put out enough money to hire a sheriff and build a proper jail.

But it appeared that like all fortune seekers everywhere, the miners in Regret didn't want to part with any of their hard-won money. Mining towns were notorious for quick trials and even quicker sentencing. Not only did the men refuse to pay for a sheriff or jail, they weren't about to waste mining time on guarding prisoners.

Jesus! Miner's court. There was no telling at all what kind of sentence would be handed down. Travis had known men to be hanged because they'd been heard planning to steal gold. The judges at that particular camp had called it a "preventive hanging." He'd also known murderers to waltz out of court free men, without any worries at all. No witnesses, no case.

A cold, hard knot of remembrance settled in his chest, and he had to fight to draw a breath. Where there was no law, there was only misery. He'd learned that lesson the hard way, and it wasn't something he was likely to forget.

"Go on down to camp," Al said suddenly, and he looked at her, blinking away the memories. "Tell Chucker you need some rope for these two. I'll stay here and watch 'em."

His hesitation must have shown on his face, because she spoke up again quickly. "The big one's unconscious, Travis." She jerked her head at the man curled up like a baby in the womb. "That one's not goin' anywhere."

"For now."

She bent at the waist and snatched up her

shotgun. The quiet *click* of the twin hammers being drawn back echoed around them.

"If they *do* try to move," she promised him softly, "it'll be the last time."

Travis's gaze swept over her, and he couldn't stop the swell of admiration that washed over him. This was some kind of woman, he told himself. She was everything Kevin had ever said and more. She deserved a hell of a lot better in life than a hole in the ground and a pretend partner.

She deserved some man to come along who would look past her temper and her strange clothes, to the woman he'd just glimpsed. She deserved to be treated like a lady and to be told—often—how pretty she was.

Travis frowned thoughtfully. Dammit, she *was* pretty, once you got past all the buckskin and temper. But even more than her looks, he admired the quiet dignity she carried herself with.

"What's wrong?" she asked, shifting uneasily beneath his steady stare.

"Nothing," he lied. "I'll be as quick as I can." Without another word, he turned and headed down the winding path toward camp.

Early afternoon sun settled over Regret like a worn blanket. Half-built structures teetered precariously in the wind, and the uneven music from several out-of-tune pianos was nearly drowned out completely by the noise of hammers being swung against wood.

Risk takers. A whole town full of risk takers.

Cutter's instincts made his palms itch to be seated at a poker table. He looked around the small, sprawling town and instead of the mud and congestion, he saw . . . opportunity.

"It's a grand little place now, isn't it?" Sean said, thoughtfully.

"I don't know that 'grand' is the word for it," Cutter said wryly.

"Well now, there's grand . . ." Sean's eyebrows danced above his sharp blue eyes. "And there's grand. I'll wager a man could make his fortune in a spot like this."

"Make it or lose it," Cutter replied.

"Aye well, that's true an' all," Sean nodded, and let his gaze slip across the crowds. "Now what d'ya suppose the two of them've done?" he said on a low whistle.

Cutter turned to look where Sean pointed. Two men, one far bigger than the other, were seated on the boardwalk outside the Mercantile, both of them tied fast to the hitching posts. The huge, bearded prisoner was shouting insults and threats at the passersby who dared laugh at his predicament.

As they rode past the prisoners, Sean shook his head. "If this is what Mary Alice has been dealin' with, it's a wonder she didn't send for us sooner."

"Al's head is as hard as the rocks in the Four Roses Mine," Cutter said thoughtfully. "I'm surprised she sent for us at all. The fact that she *did* worries me. If Al feels like she can't handle this herself—"

"Aye," Sean cut him off. "I get your meanin'." He reached up and pushed one hand impatiently through his night black hair. "We best hurry on, then, and find her."

"Yeah." Cutter threw one last look at the two

men hog-tied to the hitching posts. A nagging, troublesome feeling began to creep through him. Cutter had learned long ago to listen to his hunches. And this hunch told him that real trouble was coming.

Travis stepped out of the saloon and paused on the boardwalk. His gaze slipped over the main street of Regret, and it didn't surprise him a bit to see that a couple of new, ramshackle structures had been built overnight.

Like mining towns everywhere, Regret was growing in leaps and bounds. And it wasn't just miners flooding into the town. It was all of the vultures who made their living fleecing hard-working men of whatever gold they were able to scrape out of the earth.

Gamblers, saloon keepers, fancy women—anyone who could smell the scent of money in the air sooner or later landed in a mining town. And with those who would work for their money came men like Rafe Bennet and Thompson. Men to whom stealing came easier than working.

Travis scowled into the afternoon sun and turned his head toward the Mercantile. His gaze narrowed as he studied the two men tied to the hitching rail outside G. W.'s establishment. He might have felt better about this if he could have gotten Sikes and Taylor to talk to him about who had hired them. No doubt it was the same person behind Thompson. How many people, after all, in a town the size of Regret, would be after the Four Roses mine?

But despite his best efforts, the two men hadn't said a word about whoever was behind them.

Then again, Travis told himself, it was hardly likely that the person in charge of the attacks on Alice would be sharing his thoughts with a couple of hired thugs like Sikes and Taylor.

Actually, he couldn't imagine any halfway competent thief hiring two such inept men. Unless, of course, it was on the theory that Sikes and Taylor were expendable. Travis's eyebrows lifted at the thought of an opponent so cheerfully cold-blooded.

As he watched, Sikes shouted curses at a miner who stood nearby, laughing at his predicament. Travis shook his head and turned away. At least he knew that the two men wouldn't be escaping.

With no jail in town and no one volunteering to keep an eye on the prisoners, it had been decided to let the entire town watch over them until the miner's court presided that evening. Coils of rope wound around each of the men, binding them tightly to the thick wooden posts.

G. W. had provided the rope and assured Travis that he would call the miners together for a trial that very night.

And still Travis wasn't satisfied. He wouldn't be, either, until Sikes and Taylor were far enough away from Al that they couldn't be counted as a threat anymore. Not that getting rid of two men would end the trouble. No, there was still Thompson and his boss. But at least, he told himself, it would thin the crowd of suspects a bit.

Suspects. He laughed inwardly. Hell, he was thinking like a marshal again. Maybe it was true what folks said: "Once a lawman, always a lawman." Then a curl of memory unwound through him and Travis stiffened. No. Whatever else he was, he wasn't a marshal anymore. Hell, if it came down to it, he wasn't much of anything anymore.

Someone brushed past him and Travis heard the muffled laughter directed at him. Frowning, he stepped off the boardwalk into the muddy street and promised himself that he would get rid of his disguise. Soon.

He was going to be needing every advantage he could get in dealing with the trouble surrounding Al. And in his present disguise, he wasn't very intimidating. Travis couldn't shake the feeling that the town of Regret was a stick of dynamite with a fuse already lit and burning fast. Unless Travis figured this out pretty damned quickly, the whole place was likely to blow—taking Mary Alice Donnelly along with it.

He reached up and plucked off his derby. Holding it in one hand, he brushed the upturned brim with the sleeve of his coat. Ridiculous looking hat he told himself. Once this mess was completed, he was going to take real pleasure in dropping that damned bowler into the nearest fire.

"Travis!"

He stiffened, his fingers tightening on his hat brim, and he half turned toward the voice shouting his name.

"Hey, Travis!"

His gaze swept over the teeming crowd of people and settled on a man riding a huge black horse. The man rode steadily closer, a wide grin on his face.

"Son-of-a-bitch!" Travis muttered.

# Chapter 7

**M**ary Alice tossed the blanket off her cot and threw it to the ground. Then she picked up her pillow, looked underneath it and, disgusted, dropped it again. Muttering to herself, she turned a slow circle, letting her gaze sweep over the inside of her tent.

As a home, it wasn't very impressive. A cot, an old steamer trunk that Rose Ryan, the Donnelly family housekeeper, had given her to keep her clothes in, and a couple of crates that made do as chairs.

Briefly, she compared her living quarters to those of her sisters. Maggie's place at the saloon was grand, with silks and laces and a wardrobe stuffed with more dresses than one woman could wear in a lifetime. Frankie—or Frannie, as her new husband insisted on calling her—had a cozy room at the hotel with a fireplace, good books, and handmade quilts to throw on her overstuffed bed. And the youngest, Teresa . . . hell, she had the whole damned, family-owned ranch to call her own these days. Although, Al reminded herself, Teresa never had been happy staying on the ranch. For as long as Al could remember, the youngest Donnelly sister had been trying to come up with ways to talk herself off that ranch and into the city.

Yet even with her complaining, Teresa had more of a home than Al did. Not that she minded overmuch. In fact, living in a tent had never really bothered her. Except for the winter times, when the cold and snow forced them all to build wooden shacks that were never strong enough to last from one winter to the next. At least, it had never bothered her until lately.

But who could blame her? Everything was changing. Hell, in the last couple of months, two of her sisters had up and got married! Until two months ago, it had been the four Donnelly sisters—and their father Kevin, of course—against the world. Now, all of a sudden, Maggie and Frankie were bound to husbands.

And *who* did they marry? The very men that Kevin had sent to them as new partners in their shares of the family businesses.

This was all Da's fault. What had he been thinking, selling out his share of the saloon and the hotel? Had he been *trying* to break up the family? Al shook her head firmly. No, that wasn't it. No one believed more strongly in the togetherness of family than Kevin Donnelly. Why, it was the one thing he'd burned into his daughters' minds as they were growing up. *Family comes first*.

So it had to be something else. "Maybe," she said softly, "maybe Da is just hell-bent on gettin' himself some grandchildren."

Al frowned and glanced into the sliver of mirror hanging from the center tent pole. She studied her green eyes and noted her sunburned nose and the wild, flyaway hair that had escaped her braid.

She half laughed and sobered immediately. If that was it, she told herself, he was in for a disappointment as far as she was concerned. Not that she wasn't happy the way she was, Al thought. But she was hardly the kind of woman to send a man screaming for a preacher. And if her Da thought that sending her a new partner would end in a marriage ... well, he was doomed to disappointment. Of course, her situation was a bit different from Maggie's and Frankie's. What with all the trouble brewing in Regret, Al had finally wired her father and *asked* him to hurry up and send her some help.

"That'll teach ya," she told her reflection. "Ask Da to send ya a partner—one who's good with a gun—and who d'ya get? A fancy man who faints at the sound of gunfire."

Although, she had to admit, Travis had been handy enough when she'd needed him. If he hadn't been there to bash Sikes over the head with that rock, she wouldn't be standing in the middle of her tent right now, trying to find her blasted hairbrush.

Her gaze shifted slightly, and she spotted the carved, rosewood brush lying on the ground beside her open trunk, partially hidden beneath a spill of shirts and pants. She held it in one hand while, with the other, she untied the string of rawhide at the end of her braid. When her hair was loose and finger combed to separate the thick auburn ropes, she began to brush and tug at the knotted mess.

Bending to one side, Al let her mind wander as her hands performed the familiar chore. Much to her own disgust, her thoughts wandered only as far as Travis Deal.

An unusual man, she told herself. He looked no more than a city fella, hopelessly out of place. But occasionally she'd seen a flash of something unexpected in his eyes. Something that told her perhaps there was more to the man than he was letting on.

She scowled slightly and tugged on a particularly stubborn knot. There was his clothing to consider as well, she told herself. He looked to be a skinny thing, practically swimming in his own jacket. But she'd spent an entire night with her head on what she'd expected to be a hard, boney shoulder, only to discover that Travis's jacket had enough padding to make up a good-sized pillow.

Al frowned at her reflection. "Now why would a man want to drown himself in clothes too damned big for him? Hell, even a city man should have more sense than that." A wry smile chased the frown from her features. Except for her father and a few select others, she'd never known many men to have much sense.

And there was the way he looked at her, too. Not like most men, dismissing her with an amused glance—but almost as if he was seeing past her outside, right into her soul.

"Now's not the time to be getting fanciful, my girl," she said to the bemused woman in the mirror. Then she studied her loose, wavy hair criti-

cally. Turning her head first one way, then the
other, she watched as the unbound mass rippled
and shimmered over her shoulders.

Idly, she wondered what Travis's reaction to
seeing her hair down and soft might be. She'd
hardly had time to entertain the notion when a
shout from the camp caught her attention. Grabbing up her shotgun, Al ducked under the tent
flap and stepped outside.

"Look at you," Cutter drawled as he walked
a slow circle around Travis. "Sean, would you
believe me if I told you that standing here in
front of you was one of the most feared U.S. marshals in the country?"

"Well, now," the big Irishman hedged, rubbing his chin thoughtfully, "I'd have to say that
you were havin' me on, Cutter."

Travis gave him a sour smile.

"And I wouldn't blame you, brother." Cutter
laughed again and shook his head. "Jesus,
Travis. What in the hell has happened to you?"

"You about finished?" Travis asked tightly.

"About." Cutter laughed again and came to a
stop directly in front of him. "What's goin' on?
Why'd you drag us out of town to talk? And
why in God's good name are you dressed up like
a farm boy hitting the city for the first time?"

Travis glanced at his surroundings, satisfying
himself that the three of them were indeed alone.
Of course, any number of people—including the
gunfighter Thompson—could have seen him
leaving town with Cutter and Sean. If they had,
they would wonder, naturally, how a new man
in town happened to have friends dropping by.

But they wouldn't be able to have any of their thugs listening in.

At least, he thought gratefully, Hank and George had already returned to camp. God knew, he'd have had a helluva time trying to explain to the two miners how he knew Cutter. He gave another quick, furtive glance at his surroundings.

Here, in the woods not far from camp, they could talk unobserved. The pines were thick, with scrub brush growing up along their trunks. The only sound was the wind whipping through the needle-laden limbs of the trees and the two horses chomping steadily at the sparse grasses.

Hardly sparing a look at the man called Sean, Travis quickly told Cutter exactly why he was there and why he looked such a fool.

"It's you?" Cutter asked, clearly dumbfounded. "*You're* Al's new partner?"

Travis's gaze narrowed. "You know Al?"

"Too well, my friend," Cutter laughed. "She's my wife's sister."

"And mine," Sean echoed.

Travis looked from one to the other of the two men. The big Irishman was unknown to him, and he hadn't seen Cutter in five years. Not since the night he'd saved the gambler's life. Hell, if it hadn't been for him, Cutter wouldn't be standing there now, laughing at him.

Made a man think, he told himself wryly.

"How did you come to meet Kevin?" Cutter asked.

"About ten years ago," Travis told him. "Some drunken cowhands were trying to relieve him of his wallet. I changed their minds for them."

Cutter gave him a slow grin, then winked at Sean.

"Travis, here, has a knack for being in the right place at the right time. Saved my bacon a few years back." At Sean's questioning glance, Cutter went on briefly. "A certain poker game went my way once too often, and my opponents decided that treating me to a dance at the end of a rope was the answer." He rubbed his neck thoughtfully. "Thankfully, Travis happened to be in that saloon as well."

Sean gave Travis a long, approving look.

"It was a long time ago, Cutter."

"Not so long that I don't remember it every time I shave," the gambler shot back. "I'm real fond of this neck of mine."

Travis watched the other man and let his mind drift into the past. After escaping that saloon, he and Cutter had ridden together for a few weeks. Travis had enjoyed the company. Even for a solitary man, weeks on end of having no one to talk to but a horse gets a bit wearing. And when the two of them had finally gone their separate ways—Cutter off to the next poker game and Travis after the next fugitive—he'd discovered that he'd actually missed having a friend around.

Maybe, he told himself, *that* was when the unceasing travel of being a marshal had begun to bother him. Maybe that was when he'd first started to dream about settling down. Finding a place of his own, where he could stick his feet beneath his own table every morning at breakfast and know that he didn't have to leave.

Immediately, a voice in the back of his mind spoke up, reminding him that he hadn't quit the marshal's service because of the travel. Or the loneliness. Or the rootlessness. He'd quit because he'd failed. Failed to protect someone who had been depending on him.

Travis inhaled sharply at the sudden ache of an old pain. It wouldn't happen again. Not this time. Kevin was counting on him to protect Mary Alice. And he wouldn't disappoint the man. But even as he thought it, Travis knew that wasn't the whole truth. It wasn't Kevin he was worried about letting down.

It was Al.

"Where's your badge, Travis?"

"Don't carry one anymore," he answered shortly, ignoring Cutter's surprised expression. Immediately, he asked a question of his own. "What are you doing here?"

"Al sent for us," Sean spoke up, and Travis looked at him.

"When?"

"The wire came yesterday morning," Cutter said, all traces of laughter gone from his features.

That was something, at least, Travis thought. She hadn't taken one look at him and decided to call in her family. She'd sent for her brothers-in-law before she'd even met him.

"What's goin' on around here, Travis?" Sean asked quietly.

"I'm not sure yet," he answered. "But I mean to find out."

Cutter nodded grimly. "We'll help any way we can."

"Then leave," Travis said.

"We only just got here, man!"

Travis looked at Sean again. "I don't want to

have to be thinking about the two of you and where you are and who's following you. It'll be better . . . *easier*, if it's just me and Al."

Cutter straightened up. "We can take care of ourselves, Travis. No one's asking you to do it."

"I've not needed a nursemaid for a good long time," Sean threw in.

"I just got here myself," Travis argued. "I need time to figure out what's happening here. What I don't need is two more people tossed into this mess."

"You're good, Travis," Cutter said softly. "But no man's good enough that he can't stand some help now and again."

"Not this time."

"Look, this is Al," the gambler went on. "She's family. I've known her since she was a kid. She's my wife's sister for God's sake."

"And mine," Sean spoke up just as heatedly.

"But she's *my* responsibility," Travis told them both solemnly. "It's up to me to keep her safe. To find out what's going on around here and stop it."

"Dammit, Travis!" Cutter shoved his hands in his pockets. "I am *not* going back and telling Maggie that I just left Al here with her new partner."

"Frannie won't want to be hearin' *that*." Sean shook his head slowly. "I can promise ya."

"You said you wanted to help," Travis pointed out.

"And we will." Cutter glanced first at Sean, then looked back at Travis. Folding his arms across his chest, he asked, "Where's the best place in *any* town, for picking up information?"

Travis knew where this was leading, but he didn't see a clear way out of it. Grudgingly, he admitted, "The saloon."

"Exactly." A wide grin split the gambler's features. "And who better to spend his days in a saloon than a gambler? Hell, Travis, I can find out more in one afternoon than you could in a month of Sundays!" He waved one hand at his friend's outlandish costume. "Especially dressed like you are. It's a wonder to me these miners haven't strung you up yet, just for sport!"

Travis frowned.

"As for me," Sean put in, and waited until the two men turned to look at him. "I'll take a job in the mine. I've a strong back. And while I'm there, there'll be no funny business goin' on, I promise ya!"

"There!" Cutter nodded sharply at Travis. "It's settled. You watch out for Al, and Sean and I will help gather information and watch your flank."

"It won't take folks in town long to know that you two are related to her," Travis pointed out. Looking at Cutter, he challenged, "Just how much information do you think you'll be able to pick up then?"

Cutter shrugged, unconcerned. "Drunks still talk, Travis. They can't help themselves. Besides, even if Sean and I don't find out a damned thing, at least we'll be here. We can help protect Al."

Sean nodded grimly and crossed his huge arms over his massive chest.

Dammit, this hadn't been part of Travis's plans. But then, he hadn't actually had time to make a plan, either. Rubbing the back of his neck, he stared hard at the rocky ground. If there was a way to get rid of Cutter and Sean, he'd do it in a heartbeat. But to be honest, if they'd actually left when he'd told them to, he wouldn't have had much respect for them.

Still, Cutter was right about one thing. As a gambler he could claim a table in the saloon and stay there all day and all night. And while he was there, he would hear about everything that was happening in Regret. A western saloon was more than a place to quench a man's thirst. It was a place to talk. Men gathered, and with the help of raw whiskey and plenty of beer, their tongues were loosened. They passed on rumors. Someone, sometime, was bound to say something useful.

Even knowing that Cutter was related to Al.

And, Travis admitted silently, having the huge Irishman working at the mine would do a lot to ease his worries about Al's safety.

The tight coil of worry inside Travis began to loosen. This was probably for the best, he told himself. If he'd had Al to himself, he might have started entertaining all sorts of foolish notions. But now, with her family around her, Al would naturally turn to them, and Travis would be able to keep his mind on business.

"It's settled, then?" Sean asked abruptly.

"Well, Travis?"

He looked from one to the other of them. Slowly he nodded.

Sean sighed heavily. "That's a relief, I don't mind sayin'." He laughed. "If I'd tried to go home and tell Frannie that I'd left her sister in time of trouble, the woman would've flayed me alive!"

"Hah!" Cutter slapped the Irishman on the back. "Frankie's too new at losing her temper to be any good at it. Now, my Maggie's been at it for years, and I'm here to say, she's the most dangerous female on the Coast when her Irish is up."

Sean's deep, booming laughter shook the trees while he challenged Cutter's claim.

As he listened to the other men joke about their wives, Travis felt an unfamiliar stab of jealousy. Through the mock fear and the laughter, he heard the unmistakable thread of admiration and love that both Cutter and Sean had for their Donnelly women. The other men's obvious happiness only served to underscore the emptiness deep inside him.

Off and on over the years, Travis had run into Kevin and had heard all about the man's daughters time and again. And in each story told, Travis had listened especially for tales of Mary Alice. Strange, that even before meeting her, he'd been drawn to her. Her determination. Her stubborness.

Of course, he'd imagined her differently. He hadn't counted on her wild beauty. Or her figure. He hadn't expected her eyes to be such a deep, pure green. Kevin hadn't mentioned the soft spill of freckles across her nose and cheeks. Or the fact that her lips were full and soft and ripe for kissing. Of course, Kevin being her father, he wouldn't have noticed such things, anyway.

But even when Travis had envisioned Alice to be a rough talking, big boned, homely woman, he'd been half in love with her. Love? He laughed silently at the thought. How in the hell

could a man come to love someone he'd only
heard stories about?

But if it wasn't true, why had he jumped at
Kevin's request for help? Why had he left everything he'd known, dressed himself up as a fool,
and traveled hundreds of miles to come to the
aid of a woman he didn't know?

Curiosity. He was sure it was simple curiosity.
After years of listening to Kevin Donnelly's chat-
ter, Travis had only wanted to see if the man's
stories were true, or if it was just a case of good
Irish blarney.

And so far, God help him . . . there was no
blarney to Mary Alice.

Travis blinked away his thoughts and focused
on Cutter, when he realized the man was talking
to him.

"Let's get on to the mine, huh? I could surely
use some coffee."

"And somethin' to eat," Sean added, rubbing
one big hand over his flat abdomen. "I'm that
close to keelin' over from hunger, I am."

"Besides," Cutter broke in, "Al's expecting us.
If we don't show up soon, she's likely to go hunt-
ing us down with that shotgun of hers."

Sean shuddered dramatically. "Another good
reason for food. A man needs all his strength
when he's facin' down a Donnelly."

For the first time since meeting up with the
two of them, Travis laughed. "There I'd have to
agree with you. But before we go in, remember"—he shifted his suddenly serious gaze between the two men—"we met in town. You
don't know me except as Al's partner."

Cutter's eyebrows lifted and he rubbed his

palms together briskly. "This might even be fun," he said, flashing a quick grin at Sean.

Fun was not the word Travis would have used.

The shout came again as she stepped outside.

Al glanced up the path in time to see a cloud of dirt *whoosh* from the mouth of the mine. Five or six men raced out of the darkness and, when they were in the clear, bent over at the waist, coughing and choking.

Holding her shotgun tightly, Al ran up the path, her unbound hair streaming out behind her. Heedless of the rocks and twigs biting into the soles of her bare feet, she kept her gaze locked on the small group of miners. Several men from camp followed her, but she was well ahead of them. When she reached the still choking men, she slapped one of them on the back and shouted, "What happened?"

He lifted his head and looked at her through red-rimmed eyes. His face was covered with sweat-streaked dirt, and his bare, filthy chest was heaving in an effort to draw breath into his dust filled lungs. After a long moment, he managed to say, "Don't know for sure. Heard a creak, then a groan. We started runnin'. Think a timber snapped."

She glanced behind him at the slash of darkness marking the mine's entrance. Waving one hand in front of her face in an attempt to clear away the rest of the dust, she asked, "Is there anybody else inside?"

Another man looked up, braced his hands on his knees, and shook his head. "We went in first.

To check the drill holes. Set the charges."

Al nodded silently. That was something, she told herself. At least they didn't have to dig anyone out. But God alone knew what kind of damage had been done when the timber had given way. All it would take is one beam snapping and it could set the rest of them off. With a support beam missing, there was greater weight left on the remaining timbers. That weight would strain and push at the wooden beams until they, too, snapped, spilling thousands of pounds of rocks and dirt down into the tunnels.

Dammit, they had to get that beam replaced. Quickly.

Chucker pushed past her, carrying a bucket of water and a tin dipper. Silently, he began to move among the handful of miners, who took the water gratefully.

Looking around, Al stared into the faces of the men surrounding her. Expressions of concern, indifference, and even a few open displays of fear looked back at her. Tall, short, young, old, fat and thin. They were the faces of men she'd come to know in the last year and a half. Know and trust.

Until recently.

Who were they? she asked herself. Who were the ones only pretending loyalty to the Four Roses? Had one of them sneaked into the mine during the night and sabotaged that support timber? Did Bennet want her mine badly enough to kill to get it? And what good would the mine be to him if he caused a cave-in that shut the place down permanently?

"Al?"

She spun around and looked at Chucker.

"These men ought to go to their tents. Rest up."

"Yeah." Al nodded abruptly at the still gasping men. "He's right. Go on down to camp."

The first man she'd spoken to shook his head. "I'm all right, boss. I can help."

She wanted to believe him. A couple of months ago, she would have. Without question. But now? Now she couldn't take the chance. She'd have to go in on the repair crew herself, just to make sure no more "accidents" happened. And she would have to handpick the crew she'd take in with her.

Damn Bennet for coming to Regret. Damn him for endangering everything she'd worked so hard to build. Anger bubbled low in her stomach. She felt its warmth spread thoughout her body until the heat of it made her shake.

Her breath lodged in her throat, and the fine dust still swirling in the air burned her eyes. The group of men clustered around her suddenly seemed threatening. Al felt closed in . . . surrounded.

But she couldn't let the fear show.

Despite the uncomfortable sensations trembling through her, she forced a strained smile to her lips as she faced the men. She'd be double damned if she'd give the one responsible the satisfaction of seeing what he'd done to her. "It's all right, Mick. You go on down and rest. We'll take care of this."

A long moment later, he nodded and started slowly back down the rocky path to camp. The others followed behind him, each of them pausing long enough to glance at her. In sympathy? she wondered.

"You comin'?" Chucker asked.

"Not yet." A brief, hard wind blew up, lifting her dark red hair into a wild cloud around her head before letting it settle over her shoulders again to hang in a rippling fall down her back.

She swallowed back a choked half-laugh. Only moments ago, all she'd been thinking about was whether or not Travis would think her hair was pretty.

"No sense doin' anything today," Chucker insisted. "Might's well leave it till mornin'."

Impatiently, she reached up and pushed her hair back from her face. "Chucker, if we don't find out who's doin' all this, we might as well leave it—*forever.*"

"Hell, girl," the old man said. "Things'll work out. They always do." He frowned, and the deeply etched lines in his face shifted. "Where in tarnation's that new partner of yours? He oughta be here."

"Not much he could do," she muttered, sliding her gaze over the mouth of the mine.

"That ain't the point, girl. Hank and George've been back some time now. Where in hell is he?"

Al scowled off in the direction of town. "Still in Regret, I guess. Hell, I knew I should've taken those two into town myself."

"Ya can't do *everything.*"

"Why not?" she snapped.

He snorted a strangled laugh and shook his head until his sparse gray hair flew about his head. "Nobody never said you didn't have sand,

girl. When are those brothers-in-law of yours
comin'?"

"Should be here anytime, now."

"Good." Chucker scratched his beard thoughtfully. "Leastways then you can take it easy
some."

"Take it easy?"

"Sure. They can help and you can trust 'em."

Mary Alice shook her head. "Trust 'em, yeah.
But help? The only help they can give me is to
watch my back. They wouldn't be much good
around the mine."

"You don't know that."

"A gambler and a circus man?" Al tucked her
shotgun into the crook of her arm and started
back down the path to her tent. Chucker walked
alongside her. She studied their shadows as they
stretched out on the ground in front of them.
When she stepped on a good-sized rock, Al
winced as it jabbed into the arch of her foot, but
she didn't stop. She had bigger problems than a
sore foot.

Why had everything become so complicated?
Why couldn't her life have gone on as before?
Safe. Familiar. Mary Alice had spent her whole
life proving to people that she was as good as
any man. That she could take care of herself
without anyone's assistance.

She'd never needed anyone's help before. And
it irritated her considerably to admit that she did
now.

"Well why the hell had ya sent for 'em then?"
Chucker demanded.

Limping slightly, Al looked off into the distance. When her voice came, the old man had to strain his ears just to hear her.

"Because I don't have anybody else."

# Chapter 8

The moment he saw her, Travis felt his breath explode from his chest. She looked wild. Fierce. Like some ancient maiden warrior.

Her hair, released from its usual braid, flew out around her in a dark red cloud of abandon. Her proud features were set in a mask of grim determination, and even from a distance, he could see the rapid rise and fall of her bosom with each breath she took. Even the slight limp in her walk didn't detract from the overall image of strength.

Limp?

He frowned and hurried toward her, leaving Cutter and Sean to follow behind.

"What happened?" he asked when he was within a few feet of her.

Her features tightened. "An *accident* at the mine."

"I mean"—he waved at her right leg, and only then noticed that she was barefoot—"to *you?*"

"Oh." She shook her head and continued walking. "Stepped on something. It's nothin'."

121

Then her gaze slipped past him and he watched recognition dawn on her face. "It's about damned time," she shouted.

"Good to see you, too, Al," Cutter countered.

"We came as soon as we got your wire," Sean put in.

"She knows that," Cutter told him.

Travis listened to them for a moment, watching Alice try to hurry the rest of the way down the rock-strewn path. He watched her lips tighten with every step, and he knew her foot was bothering her more than she was saying. He also knew that she was going to go on, whether she was in pain or not.

Stubborn woman, he told himself as he stepped up beside her, bent low, and caught her stomach across his shoulder. As he straightened up, lifting her off her feet, she slammed her knee into his chest.

"Put me down, you fool!"

"At your tent," he told her on a groan, and locked one arm around the backs of her knees in self defense.

"Goddammit, Travis!" Still clutching her shotgun in one hand, Al braced her other palm flat against his back and pushed herself up. "I ain't some soft female that has to be fetched and carried everywhere."

He would have to argue with her there, he thought. The parts of her body now pressed against him certainly felt soft enough. And the faint scent of soap and woman enveloped him, making parts of his body feel as hard and unyielding as the ground beneath his feet.

"What about you two?" she demanded hotly.

"Ah, no, lass." Sean chuckled. "I wouldn't want to be crossin' such a mean lookin' man as that!"

A couple of the nearby miners hooted with laughter at *that* ridiculous statement. Grimacing, Travis kept going, ignoring everyone around him.

Alice slapped her palm flat against his back and shouted, "And you, Cutter! Are you just gonna stand there?"

Travis heard Cutter laugh quietly. "I never come between a woman and her partner, Al."

"Shoulda known you wouldn't be any good to me!" She plowed her elbow into the center of Travis's back and he grunted. "You always were more trouble than you were worth, Cutter! Never did see what Da saw in ya!"

By this time Travis was well past the crowd and headed for her tent. When he got there, he stepped under the flap, walked inside, and dropped her inelegantly onto the cot.

She landed heavily as the wooden legs snapped, sending both woman and cot crashing to the dirt.

"That's just fine, Travis," Alice said, throwing her hands high in the air and letting them drop into her lap. "Now where do I sleep?"

Green fire snapped in her eyes, and Travis met her glare for glare. He took note of her flushed face and rapid breathing and only just managed to keep from blurting out, With me.

His brain reeled at the idea. Hell, he was in no position to even be *thinking* such things. Once this job at the Four Roses was finished, he was leaving. There were other jobs. Other obligations waiting on him. Besides, she surely wasn't showing any interest in *him*.

He took a mental hold on his sudden desire and reached for her injured foot. "I have a spare cot," he said through clenched teeth.

"Let go!" She tried to pull her leg free, but he only tightened his grip. "Goddammit, I've got things to take care of, Travis. There's some kind of cave in at the mine. I've got to pick a crew to go in there tomorrow and sort things out."

"It will wait a minute or two," he said quietly, and took his time inspecting the bottom of her foot. There was no blood, so she hadn't been cut. But there was a huge bruise forming on her highly arched instep.

His thumb moved over her delicate anklebone, smoothing across her soft skin.

She gasped and Travis dropped her foot, reminding himself once again that he wasn't there for *his* sake. But he had to wonder why it was that he was suddenly so much more aware of the woman hidden beneath her brash exterior.

Alice pushed herself to her feet and hobbled across the tent to her boots. "You finished, Doctor?"

He half turned to watch her and rubbed his jaw viciously. He wanted to bury his fingers in her hair and draw her mouth close to his. His breath caught as he imagined Al Donnelly's lips parting for him, and he could almost feel the brush of her breath against his cheek.

Deliberately, he shoved his hands through his own hair and squeezed his skull in an attempt to rid himself of the suddenly overpowering desire to touch her.

Al sat on the corner of her trunk to pull her boots back on. He could feel her watching him.

"Mister, you just keep on surprising me," she said as she stamped her foot to adjust the fit of her boot.

"How is that?"

"The way you dress. The way you talk." She pulled her other boot on and stamped her injured foot into the worn leather. This time she sucked in a breath at the resulting pain. "And now this. I wouldn't have guessed you were strong enough to pick me up. Let alone carry me down that path."

That had been stupid, he had to admit. But dammit, when he'd seen her limping, he'd just naturally stepped in. He hadn't even stopped to think about what he was doing. Now, half the men in camp were probably wondering about him, too.

As she walked up beside him, Travis turned his head to meet her direct stare.

"Guess that means things ain't always what they seem, huh?" she asked.

Travis studied the suspicious gleam in her eye and knew he'd have to be more careful. This wasn't a woman who would blindly place her trust in any man. Partner or not.

Alice waited another half-second or so, then spun around and headed for the tent flap. Over her shoulder, she said, "I got a few things to say to my sisters' husbands. If you're comin' . . . come on."

Travis swallowed back his anger at being so handily dismissed, and tried to turn the tables on her. "Al?"

"Yeah?" She stopped dead and looked at him.

"Your hair looks very pretty like that."

Stunned, she blinked at him mutely.

Travis hid a smile as he passed her and stepped outside.

Bennet stood at the window, staring down at the two men still tied to the hitching post. He frowned thoughtfully as the bigger of the two shouted curses and insults at passersby. It seemed as though every miner for miles around had chosen that day to stroll the main thoroughfare of Regret.

How thoughtful of them to create such a noisy, confusing scene.

Behind him, the door opened. Rafe Bennet didn't even turn. He knew who it was. The man he'd sent for.

"Thompson?"

"Yes sir?"

"See to it that those men are gone before the miner's court convenes tonight."

"Gone, sir?"

"Gone." Bennet ran the tip of one finger along the windowpane, then checked it for dirt. Shuddering slightly, he reached inside his coat for a handkerchief, then scrubbed his fingertip clean again. "Arrange for their bonds to be cut and for them to escape into the crowd."

"You want them gone, *permanent*?"

Bennet shook his head once. "I want nothing to do with a killing. *Yet*. Death has a way of becoming very . . . untidy." Stepping away from the window, he walked slowly toward his desk, sparing only a quick glance at the man watching him. "Just make sure they are far away from here before this evening."

"Yes sir." The gunman stepped through the still open door into the hall and stopped abruptly at Bennet's calm voice.

"Oh, and Thompson . . ."

"Yeah?"

"You showed exceptionally poor judgment in hiring those two."

The man's features tightened slightly. "I picked 'em on purpose. Figured if anything went wrong and they ended up dead, nobody would miss 'em."

"You *figured* wrong."

"Yessir."

"Don't let it happen again."

The gunman looked into Bennet's cold dark gaze and felt something he hadn't felt in years.

Fear.

Shadows danced across the features of the four people gathered around the campfire. A mountain wind skittered through the flames, tossing a small shower of sparks skyward.

Cutter reached for a dry branch, snapped it against his bent knee, then carefully fed the fire. "Anybody could have cut those two loose, Al. The crowd in town was so blasted thick, it could have been any one of a hundred people."

"Nope," she said, staring hard at the fire. "It was Bennet."

"And ya say this Bennet fella is the one behind all the troubles plaguin' ya?"

Al glanced at Sean briefly and nodded.

"What makes you so sure?"

She frowned at Travis. "I told you what's been goin' on in Regret lately. And until Rafe Bennet showed up, there was no trouble. Well," she allowed, "except for some bar fights and a couple of shootings. But ever since Bennet got here, he's been busy stickin' his nose into everybody's business. He's got that hired gun of his, Thompson, scarin' off those he can't buy. He bought up all the land outside of town, waitin' for Regret to grow so's he can drive up the prices to whoever wants to buy a town plot for a store or somethin'."

"Buyin' up land's not illegal," Sean said softly. "Just a gamble."

"He's gambling that Regret will grow. And if it does, he has a right to make money off that land." Cutter shook his head and looked at her. "As for scaring people off . . . you don't know that he's behind that, Al."

"I do know it," she insisted, and shook her hair back from her face. "I just can't prove it."

"I'll admit," Travis said quietly, "your Mr. Thompson does seem the kind of man who wouldn't have a bit of trouble frightening people."

"He ain't my Mr. Thompson," she shot back.

Travis felt a swell of admiration rise up in him. How could a man not admire a woman like this? Backed into a corner, she stood her ground against all comers.

"But unless you have proof that he's working for Bennet, there's not much you can do about it."

"So this is why you're all here?" she demanded, and jumped to her feet. "To tell me what I can't do?"

"Sit down, Al."

"Shut up, Cutter!" Jamming her hands into the pockets of her buckskin pants, she kicked at the dirt around the campfire, sending a cloud of dirt flying up in Cutter and Sean's direction. "I don't know why in hell I sent for you two! Should have known you'd be no good to me."

"Dammit, Al," Cutter grumbled, and waved one hand in front of his face. "If you'll sit down so we can talk about this—"

"There's nothin' to talk about!" she snapped. "You don't believe me!"

"We believe ya, lass," Sean said on a cough. "We're only sayin' that we can't go marchin' into Bennet's office callin' the man a thief without proof."

Travis watched the three of them. Jesus, he told himself, if this was how the Donnelly family worked together, it was a wonder they had any businesses to run!

Alice and Cutter had been at each other's throats for nearly an hour now, and Travis saw no sign of it letting up any. At least, in between battles, Al had told them all about what had been going on in Regret. Her suspicions about this Rafe Bennet sounded pretty damned well founded, he thought.

Apparently, until Bennet had shown up in town, Regret and the mines surrounding it had been fairly quiet, all things considered. Of course, any mining town was going to be a lot wilder than some settled little farming community. But taken as a whole, Regret had been as law abiding as most, and a helluvalot better than some.

Until Bennet.

Before he'd hung up his badge, Travis had seen plenty of men like Bennet. Rich, unscrupulous, hungry for more money, more power, and not much caring how they got it. It was men like Bennet that made men like Thompson possible.

And men like Thompson made their own rules. Generally, they would take orders from whoever was paying them. But most of them had their own, private codes that they lived by. Travis had arrested men who wouldn't have thought twice about shooting a man in the back. But those same men wouldn't speak rough in front of a lady.

He frowned as Thompson's image rose up in his mind. What kind of man was this gunhand? Was he likely to get sick of Bennet and ride on? Or was he more liable to set up shop on his own and start making his own plans for Regret?

Hard to say, Travis knew. Hell, for a short time after he'd quit the marshals, Travis himself had hired his gun. Of course, he'd like to think he'd been a bit more particular about the wars he'd signed on for. But who knew, really? Maybe he'd only convinced himself of that to help him sleep at night. Not that he slept that well, anyway. He shifted uncomfortably as another, older memory intruded on his thoughts.

Forcefully, Travis pushed those ghostly images aside. He couldn't afford to remember. Not now. When the job was done, and he was satisfied that Alice was safe, he would ride on. Then the memories could return and show him the way back to hell.

"You are the hardest-headed woman I have ever met," Cutter shouted. "Why, Maggie's not a shade on you, and that's saying something, believe me!"

"Leave my sister outa this, Cutter," Al snapped. "This is between you and me. Like always."

"If ya want to know what I'm thinkin'—" Sean started.

"I don't!" Cutter and Alice spoke together, then turned to face each other over the fire again.

Ever since going into Regret for the trial, only to find out that the prisoners had escaped, Mary Alice had been a one-woman fireworks show. Her temper was on the boil, and she made no attempt at holding it back.

Travis glanced up at her and couldn't quite stop himself from thinking just how magnificent she looked. Fury etched into every line of her body, the firelight played over her features and glittered in her eyes, making her look like some mythic goddess wreaking vengeance on the non-believers.

But as much as he admired her guts, he knew that to keep her safe, he was going to have to find a way to calm her down. A wry smile lifted one corner of his mouth. Trying to cool her temper would be a lot like trying to throw a saddle on a cyclone.

But it might be interesting to give it a try.

"Somethin' funny, Travis?"

He looked up into her eyes and shook his head slowly. "Not funny, I assure you," he said, remembering to keep the hated, reedy note in his voice. "But as your partner, I must say I am disappointed in your emotional reaction to this situation."

"*What?*"

He felt Cutter's and Sean's gazes on him as he pushed himself to his feet. Ignoring both of them, he concentrated instead on the woman. If he was going to have to deal with Mary Alice, he preferred to do it standing. At least then, *she* would have to look up at *him*. Though tall for a woman, she was still a good deal shorter than his own six foot two. The top of her head hit him about chin level, and for the first time, he thought how she was just the right height to hold close in a heart-stopping kiss.

But as he looked into those eyes of hers, all thoughts of kissing her slipped away. At the moment, she looked as though she'd rather take a gun to him.

"Emotional, you said?"

"That's right."

"Well, goddammit, Travis!" She set both balled fists on her hips and leaned toward him. "Twice now, I had those sons-of-bitches come at me. The first time, I walked away 'cause I had a shotgun. The second time, if you hadn't been there, Lord knows what would've happened."

A brief spark of pleasure shot through him. At least she was willing to give him a little credit, here. The spark died in the next instant.

"Of course, you took your own sweet time about it," she snapped. "Now, *somebody* turned 'em loose and those fellas are out there." She waved one hand at the dark pines beyond the fire. "God knows where, doin' God knows what. I'll have to set up extra guards around the mine and be watchin' my back for who knows how long, and you don't think I should be so emotional?"

"We'll be watchin' your back, darlin'," Sean piped up.

She snorted derisively.

Cutter shook his head.

"If you want to stop what's happening around here," Travis pointed out quietly, "then you're going to have to stop shouting and start thinking."

"About what?"

"Your brothers-in-law and I"—he glanced at the two men briefly—"believe we've come up with an idea."

"Is that right?" Mary Alice, too, glanced at the other men before turning back to Travis. "And just when were you goin' to tell me about it?"

"Just as soon as you shut up for a minute," Cutter said.

She scowled at him.

If they waited for her and Cutter to stop sniping at each other, they'd be there all night. Determinedly, Travis started talking.

"Sean will work in the mine, keep an eye on things in there and try to discover who might be behind sabotage like what we experienced today."

Sean grinned and nodded when Al looked at him.

"What about you?" she asked, letting her gaze slide over to Cutter.

"I shall work the saloon," he told her.

"Figures."

He ignored her comment and went on. "I'll ask questions, listen, and hopefully come up with something on this Bennet you told us about, and his man Thompson."

"And just who's goin' to be willing to tell my *brother-in-law* anything?"

"With enough liquor in him . . ." Cutter smiled and inclined his head. "Or with enough luck at a card table, a man will talk to anyone about anything."

She scowled at the smug look on his face, but then said, "All right." Al turned back to Travis then, arms folded over her chest. "That leaves you, partner. What job do *you* get?"

"The toughest one," Cutter mumbled.

Travis smiled, tugged at the lapels of his hideous coat and gave her a half-bow. "My job is to be with you. To watch over you. In short, to do whatever you're doing. Be wherever you are."

She was quiet for a long moment. The snap and hiss of the fire sounded unnaturally loud in the hushed stillness. Travis felt Alice's thoughtful gaze and knew that in her mind he didn't shape up to be any sort of bodyguard. Well, he told himself, he was going to be guarding her, whatever she thought. But Lord knew, it'd be a sight easier if she went along with the plan.

At last, she nodded.

Travis thought he heard a sigh of relief from either Cutter or Sean, but he couldn't be sure.

"I guess I don't have much choice anyway," she said, completely shattering his pleasure in her agreement. "You *are* my partner."

It wasn't much of an agreement, Travis told himself. But he'd take it.

"Well, now," Sean said much too loudly, "as we have that settled, I'm off to bed." Clapping one hand to his behind, he admitted, "It's been awhile since I've spent so much time in the saddle." He glanced down at the man still seated by the fire. "You comin', Cutter?"

"Yeah." He pushed himself to his feet, but before following Sean to the tent they were sharing with a few of the miners, Cutter stopped beside Mary Alice.

She waited, poised as if for another battle.

Cutter gave her a smile and shook his head. "No more tonight, Al. I'm too tired to fight fair."

Travis watched as Alice slowly returned the gambler's smile.

"All right, then," she said. "We'll start fresh in the mornin'."

"Deal." Cutter bent forward and left a quick kiss on her forehead. "G'night, Al. Travis."

As he walked away, Mary Alice said softly, " 'Night, Cutter. Thanks for comin'."

He lifted one hand to let her know he'd heard her, but kept walking toward the line of tents.

Alone with her by the fire, Travis watched as Mary Alice tore her gaze from her brother-in-law, then tipped her head back to stare up at the night sky.

"It's a fine night," she said softly.

Travis didn't even glance at the stars. He preferred looking at her profile and the long, elegant line of her throat. "It is," he agreed.

"You prob'ly think we're half-wits, don't ya?" she whispered.

He chuckled, then answered her in a voice as soft as her own. "Perhaps not half-wits," he allowed.

Alice smiled, her gaze still locked on the heavens. "Just a bit demented, huh?"

"I think maybe 'different' is a better word."

She straightened up, inhaled sharply, then blew the air out of her lungs in a rush. "Different. Yeah, I suppose you could call us different." Turning her head slightly to look at him, she asked, "What's your family like, Travis?"

"I don't have a family," he admitted, and was surprised to hear that small truth slip out.

"No one?"

"No." He hoped she would let the subject end there. It might be hard to explain how an eastern man's relations came to be killed in a Comanche uprising in Texas. Besides, just thinking about the family he'd lost brought a sharp stab of pain that jarred the loneliness within him.

"I'm sorry," she said quietly, as if reading his mind. "Strange, but I can't even imagine how my life would be without my sisters and Da."

Inwardly, he admitted that his life, too, would have been emptier without his sharp-tongued sister. He imagined that he and she could really exchange some interesting stories. But this wasn't the time or place for that. Instead, he was thankful that she was apparently not going to question him further. Travis asked, "And Cutter? Can you imagine your life without him? Or Sean?"

She laughed shortly and lowered her gaze to the fire again. "Cutter. Seems we've been lockin' horns since I was a girl."

"You both appear to enjoy it."

"Now, maybe." She shrugged and tossed him a quick glance. "I guess the fightin' is more habit now than anything else. Of course," Alice confessed with a small smile, "we don't see each other too often anymore, either."

"He cares about you," Travis told her.

"Hell, I know that." While she talked, Alice reached up and began to twist a long, loose lock of hair around her finger. "But it doesn't make it any easier to listen to him when he starts in telling me what to do."

Travis watched, fascinated as her fingers slowly began to comb through her thick hair until it fell in long, rippling waves of dark fire down her back. He jammed his hands into his pants pockets to keep from reaching out and threading his own fingers into the shining mass. Silently, he asked himself what the hell he was thinking.

"Da didn't do you any favors when he sold you a share in this mine, Travis."

He pushed his wayward thoughts to the back of his mind. It sounded to him as though she was going to try and talk him into leaving again. And if that was her plan, it was better she find out right away that he had no intention of leaving.

"It doesn't matter. All that matters now is that I'm here and I'm staying."

She smiled to herself and shook her head gently, sending her hair into a dance of movement just above her hips.

"You're stubborn," she said. "I'll give ya that. And you've got nerve enough to stay put when your brain must be telling you to run for cover.

But you're staying here? That's not all that matters," she countered, and turned to face him. "Look, Travis, a man like you don't belong in a place like Regret. If you stay, you'll probably end up gettin' shot. Or run down in the street. Or beat up."

"Al—"

"All right," she cut him off, and held both hands up in mock surrender. "It seems you're no more likely to listen to me than I am to listen to Cutter. But, Travis, if you're dead set on staying, at least promise me you'll watch out for yourself."

He swallowed back a smile at her concern.

She frowned at him. "Da will never let me hear the end of it if something happens to you."

# Chapter 9

*Four Golden Roses Saloon*
*San Francisco*
*Two weeks later*

**E**lbows on the table on either side of the cup, Maggie propped her head in her hands and leaned over the coffee the bartender had just set in front of her. The rich aroma of freshly brewed coffee slowly began to sweep away the last of the cobwebs in her brain.

Warily, she lifted her head and opened one eye to glare at her sister, seated opposite her in a brilliant spill of sunlight. Frankie Donnelly Sullivan looked even more bright-eyed than she usually did. Her cheeks were flushed a deep rose, almost matching the color of the pink lace trimming the high collar and sleeve cuffs of her simple, dove gray dress. Her strawberry blond hair was styled in the fashion her husband, Sean, preferred—a loosely secured topknot with a few stray curls allowed to bounce around her smiling face—and there was a definite sparkle in her soft green eyes.

She stifled a groan. Even at this unholy hour. Frankie looked wonderful. Maggie knew bloody well what she looked like in comparison: Her copper colored hair, wild and tangled around her shoulders; her sea green silk wrapper, haphazardly tied around her waist; and her own green eyes, undoubtedly lined with red streaks caused by a lack of sleep.

"What have I told you about coming to the saloon this bloody damned early?" Maggie finally managed to say, and winced as the words scraped against her throat.

"I know, I know." Frankie grinned and reached across the poker table to pat Maggie's hand. "But, it's not that early, Maggie. It's nearly nine A.M."

Maggie snarled.

"What's going on down there?" a woman called out from upstairs.

"Fine," Maggie muttered as she hesitantly lifted the coffee cup to her mouth. "Just what I need. Another voice."

"It's only me, Teresa," Frankie yelled, ignoring Maggie's flinch at the shout. "I've got a letter from Sean."

Maggie blinked, swallowed a mouthful of coffee, and tried to sit up straight. Pushing her hair back from her face, she squinted into the sunlight streaming through the saloon's wide front windows. "Why didn't ya say so?"

Frankie's lips pursed. "You didn't give me a chance."

Light, quick footsteps sounded out on the

stairs leading to the second story living quarters above the saloon. "What does he say?" Teresa called out while she ran, "How is Al?"

"Quietly," Maggie murmured. "Speak quietly."

"She's fine," Frankie answered in, what seemed to Maggie, a deliberately loud voice.

"Joe, can I have some coffee, too?" Teresa shouted as she slid into a chair between her older sisters.

Maggie glanced at the youngest Donnelly daughter. Teresa had only been in town for a few days, with the excuse that she had wanted to be in San Francisco when word came from Mary Alice. But Maggie knew that wasn't the whole truth. Her youngest sister snatched at whatever reason she could find to leave the family ranch. It was a shame Teresa hated ranch life so much— she had a real talent for running the place.

Heaven knew, she kept country hours even while she was in the city. An early riser, she had the despicable habit of being cheerful in the mornings. Frowning just at the thought of it, Maggie let her gaze sweep over the youngest Donnelly. Dressed in a white silk blouse tucked into her dust colored, split riding skirt, Teresa wore her night black hair tied at the base of her neck and hanging loose down her back. Her deep blue eyes had the shine of a mountain lake, and her skin was tanned to the color of a ripe peach.

God, Maggie thought, it was enough to make her feel as old as the hills.

"You look dreadful, Maggie," Teresa commented as Joe brought her a cup of coffee.

The bartender snorted a laugh, and Maggie glared at him.

To her sister, she said only, "To look my best, I usually require more than four hours sleep."

"What's happenin'? Who is that down there? Is somethin' wrong? Oh, God save us, it's Al. Or no!" The new voice paused dramatically, then moaned gently, "It's himself. Kevin, your Da. He's dead."

"Not yet," Maggie said, more to herself than anyone else.

"It's me, Rose. Frankie. I've a letter from Sean."

"Praise the saints!" Rose Ryan called out. "I'm comin'. Don't say another word till I get there!"

Heavier footsteps sounded out on the stairs, and Maggie's head pounded with each one. Out of the corner of her eye, she saw Joe striding toward them, carrying yet another cup, but this time bringing the coffee pot, too.

He set it down in the center of the table atop a bar towel, then went back to work.

By the time Rose sat down, Maggie had poured herself more coffee and resigned herself to waking up.

"So what does the boy-o have to say for himself?" Rose asked. " 'Twas good of him to write." Rose glanced at Maggie and her eyebrows lifted. "Not like *some* I could mention . . ."

"Cutter doesn't write letters," Maggie said for what must have been the tenth time since both her husband and Sean had left for the mine.

"What about Al?" Teresa asked, ignoring the others. "How is she? And what about the partner Da sent her?"

Maggie flicked her a quick glance. Teresa had made no secret of the fact that she wouldn't stand for their father sending her a partner. Maggie and Frankie had each married the men Kevin had sent them, and Teresa wanted no part in their father's matchmaking.

"If you'll be still a minute," Frankie said, and pulled an envelope from her skirt pocket, "I'll read the letter to you."

A soft smile curved Frankie's lips as she pulled a single sheet of paper free and unfolded it carefully.

"Not much to say, has he?" Rose commented.

"Shh . . ." Maggie told her. "Go on, Frankie."

"Before I start . . ." Frankie paused and pulled another folded sheet from the envelope and held it out to her sister. "Cutter sent you a note, Maggie."

Stunned, Maggie reached for it. Slowly, she unfolded the paper and grinned down at its contents.

"What's he say?" Rose prodded.

"Everything," Maggie replied and showed the others what her husband had sent her.

"The King and Queen of Hearts?" Teresa asked.

Rose sniffed pointedly. "With all the schoolin' the man's had, you'd think he could take pen in hand and . . ."

Maggie shook her head, picked up the cards, and held them tightly between her palms. "He didn't have to." Meeting her sister's gaze, she smiled softly and said, "Go ahead, Frankie. Read the letter."

Still smiling, Frankie nodded, bent her head, and began to read.

" 'Frannie Darlin'—' "

"Why can't he call her Frankie like the rest of us?" Teresa wanted to know.

"Hush!" Rose snapped.

" 'Every day away from you seems a lifetime. Your sister's fine, though the way she and Cutter carry on, it makes me long for the peace and quiet of wartime. Cutter's working in the saloon, trying to find out who's behind Al's troubles. As for me, I'm lumbering about in the mine like a great bloody elephant, trying to stave off another cave-in.' "

"Another cave-in?" Rose interrupted.

Frankie went on. " 'Al's new partner Travis seems a good sort, though there's more to the story than I can say right now. One thing, though, it looks to me like Al's taken a shine to the man. Maybe good ol' Kevin has done it again, eh?' "

"Al?" Teresa gasped. "Taking a shine to her partner, too?"

"Quiet, Terry Ann!" Maggie said sharply. "I want to hear this."

"Don't call me that!" Teresa snapped.

"Shh . . ." Rose frowned at her.

"What else does he say?" Maggie wanted to know.

"Uh," Frankie hesitated and her cheeks flushed a deep, dark red. "Most of the rest is . . . personal."

Rose smiled fondly. "A good lad, Sean is."

"Is there nothing else?"

Frankie looked at Maggie and nodded. "At the end here, he says, 'We hope to finish up soon, love. Tell Maggie that Cutter's missing her, and say hello

*for us to Teresa and Rose. I'll write again soon. All
my love, Sean.'"*

Rose lifted one corner of her apron to dab at
her eyes. "Haven't I always said he's a fine lad?"

No one answered her.

"So they'll be gone still longer," Maggie said
thoughtfully.

"Certainly sounds like it." Frankie sighed.

Teresa jumped to her feet so quickly, her chair
toppled over and clattered to the floor. The three
women at the table stared at her.

"Didn't you hear what he said? Al has 'taken
a shine' to her new partner!"

"He didn't say she was going to marry him,"
Maggie pointed out.

"That doesn't matter," Teresa answered hotly.
"All that matters is that Da sent three men to
three sisters and each of them 'took a shine' to
their new partners."

Frankie and Maggie shared a quick, helpless
look before turning back to Teresa.

"Well, he won't do it to me," the youngest
Donnelly swore. "I'm not going to hog-tie myself
to a man and spend the rest of eternity on that
ranch!" She took two steps back from the table
as if distancing herself from her family could
keep the threat of marriage at bay. "I want to
travel. See things. Meet people." She turned
around sharply and headed for the front door.
"Dammit, I won't let Da pick out a husband for
me!" As she opened one of the stained-glass
double-paned doors, she looked back over her
shoulder and vowed, "I swear I won't!"

Then she was gone, and the only sound was

the slamming of the door and the rattle of the glass.

Maggie, Frankie, and Rose sat solemnly at the table for another few seconds. The sunshine slanting through the windows fell across the table and glittered on the polished silver coffee pot. Frankie refolded her letter and slipped it back into the envelope. Gripping it tightly with both hands, she chewed at her bottom lip.

Maggie tapped the cards Cutter had sent her against the tabletop and stared off into space.

"Teresa will be back," Rose said as she slowly stood up. "Mark my words, now. She'll be back," the housekeeper repeated sternly as she left to go about her work.

She didn't look back and so didn't see the doubts on the other women's faces.

*Regret*

"Two weeks," Al mumbled, and held out her empty tin cup toward Chucker. As the old man poured steaming hot coffee into it, she spoke again, more to herself than to him. "Two weeks and not a damned thing has happened."

"A body would think you'd be pleased about that," the cook muttered, and set the battered coffee pot down on a flat rock near the fire. His weathered features wrinkled even further as he sniffed the air.

She shot him a disgusted glance. "Well, of course, I'm glad nothin's gone wrong! It's just that, how the hell can we catch Bennet up to no good if he doesn't do anything?"

Chucker straightened up, his palms at the

small of his back. Pointing his nose straight up at the sky, he sniffed again, shook his head, then scratched his chin. He took his time stretching the kinks out of his muscles before speaking. "So you're hoppin' mad when he's doin' somethin', and you're even madder when he ain't."

Put like that, it did sound a bit ridiculous, Al acknowledged. But dammit, she was nearing the end of her rope. Soon even *she* would stop believing in her suspicions. She could already see the doubts in Cutter's eyes.

The blasted man spent every damn day in the saloon, and the only thing to come out of it was his wallet getting thick enough to choke a mule. Oh, he'd admitted to hearing bits and pieces of conversations. Tidbits of information that amounted to no more than Al's own suspicions.

Cutter was of the opinion that everyone in town blamed Bennet for whatever went wrong. Whether it was his fault or not. He kept insisting that it was the way of things. Folks always pinned the blame on the man with the most money.

And that was surely Bennet.

Although, Cutter was willing to admit that he'd had about enough of feeling Thompson's blank stare boring into his back.

Sean was no better. Daily, the big Irishman went into the mine with the men. He'd seen no sabotage and hadn't heard a whisper of gossip from the men. Not surprising, that, considering that all of the miners at the Four Roses knew damn well that he was Al's brother-in-law.

But at least, she told herself, while Sean was

in the mine, she was less concerned about "accidents" happening.

Chucker sniffed again and Al snapped, "What's wrong with that nose of yours, anyway?"

"Nothin'. It's just..." He turned his head slightly as if hoping to catch a breeze. "Don't you smell nothin' ... odd?"

Al shifted, frowned, and lowered her gaze to her coffee. "Like what?" she muttered.

"Like..." The older man scratched his chin again, sniffed loudly, and said, "Flowers. Some kinda flower I ain't never smelled around these parts before." He shook his head again, shrugged, and added, "First off, I figured some skunk or other up and died too close to camp. But it ain't that at all. Don't you smell it?"

*Oh, Lord.*

"I don't smell a thing," she lied. This is what happens, she told herself, when a body tries to be something she's not. Imagine her trying to douse herself with sweet smells just so some dude would notice her! Well, that was the last damned time she'd be wearing that french perfume her sister Frannie swore by.

Hell, she wasn't even sure why she'd worn it. Another lie, the voice inside her head argued. She knew good and well why she'd worn it.

Travis Deal. This was all his fault. Making her think about things like smelling good and what her hair looked like and all. What did it matter what he thought, anyway?

Too damned much, that's what.

Chucker wandered off, still muttering to himself about flower gardens in the pines, leaving her alone at the fire. She shivered slightly as the nightwind blew up around her, twisting the dying flames into one last burst of blazing light.

Mary Alice sighed, folded her hands around the warm coffee cup and took a quick look around her. Most of the miners were busy with whatever nightly chores they'd set for themselves. From washing out their socks to readying their tools for the next day's work. Lamplight gleamed through canvas walls, and a low murmur of conversation rippled over the claim site like a high-running stream.

She turned back to stare into what was left of the campfire. Glowing chunks of wood splintered under their own weight, and sparks flew like half-finished dreams at dawn.

She shivered slightly and told herself she should be getting to bed. But even if she lay down, Al knew she wouldn't sleep. Lately, the minute she closed her eyes, her brain dredged up thoughts of Travis.

"Fool," she muttered thickly, and shifted her gaze to the rocky ground between her booted feet. "There's nothing there for you," Al told herself in a whispered rush. "You share nothing with the man. You've not a damned thing in common."

"Is this a private conversation?" Travis asked as he stepped up behind her. "Or can I join in?"

She jumped, startled, then tossed him what she hoped was a negligent glance. Settling back on her log again, she asked herself frantically how long he had been standing in the shadows? How much had he heard?

And, oh Lord, why did the low-pitched rumble of his voice create such skittering sensations inside her?

"You looked cold," he said as he draped a blanket around her shoulders.

Maybe she had been, before. Now, though, an incredible heat was beginning to work its way through her bloodstream. And that undeniable fact irritated the hell out of her. As Al instinctively caught the ends of the wool blanket with one hand and pulled them tight around her, she took a deep breath and started talking.

"Why do you do things like that?"

"Like what?" he asked, taking a seat beside her on the log.

"Like this!" she snapped, and waved one corner of the blanket at him. "Why would you go get me a blanket, for God's sake?"

"I told you," Travis shrugged and gave her a half smile. "You looked cold."

"That ain't the point, Travis."

"Fascinating," he said slowly, that half smile spreading across his face, "just what is the point?"

"You're about to drive me out of my mind, that's what."

When he had the nerve to chuckle, it was all Al could do not to punch him dead in the nose.

"I don't see what's so damned funny."

"No," he allowed, shaking his head. "I suppose you don't."

"There you go again," she snapped. "Why can't you just give me a straight answer?"

He stared at her for a long minute, and Al found herself drifting into the icy coolness of his pale blue eyes. The men, the mine, and all the other worries that had plagued her for weeks faded away as she faced her most confusing problem.

Travis Deal.

This whole thing was ridiculous. Laughable. Hell, if anyone had told her a month ago that she would be having disturbing kinds of notions about a fancy man in a derby who fainted at the sound of gunfire, she would have fallen to the ground in a fit of laughter.

So why wasn't she laughing?

"It's not the blanket bothering you, Alice," he said quietly. "So what is it?"

No, it wasn't the damned blanket. It was everything. Everything about him. But she couldn't very well say *that*, could she?

"For one thing," she snapped instead, "like I keep telling you, my name's *Al*."

"And I've been calling you that, haven't I?"

"Until now."

"Ah, but now is different."

"How's that?" she asked warily.

"We're alone here," he said. "By the firelight." He leaned in a bit closer. "And your perfume smells much too good for me to call you Al."

He'd noticed. She swallowed heavily. Of course he'd noticed, she thought. Hell, even Chucker had noticed. But leave it to Travis to know that the scent in the air was perfume. And that she was the source.

That was the whole problem here, she wanted to shout. Him setting himself apart from everyone else in her world. Him treating her . . . different. It was damned disconcerting.

And if she was to be completely honest, it was

exciting, too. A tiny curl of pleasure ignited low in her belly, and Al had to force herself to ignore it.

Deliberately, she returned his smile with a frown. Leaning forward, she set her coffee cup down on the ground, then clutched the ends of the blanket even tighter around her. Al knew she was using the worn wool fabric like a shield to hide behind, but she was past caring. To protect herself from these strange feelings creeping over her, she was even willing to look like a coward. Momentarily.

Of course, if she hadn't wanted his attention, she should have left the damned perfume alone.

Travis reached down, picked up a branch, and snapped it across his bent knee. As he slowly fed it to the dying embers, he asked, "What are you thinking?"

"I'm wonderin' why you don't treat me like everybody else does. Why you don't treat me like you would if I was a man."

"But you're not," he pointed out, and tossed her a look that swept over her form in an instant, leaving small fires of excitement in its wake.

Al's heartbeat staggered a bit, but she steeled herself against her body's response to him.

"I know that," she told him. "But Travis, I've spent most of my life trying to prove that I'm as worthy as any man. That I can run this mine and take care of myself as well as a man could."

"Don't you think you've already accomplished that?"

"Hell yes, I have!" She bent over, picked up a nearby twig, and tossed it onto the fire. "But everytime you go and fetch me a cup of coffee, or bring me a blanket, you ruin it all!"

Travis glanced at her quizzically. "I had no idea. But, in my own defense, not many men wear French perfume."

She scowled. Al had a feeling that he was amused by all this. But if he was, she told herself, he at least had the good sense to hide it from her. And amused or not, he was going to listen to her.

"Nobody around here tips their hat to me," she went on quickly, in a rush to say everything that needed to be said. "No one watches their language in front of me or opens doors or carries heavy things for me, either!"

"I do."

"That's what I'm talkin' about!"

At first she hadn't thought much of the little gestures Travis performed. Pouring coffee for her in the mornings. Easing her to one side and pushing a heavy ore-car himself. Setting up a new cot in her tent to replace the broken one.

Little things, all. But she'd begun to enjoy them. Just as she enjoyed how he watched her when he thought she was unaware of him. When Travis's gaze moved over her, Al felt something she'd never experienced before. A deep, inner warmth that spread throughout her body, leaving her trembling and almost breathless with anticipation. Her heartbeat thundered and every drawn breath was a triumph.

"So my treating you like a lady upsets you?" His voice seemed deliberately low, intimate.

"Well, *yes!*" Hell, she wasn't even used to being treated like a woman, let alone a *lady*.

Never mind that she was beginning to like it.

He scooted a bit closer to her on the log, and Al felt his thigh press against hers. Heat exploded at the spot where their bodies met and raced through her veins. Al's breath caught, and she forced herself to inch away from his touch.

"I'm sorry," he said and kept his gaze fixed on the smoldering fire in the circle of rocks. "But you *are* a woman. A lady."

She should be furious. And dammit, she *was* mad. But there was also a small, hidden corner of her heart that was glad he saw her as a woman. Sweet Jesus, Al thought. How had everything gotten so bloody damned confusing?

Why was it that even while she was telling him one thing, she wanted another? Why was it she was feeling so uncertain about everything that had always been so clear before? And why had Kevin sent such a man to her in the first place?

Why hadn't her da sent her a partner as old as the hills with a hunched back, crossed eyes, and grizzled features?

In the moonlight, Al studied his profile. The streaks of blond in his light brown hair seemed to shine like silver. His neatly trimmed mustache quirked with his half smile and for the first time, she noticed the fine lines at the corners of his eyes, usually caused by years of squinting into the sun.

"Now, why is that, I wonder?" she said softly.

"Hmmm?" he turned to look at her directly. "Why is what?"

Al reached out one hand and touched the tip of her index finger to the web of creases by his right eye. "How is it," she asked, "that a city man like you has all these lines here?"

He dipped his head slightly, pulling away from her touch. "Guess I'm looking my age, eh?"

"Those ain't *old* marks, Travis," she argued. "Those are squint lines. The kind you get from starin' into the sun for hours on end." Cocking her head, she asked, "Just how would a city man like you come to get those?"

He cleared his throat. "The sun shines in the city, too, you know."

"Uh-huh." Al frowned thoughtfully, and let her gaze move over him carefully.

Travis dropped another stick into the fire and dusted his palms together. As she watched him, she noticed something else. Quickly, she reached out and grabbed his right hand. Before he could pull away, she turned his palm toward the dying firelight and ran her index finger over his calloused, scarred flesh.

"How do ya explain away these scars, Travis?" she asked wryly. "Paper cuts? Or maybe holdin' a pencil too tight?"

He yanked his hand free of her grasp and stood up. She jumped to her feet, too, and grabbing hold of his arm, turned him around to face her. Looking up at him, she saw the haunted expression on his face and was immediately sorry for bringing up what was obviously a painful memory.

"Travis?"

"It was a long time ago," he whispered, keeping his gaze fixed on the shadowy pines surrounding camp. He didn't trust himself to look down at her. She might see too much in his eyes.

Hell, she'd seen too much already.

If he had any sense at all, he would walk away. Go to his tent and stay there until morning, when there would be enough people around to help him keep this raging desire for her in check.

Being here with her . . . alone in the dark . . . was dangerous, he knew.

Sitting beside her, talking with her, only served to whet his appetite for more. She was so unlike every other woman he'd ever known. Strong, confident, Alice gave the impression that she was in complete control. But Travis sensed more in her. He felt her untapped desire. Her hunger.

And he shared it.

His body ached with the need to possess her even as his mind told him daily that he shouldn't. His imagination continued to conjure up images of him and Alice wrapped together in the darkness, despite the rational voice in the back of his mind that kept warning him to keep his distance.

Hell, rationally, he knew he should never have come to Regret. He should have stayed hundreds of miles away from Mary Alice. He should have kept his dream images of her just that—dreams. Now he would have to carry a mental image of her inside him wherever he went. And he would be leaving. Eventually. Travis had known all along that he wasn't the man for her.

Why wasn't that knowledge enough to make him back off?

"Travis . . ." she said again.

"What?"

"What kind of 'city man' are you, anyway?"

Questions. Too damned many questions. Especially since he wasn't prepared to answer them. He ground his teeth in frustration. If there was one thing he'd learned about Alice in the last couple of weeks, it was that she didn't give up. And, except for gagging her with her own bandanna, he could think of only one way to silence her.

He looked down into the fathomless depths of her green eyes, and the last of his resolve disappeared. Instinctively, he grabbed her and pulled her close. Travis dipped his head and pressed his lips to hers. Alice gasped in surprise and Travis's tongue swept past her parted lips to caress the inside of her mouth, to feel her warmth, to taste her very breath.

After a moment's stunned hesitation, her hands slid up the length of his arms and finally clutched at his shoulders. Her breath dusted his cheeks and he held her tighter, closer. He felt her rigid nipples pressing into his chest, and Travis groaned in quiet desperation. His right hand slipped slowly up to cup her breast, and when he claimed his prize, he rubbed his thumb gently over the blue cotton shirt separating him from her tender, distended flesh.

Then he saw stars.

Alice stomped her bootheel down on his toes once more for good measure, before shoving herself back and away from him.

"Holy . . ." Wobbling unsteadily as he favored his injured foot, Travis stared at her in dumbfounded surprise. "Why'd you do that?"

"Me?" she said, and lifted one hand to cover

her swollen, well-kissed lips. "What do you think *you* were doin'?"

"I *thought* I was kissing you," he snapped. Travis glanced down at his injured foot and carefully put all of his weight on it to test for broken bones. Then he glanced back at her. "I also thought you were kissing me back."

"Well, I wasn't."

"My mistake," he nodded, and mentally decided that nothing was broken. It just felt like it.

Alice crossed her chest with her arms and lifted her chin, looking him directly in the eye. "And, mister, *nobody* touches my—my . . . *me* without askin' first!"

"I assure you," he said tightly, "I'll make a point of remembering that."

"Good." Color so deep it was plain even in the moonlight filled her cheeks. "See that ya do."

As she turned to leave, Travis knew he'd botched everything. Dammmit, he shouldn't have grabbed her like she was the last flapjack at a lumberman's breakfast. But Christ, she did try a man something fierce.

Now he had to find a way to reassure her despite the fact that his desire hadn't cooled one bit.

He took a few quick steps and closed the distance between them. Grabbing her upper arm, he released her quickly when she glanced down meaningfully at his fingers.

"Would you have supper with me tomorrow night?" he asked before he could change his mind.

A small frown crossed her face briefly. "We eat together every night, Travis."

"Everyone eats together, Alice." He moved in even closer, until she was forced to tilt her head back on her neck to look at him. "Tomorrow night, I'd like it if you and I could share a meal together. Just the two of us. Perhaps in my tent?"

In the dim light, it was impossible to read the expression in her eyes. But she hadn't refused him outright, so Travis pressed his advantage.

"It would give us a chance to talk some more. Privately."

"*Talk?*"

She took a deep breath, and Travis's gaze dropped to watch the swell of her breasts. His hands clenched into fists to keep from touching her again.

"Yes," he said. "We can talk about our ... plans."

"Cutter and Sean—"

"Will no doubt be spending the evening at the saloon as they are tonight," he finished, and promised himself he would find a way to ensure that fact.

"I don't know ..."

"To talk, Alice." Travis inhaled deeply and prayed for strength. "Nothing else will happen unless we both want it to."

Her dark red brows arched above her eyes, and she folded her arms across her chest defensively as if telling him silently what the chances of *that* were.

"Then," she said hesitantly after a long, thoughtful pause, "I suppose it would be all right."

"Good."

"As long as you remember what I told you."

"Don't you worry, Alice. The next time, I'll ask. I can't afford to have *both* feet broken."

She nodded stiffly.

Travis grinned at her. "I'll see to everything," he said quickly. "We'll make this a special dinner. All you have to worry about is wearing your nicest dress. Leave the rest to me."

# Chapter 10

**M**ike Thompson shifted uneasily from foot to foot, waiting for his employer to ask him to sit down. He'd learned that Rafe Bennet was a stickler for what he called "The Proprieties." Thoughtfully, Thompson kept his cool, gray gaze locked on the man across the desk from him.

Bennet.

A few months back, when he'd hitched his horse to Bennet's wagon, Thompson had thought big things were going to be heading his way. So far, all he'd done was to roust a few small-time hard-rock miners. Mainly, he sat in the Hopeless Cause Saloon and waited.

Waited for what . . . only Bennet knew.

But Thompson wasn't a waiting kind of man. Inaction grated on him. Made him jumpy. Careless.

And a careless gunman usually ended up dead.

"Sit down, Mister Thompson," Bennet finally offered, and Mike plopped down onto the

161

leather chair on the customer side of the wide desk. Silently, he watched as his employer poured them each a drink of expensive whiskey, then he took the glass the other man handed him.

Lifting it to his lips, Thompson tossed the good liquor down his throat. Smoother than the rotgut he usually drank, the fine liquor left behind a warm glow that filled his insides, rather than the strip of fire that raw whiskey ignited in a man. He set the empty glass down on the edge of the desk. Even when he could afford it, Thompson didn't spend money on good liquor. What was the point? he'd often asked himself. The cheap stuff got a man just as drunk—and usually a helluvalot quicker.

Not that he allowed himself to get drunk very often. A man in his position couldn't afford to be in a stupor. There were far too many men who would be more than willing to take advantage of an opportunity like that and send him to hell.

Thompson smiled grimly. He had no doubt that there was a special corner in hell waiting on him. But the Devil, like everyone else eager to see his soul burn—would just have to wait his turn.

Bennet leaned back in his chair, propping his elbows on the walnut arms and steepling his fingertips. "So, what have you to tell me today?"

The same thing as yesterday, Thompson thought, but wisely didn't say so out loud. "Nothin' much. That gambler Cutter is still in the saloon most every day and night. Him and that big Mick, Sullivan."

"Still?"

"Yeah." Thompson crossed his legs, resting his right ankle on his left knee. Absently, his fingers plucked at the leather embossing on his boot. "They're laughin' and talkin' with those miners all the time. Cutter gathers up pieces of information like most men look for gold."

"And has he found anything interesting?"

"No. No one's talkin'."

"Good." Bennet took a small sip of whiskey, swishing the liquid around his mouth to enjoy its flavor, then swallowed and held the glass up to the light, admiring the rich, amber color of the liquor. "You told me a few days ago, I believe, that these two men are relations of Mary Alice Donnelly?"

"Yeah. They're kin."

"Kin." Bennet chuckled at the word.

Thompson stiffened. He didn't like knowing that Bennet was amused by him. Hell, he'd killed men for less offense than laughing at him. But most men weren't paying him as much as Bennet. For that kind of money, Thompson was willing to overlook a few things.

For a while, anyway.

"I suppose, then," the other man said softly, "she called on them for help?"

"I guess." Now Thompson laughed quietly. "Hell, when I'm good and ready to do what needs doin', she'll need a damn sight more help than those two!"

"Of course."

Thompson suddenly straightened up, planting both feet on the floor and leaning toward his employer. Just looking at his cool, unflappable features and perfectly combed blond hair was enough to make Thompson want to leap up and shake him. The only reason he hadn't already was that Bennet was paying him too much to walk away from. But dammit, even his patience was beginning to stretch a mite thin. "How long do you expect me to just keep sittin' around doin' nothin'?"

Bennet's dark brown gaze locked on him. There was nothing in his expression to give a man cause to worry, but it was that very lack of emotion that forced Thompson to lower his voice respectfully.

"I mean, if you'd just let me kill Al Donnelly in the first place, none of this would be happenin' now."

"I've told you before," Bennet started.

"I know. You don't like killin'."

Bennet nodded, reached up, and smoothed the tip of one finger back and forth across a small scar over his right eye. "Not unless every other option has been tried first."

"We *did* try the other option. You wanted her kidnapped, but she got free."

"Because you sent idiots out to do the job."

His voice was quiet, steely, like the edge of a razor-sharp knife.

All right, Thompson conceded. Maybe he shouldn't have used Fat Jim Sikes. But hell, all the halfwit was supposed to have done was hit her over the head, cart her off, and stash her somewhere!

"You should've gone after the Four Roses right when we hit town," Thompson muttered without thinking. "By taking over all those small mines first, *then* goin' after her, you gave Al time to get suspicious. And to get set for trouble."

Bennet's chair legs scraped against the floor as he pushed away from the desk. Standing up, he looked down at Thompson and actually sneered at him.

"I don't expect you to understand my business, Mister Thompson," he said stiffly. "I *do* expect you to keep your opinions to yourself. I'll thank you to remember that I am paying you to do exactly what I tell you, when I tell you to do it."

A sliver of alarm sliced through Thompson. In the last ten years or so, he'd faced countless men in gun battles and always come out the victor. But there was something about Bennet—a coldness—that set him apart and made Thompson wish he'd never agreed to work for the man.

"Is that clear?"

"Yes sir," he answered, and a voice in the back of his mind said that he couldn't really blame Bennet for guessing wrong about Al Donnelly. Hell, the man had probably figured that stealing a mine from a woman was going to be a lot simpler proposition. But, Sweet Jesus! Al Donnelly was no ordinary woman! Why, if ever there was a woman who tried a man's gentlemanly notions about not killing women . . . it was the Donnelly bitch.

"What else are this Cutter and Sullivan up to?" Bennet wanted to know.

"Not much, except that the gambler's gettin' richer every day."

"How so?"

"These damn fool miners are lining up to get fleeced by that well-dressed sharpy."

"A sharpy?" Bennet strolled over to the window and glanced back at the other man. "He cheats, then?"

"Well, nobody's called him on it." Apparently, Thompson told himself, this Cutter was good enough that he didn't have to resort to trickery to win.

"Perhaps it's time someone did," Bennet murmured.

Hmmm. Thompson smiled slowly. Now there was a real interesting idea. Why, men had been known to get shot real bad over a bad card game. And if enough of the miners were convinced Cutter was a cheat, they'd string him up themselves and save Thompson the trouble.

"But no killing—not unless I order it."

"Sure." Hell, a couple of bullets, nicely placed, could be even more fun than killing Cutter outright.

Bennet continued talking, forcing Thompson to cut his pleasant thoughts short. "Afterward, I want you to snatch the Donnelly woman." He narrowed his gaze meaningfully. "This time, *you* do it. Personally. I want no more mishaps."

"All right, boss." Thompson smiled to himself. Shooting Cutter and kidnapping Al Donnelly. Finally. He was going to be allowed to do what he did best. Then he thought of something. "What about her new partner? Want me to carry him off, too?"

Bennet shook his head. "It's not necessary. Of course, if the opportunity presents itself, that's one thing. If not"—he shrugged—"Mister Deal doesn't belong here. I have no doubt that if given a chance, he would quite happily sell his share in the Four Roses to me."

"Mister Bennet..." Thompson nodded and reached for the whiskey bottle. "I believe this'll work out just fine. And to celebrate, I'll just have one more drink, if you don't mind."

"Please," Bennet waved one hand negligently at the liquor bottle.

Not tonight, Thompson told himself as he splashed three fingers of whiskey into the glass. Tomorrow was soon enough. When he sat down at a poker table with Cutter, he wanted his wits about him.

Travis groaned quietly, his legs kicking at the rough wool blanket covering him. His head tossing from side to side on the flattened pillow, he mumbled a soft, almost inaudible, "No . . ." just before the dream came again.

*The cabin was on fire. Smoke curled through the tiny rooms like a venomous snake, promising a slow, painful death to whomever made the mistake of crossing its path. The stench of burning wood stung his nostrils as he dragged himself on his belly across the floor, searching for the woman.*

*She was there. Somewhere. She had to be. He'd told her not to leave the cabin's safety. Safety! Even now that word stung more viciously than the flames licking at his clothing or the smoke blinding him.*

*Then he heard it. A quiet moan that rose into a soul-chilling scream. The hairs on the back of his neck stood straight up. The wall of flame in front of him seemed to part for an instant, and Travis scooted across the hot floorboards, determined to reach her.*

*She was in a corner of the room. If she'd been hid-*

*ing before, that was finished now. Standing before him like a biblical pillar of fire, she spun helplessly in a tight circle, unconsciously fanning the flames already engulfing her. Without hesitation, Travis drew a deep breath, ignoring the burning pain lancing through his chest, held it, and launched himself toward her.*

*He saw the pain, the terror in her eyes a split second before his momentum carried them both toward the window and through the glass. They landed on the hard-packed dirt, and Travis began to roll with her, trying to smother the flames between his own body and the earth.*

*And still, her screams filled him.*

"No!" Travis shouted and bolted upright. Shivering uncontrollably, he sat up, struggling to draw breath into his heaving lungs. His gaze shot around the interior of the tent as if searching for the flames he'd so recently experienced again.

But there was nothing.

Only the darkness and the faint sounds of the surrounding night.

His brain racing, Travis forced himself to draw one breath after another into his body. He told himself that it was over. The fire was in the past. Her suffering was over.

Sighing heavily, he reached up and rubbed his face viciously with both hands. Old scars on his palms scraped against his features, refusing to be ignored.

"Dammit!" he whispered, and dropped back onto his cot.

Staring up at the canvas roof, he lay perfectly still. His eyes burning with weariness, he desperately wanted to close them and escape into sleep. But there was no escape for him.

Resolutely, Travis kept his eyes wide open.

Mary Alice paused on the boardwalk just outside the general store. An eerie sensation crawled up her spine and she tried to shake it off, but it wouldn't leave her. Someone was staring at her. Someone was watching her, and the force of his gaze was enough to shake her despite her distraction.

Instinctively, she knew who that someone was.

She drew one long, deep breath and, slowly, half turned until she was facing the telegrapher's office. Then she looked up to the building's second story and the window facing the street.

She saw Rafe Bennet. Their gazes locked.

Through the dirty glass, she looked into her enemy's eyes and deliberately straightened up. Lifting her chin slightly, she squared her shoulders and stared into the face of the man behind all of her problems.

In disbelief, she watched as Bennet slowly tipped his head to one side in a mockery of a bow. Her temper, already sorely tried, began to bubble and boil in the pit of her stomach. If it wasn't for *him*, everything in her life would be running just as it should. It was *his* greed, *his* hired thugs who were making all the trouble in town, and there didn't seem to be a damned thing she could do about it.

But, she told herself firmly, she would be blasted if she'd stand there on the street and pretend to be civil. Shouting at him was out of the question. It wouldn't do any good, and besides, he wouldn't be able to hear her anyway. Shooting him . . . no. She couldn't do that, as much as it pained her to admit it.

With her choices limited, she did the only thing she could do to show Bennet her contempt. She looked at him long and hard, then defiantly spit into the dirt. When Al looked at the window again, he was gone. Disappeared back into his rat hole.

At least, though, she was sure she'd made her point. A small, victorious smile curved her lips as she stepped up to the Mercantile's front door and walked inside.

"Mornin', Al," G. W. said, giving her a brief wave from his perch at the far end of the counter. Leaning to one side, he spat a stream of thick, black tobacco juice into a nearby spittoon.

"G. W." She grimaced at the sight, nodded, then shifted her gaze to the stacks of merchandise cluttering up his store.

Not for the first time, Al wished that there was more than one mercantile in Regret. She hated like hell to come to G. W., but she really didn't have a choice in the matter, did she?

*Wear your best dress*, Travis had said.

Al scowled and began to walk toward the back of the store. She wondered what he would say if he knew that her "best dress" was a brand-new pair of Levis?

Hell, she hadn't owned a dress in she didn't know how long. It hadn't been necessary. She'd never been invited anywhere that required her to wear a dress. And if she had been, she would have refused the invitation.

But if that was true, why hadn't she turned

Travis down when he'd suggested this supper of his?

She pushed that silent question away for the simple reason that she didn't have an answer.

"Lookin' for somethin' in p'ticular?" G. W. called out around a wad of tobacco, his head swivelling to follow her progress through the maze that was his store.

She damned sure wasn't going to tell *him* what she was looking for. Bad enough that she'd have to face him and pay for it—if she actually found a dress buried somewhere in the monstrous piles of merchandise.

"I'll know it when I see it," she told him, hoping it would shut him up.

She should have known better.

"Got some nice new work shirts in," he offered eagerly.

"No thanks."

"How 'bout some boots? Yours look about done in."

She glanced down at the toes of her battered boots and told herself that the man might have a point. Then she shook her head. Not today.

G. W. spit again, and she heard the metallic *thunk* when he hit his target.

She stopped at the first mountain of clothing stacked on a table that was bowed under the weight of it all. Her gaze moved over the shirts, long underwear, and socks. She saw bandannas, white linen handkerchiefs, and a few dozen pairs of work gloves. There were wool scarves and rain slickers, brocade vests, and black suit-pants jumbled in with everything else, so when she spotted a corner of calico material, Alice grabbed at it.

Keeping one hand firmly on the stack of clothing to keep it from tipping over, she used her right hand to tug at the material clenched between her fingertips.

"Whatcha got there?" G. W. asked, but was still not curious enough to climb down off his high stool behind the counter.

Alice ignored him and held her breath. Still pulling at the bit of sky blue, flower-sprigged calico, she sent up a quick, heartfelt prayer that this would be a dress. And that the dress would fit. A lot to ask for, she knew. But if you're going to wish, she told herself, wish big.

Giving one last yank, she pulled the calico from its nest, and her heart dropped like a stone into the pit of her stomach.

An apron.

Worse yet, a *child's* apron!

Why the hell would G. W. be stocking children's clothes? There wasn't a kid within ten miles of Regret. Of course, she thought dismally, there weren't any women around, either. Except of course, for the whores at the Hopeless Cause, and they sure wouldn't be looking for calico dresses anytime soon!

"Ya find somethin'?"

"No," she grumbled, and stuffed the apron back into the crevice where she'd found it.

"Well, now, if you'll tell me what you're lookin' for exactly, mayhap I can help."

There was no way to avoid it, she supposed. Unless she wanted to spend all day in the mercantile, burrowing through stack after stack of clothing. Al took a deep breath and frowned at the foul smell hovering in the room. Another reason for completing her business quickly.

"All right," she said, and turned slowly to face the florid faced man. "But G. W., I don't want to hear you've been talking about whatever it is I buy in here. You understand me?"

G. W. pulled his head back and stared at her as if he was mortally wounded. Lifting one hand to slick down his greasy black hair, he huffed, "Now Al, I ain't a talker. You know that."

Well at least he wasn't a mover, she told herself. G. W. rarely roused himself to actually leave the Mercantile. The only way he'd be able to tell anyone anything is if they came in the store. And God knows, with the stink in there, no one stayed around long enough to chat with the big man. They did their business, then ran for fresh air.

She should be safe enough.

"I need a dress."

G. W. inhaled sharply, and his small blue eyes bulged and teared up as he began to cough and choke on his wad of tobacco. Arms flailing wildly, he blinked frantically, then Alice saw his Adam's apple bob once, hard. He gasped, twisted his neck, then whined, "God almighty, you made me swallow my chaw!"

To her credit, Alice didn't even smile. Although, she was of the opinion that since G. W. obviously ate anything and everything—in great quantities—that chaw wouldn't even be noticed.

Smacking his thick lips together, he rubbed the flat of one meaty hand across the mound of his

stomach. "Lord only knows what chewin' tobacco's gonna do to my insides!"

"If you die, I'll see you're buried proper," Al
told him solemnly.

He squinted at her as his lips twisted at the
lingering distaste. "No call to go gettin' so
snippy, Al. Oooh, my guts're already chur-
nin' . . ."

Alice sighed, rested her right hand on the butt
of her hip pistol, and waited. Sooner or later
G. W. would tire of complaining.

True to form, when she didn't commiserate
with him, his groans quietly faded. At last he
cocked his head, fixed one eye on her, and asked,
"Did you say you was lookin' for a *dress*?"

Alice folded her arms over her chest, braced
her feet wide apart, and jerked him a nod.

Shaking his head slowly, he said, "I was pretty
sure that's what you said—but I still don't believe it."

"I don't care what you believe, G. W.," Al shot
back. "Do you have a dress or not?"

With his head tilted back, he stared thoughtfully at the ceiling for a minute or two before
saying slowly, "As I recall, there was a couple of
ladies things once upon a time." G. W. glanced
at her out of the corner of one eye. "Ya know, I
ain't had a lot of call for that sort of thing."

Alice sighed. "I know. Do you still have 'em?"

"Reckon so," he allowed. "Don't recall
throwin' nothin' away."

Now *that* she believed.

"Where do I look?"

"Ya might commence over to the back, there
in the corner."

He waved one hand in a general direction, and Alice resolutely headed for the far corner.

Even before she attacked the mountain of merchandise, she began mumbling to herself.

"This whole thing is just plain stupid. Why in the hell do I need a dress to eat supper?"

"Havin' supper with some fella?" G. W. called out.

"Dammit, G. W.," she snapped, "keep your ears to yourself."

"Can't hardly help but hear, Al," he whined. "'Sides, this here is my place. I reckon I can listen to whatever I have a mind to."

"Then listen to this, you old goat," she muttered as she poked and prodded at the different fabrics towering in front of her. "This may be your store, but it's *my* business. And if I hear my business bein' talked about from here to creation, I'll go after you like a hound on a bone."

"You maybe goin' to see Bennet? Sweet-talk him into leavin' your place be?"

An icy calm settled over Alice. The scene she'd played out with her enemy only moments before rolled through her mind again. Slowly, she looked over her shoulder at the fat man. Even the idea of tarting herself up and trying to sweet talk the man responsible for destroying her peace and quiet was enough to get her blood boiling. Hell, the only way she'd go to see Bennet was if she took her knife and gun with her. And dammit, if something didn't happen soon, she just might.

G. W. shifted uneasily on his stool, and it pleased her to see him swallow convulsively. Those tiny, sharp blue eyes of his slid away from her gaze, and Alice turned back to continue her search.

Then, finally, just as she was beginning to give up hope, her fingers came to rest on a soft, dark blue fabric. Holding her breath, Al pulled it from the stack carefully.

It was ugly.

Al knew nothing about ladies fashions, but even *she* knew ugly when she saw it.

As she held the dress up by its shoulders, the wrinkled skirt fell, its hem lying on the floor. Al studied it critically, hoping she was wrong about the thing. After all, she didn't know much about dresses.

A high neck, studded with decorative jet buttons had Al stretching her neck, as though she could already feel its confining grasp around her throat. Its long sleeves were edged with what had once been white lace. Now the delicate strands of thread were more of a sickly yellow color. That yellow lace also ran down the front of the dress, with tiny black buttons dotting its length.

Nope, she told herself grimly, she wasn't wrong.

"There ya go," G. W. shouted triumphantly. "I knew I had some ladies finery in stock."

"*Finery?*"

"Shoot, yes. That there's Irish lace on that dress, ya know."

What was left of it maybe, Al thought dismally as her fingers trailed over a few loose threads.

G. W. must have sensed her doubts, because his merchant's tongue swiftly went into action.

"That blue wool," he pointed out, "comes

from the finest durn sheep in England, too, ya know. Raise 'em special. Only shear 'em once every couple of years or so. Live like kings, the little beggars do."

While he talked, Al inspected her prize. All right, maybe it wasn't the fanciest dress in the country. Hell, in the world. But it was here. It looked like it would fit. And she didn't have a helluvalot of choice.

"All right," she said abruptly, cutting G. W. off in the middle of him telling her how wool from English sheep didn't even have to be carded—it just came off the animal soft and ready to use. If he kept talking, he'd probably try to convince her that those damned English sheep weaved their own wool into dress lengths.

"I'll take it. How much?"

"Oh, well, now," the man said thoughtfully. "That's gonna cost ya dear."

"Why the hell should it?" Al said, and stomped over to the counter. "It was buried under a pile of stuff that probably hasn't even been moved in ten years!"

"Kept it there for safekeepin'."

Al balled the dress up, stuffed it under her arm, and glared at him. "I'll give ya two dollars for it."

"Ten."

"Three."

"Eight."

Al didn't mind the haggling. And actually, she was pretty good at it. But at the moment, she didn't have the patience to play the game. All she wanted to do was get out of that store and get back to the mine.

"Three-fifty, not a penny more."

"Done." He reached out one hand and turned it palm up so she could count her money onto it. "But you done taken advantage of my soft heart, Al. Knowin' as how you want that fine dress to meet up with a beau."

She stiffened, but continued counting out coins.

"Ya want to see if we can find ya some new shoes, too? Or are ya just gonna wear your boots?"

The last coin fell onto his palm, and his fat fingers closed around the money like a hawk's talons.

"Shut up, G. W."

Lamplight seemed too harsh somehow, so Travis lit a few of the candles he'd bought at the Mercantile. Hell, what *hadn't* he bought at the Mercantile?

The small, makeshift table—an upturned crate covered by a square of dark brown cotton—held two place settings and a mason jar stuffed with wildflowers. Two small candles stood on either side of the homely vase, their flames flickering in the breeze sneaking in under the tent flaps.

Travis reached for the bottle of wine he'd managed to buy from Sam, the bartender at the Hopeless Cause. He'd paid quite a bit for it, too, since Sam himself preferred wine to whiskey and always hoarded a few bottles for his own use. He poured the rich, deep red liquid into two tin cups.

Right or wrong, trouble or not, he had to have this one evening with Mary Alice Donnelly.

When this situation with the mine was finally settled, he would be moving on. Going back to the solitary life he knew all too well. Over the last few years, he'd grown accustomed to hearing nothing more than the sound of his own voice. To not belonging anywhere. To owning no more than his horse, saddle, and guns.

Long ago, Travis had accepted the knowledge that no other woman would ever live up to the stories he'd heard from Kevin about Alice. And since he'd never expected to actually meet her, he'd resigned himself to the fact that he would probably never know what it was to have a wife. A family.

Now, though, now that he'd actually met her, it would be harder than ever to let go of the dreams.

He inhaled sharply and stared down at the candle's flame. Soon this little slice of time with Alice would be over. All he would have to take with him were the memories.

And, dammit, he wanted to build some memories with her that would warm every lonely night that loomed ahead of him. He wanted to be able to close his eyes and have her come to life in his mind. He wanted to be able to recall everything about her.

Oh, he admired her fighting spirit and her sheer stubbornness, but Travis wanted more. He wanted to hold her close again. He wanted to kiss her again. To touch her. He remembered her body pressed along the length of his. Once again, he felt her heartbeat pounding in tandem with his own. He felt the soft puff of her breath on his cheek and heard the low moans of pleasure escaping her throat.

Travis's hands fisted helplessly at his side. Lord, he wanted to feel like that again. He wanted to feel the rush of delight sweeping through him when she clung to him. He *needed* to feel the sense of completeness that had been his so briefly.

Slim chance of that, he knew, judging from her reaction the night before. Of course, he told himself, until he'd caressed her breast, she hadn't seemed to mind his attentions any. In fact, he thought suddenly, as he concentrated on the feel of her in his arms, he remembered clearly that flash of eager innocence in her kiss. The feel of her fingers digging into the padded shoulders of his jacket.

As that thought took hold, Travis frowned and dropped down onto his cot. Briefly, he glanced at his trunk. Inside that trunk, his familiar Levi's and buckskins lay waiting, along with his holster and pistols, his hat, and his worn, comfortable boots. In fact, he told himself, it was actually Travis Delacort himself buried beneath an assortment of loud, vulgar clothing that he'd purchased specifically for his stay in Regret.

Travis shifted his gaze to the pale green jacket he wore over a bright orange vest and plain white shirt. He rubbed his palms on the knees of his wheat-colored pants and stared into the twin candle flames on his makeshift dining table.

He was a damn fool. For the last few minutes, he'd been telling himself that a part of Mary Alice Donnelly cared for him as he cared for her.

But that wasn't true at all.

The night before, when they'd stood outside kissing under the stars, Alice hadn't been kissing Travis Delacort.

She'd been kissing Travis Deal.

Derby wearing, gunshot fainting Travis Deal. Good Lord.

He didn't know whether to be pleased or insulted.

# Chapter 11

*Hopeless Cause Saloon*

**T**he out-of-tune piano sounded hideous. A
thick layer of smoke lay over the noisy,
drunken crowd. And there was an overpowering
odor of cheap perfume, rotgut whiskey and unwashed bodies clinging to the saloon's shaky
walls. The crowd was too big, the tables too
small, and a fistfight broke out every few
minutes.

Cutter loved it.

He should feel guilty about that, he knew. After all, he was only in Regret to assist Al. And
the whole point of going to the saloon, day in
and day out, was to keep his ears open for information that would help solve the problems
facing her.

But, dammit, who said he couldn't enjoy himself while he was doing it?

Oh, he didn't prefer the Hopeless Cause to his
and Maggie's place in San Francisco. There was
really no comparison. The Four Roses on the Bar-

bary Coast was a splash of elegance on a dirty wharf. It was quiet, refined, specializing in entertaining San Francisco's finest. He had his own polished walnut card table there, and the bartenders were trained to mix the best damn drinks in the state.

And, of course, Maggie was there.

But, he gave a quick glance to his surroundings, there was something to be said for the energy found in this raw, uproarious place. Cheap whiskey flowed like a river, eager miners traded gold nuggets for a game of cards, and there was no local law stopping by to ride herd when things got a bit rambunctious.

Cutter tucked his cigar into the corner of his mouth and smiled. Just being in Regret reminded him of his younger years, when he'd move from town to town with nothing more than a deck of cards in his pockets. He spared his memories a brief, wistful smile, then turned his attention back to the game facing him at the moment. His gaze shot to the poker hand he'd thrown down onto the table a moment ago.

Three Queens.

The Queen of Hearts seemed to call to him, and he admitted silently that although he was enjoying his stay in Regret, he could hardly wait to get back home. To his own Queen of Hearts. Maggie. Just the thought of his wife brought a familiar tightening to his body, and he shifted in his chair.

Oh, yes, he told himself uncomfortably, he'd do well to get Al's mess settled so he could get back where he belonged.

In Maggie's arms.

"Ah, Cutter me lad." Sean grinned and slapped his brother-in-law on the back. "It's a rare treat watchin' you play poker."

Cutter smiled and gathered up the playing cards. As he tapped them on the table, his deft fingers straightening the deck, he asked, "Why don't you try playing a hand or two, Sean? You've come to the saloon with me every night the last couple of weeks, and you've yet to play a single hand."

"Ah, no, man," Sean answered, lifting his beer mug to drain the last of its contents. "You'll not catch me that easy. I'm a man who knows what he's good at and what he's not."

"Are you gonna deal or talk?" One of the miners at the poker table complained.

Cutter ignored him.

"Besides," Sean went on as if the miner hadn't spoken. "There's an old sayin', 'Unlucky in cards, lucky in love.' That's me."

Cutter laughed and began to shuffle the worn, frayed deck. "And how do you explain me and Maggie, then?"

Sean scratched his cheek thoughtfully, then winked one deep blue eye. "Ah, well, with a Donnelly, *anything's* possible!"

"True, true," Cutter muttered with a smile, and shuffled the deck one last time.

"Can we play, now?" A different miner spoke up, his dirt encrusted fingers idly fondling his dwindling stack of chips.

"Certainly." Cutter glanced around the poker table and announced, "Ante up."

Instantly, four blue chips followed Cutter's

own into the center of the table. A heartbeat later, a fifth chip was tossed onto the pile.

Slowly, Cutter glanced to his right. The tall man with iron gray eyes stood waiting behind the only empty chair.

"Mind if I sit in?"

Mike Thompson. A gunfighter and, according to Al, the man who carried out Rafe Bennet's orders. Cutter had seen Thompson in the saloon off and on for the last two weeks. He'd watched how the miners walked a wide path around the gunfighter and had wondered how long it would take the man to make a move.

Apparently, tonight would be the night.

Cutter shot a quick glance at Sean and was pleased to see that the big Irishman was alert and watchful. They exchanged an almost imperceptible nod before Cutter looked up at Thompson again.

Waving at the chair, he said, "Take a seat."

The other man pulled the chair out, sat down, and scooted a bit closer to the table. Setting a tall stack of chips down in front of him, he asked "What's the game?"

"Same as always," Cutter answered. "Five card stud, Jacks or better to open."

The miners on either side of Thompson quietly moved their chairs a bit further from the man. If he noticed, he showed no sign.

Cutter's fingers smoothed the edges of the cards as he slanted another look at Sean from the corner of his eye. The Irishman's hands were out of sight, beneath the table. Cutter smiled to himself. He was ready.

\*    \*    \*

The pinpoints of candlelight shining through canvas guided her.

Al took the back way, around the tents, clinging close to the shadowed line of pines. In each fist she clutched a handful of material, hitching the hem of her dress up past her knees. Muttering viciously with every step, she wondered how in hell women actually *walked* in long skirts. Before she'd yanked the damn dress out of her way, the yards of fabric had entwined themselves around her legs like determined hands, trying to push her back into her tent.

She glanced down at her legs and scowled. Jeans and boots, she supposed, shouldn't be worn beneath dresses. But she hadn't realized until after she'd left G. W.'s place that she didn't have any petticoats to wear under the damn thing, and she surely wasn't about to go back into that mercantile to try and find one.

Even at that, she wouldn't have worn her jeans. But for one thing. The wool dress that felt so soft on the outside, itched like hell on the underside. This supper with Travis was going to be strange enough. She sure didn't want to spend the entire evening scratching herself like some neglected old hound.

Al stopped suddenly, sighed, and glanced down at her filthy boots and mud-spattered jeans. She looked ridiculous. Not that the right kind of shoe or a petticoat would have made any difference, she told herself. If she'd had a full length mirror, and had been able to get a good look at herself in that get-up, she probably wouldn't have had the nerve to keep this supper appointment.

Her new dress felt . . . wrong. Not just because it was a dress. Not even because of the way she wanted to scratch wildly at her arms and the parts of her back not protected by a cotton chemise.

It was worse than that. It felt as though the sleeves were different lengths. She had to hold her shoulders in a half-shrug, cocked to the right, just to be comfortable. Plus, the dress had been designed to wear with a bustle. Something else Al didn't have. So now the hem in back hung about six inches longer than in front. Al glanced over her shoulder at the length of blue wool stretched out across the muddy ground. She looked as though she was dragging a blanket behind her.

Turning back to face front again, Al frowned and stretched her neck. That was another thing. The old, decaying lace around the collar scraped against her throat. But she refused to scratch. "Ladies," she knew, never admitted to an itch, let alone surrendered to the urge to scratch.

Then there was the smell.

Al sniffed again, but wasn't surprised to find that her nose had somehow become accustomed to the odor wafting up from the dress. After years of lying stacked in G. W.'s place, it would have been a miracle if the fabric didn't stink. But she hadn't really noticed it until she'd returned to her tent. Then it was too late. Thankfully, the Christmas before last, Frankie had given her a small bottle of French perfume. Though she'd laughed at the time, Al had been grateful for it today. She'd dumped half the bottle's contents

on the blue wool, hoping to mask the mildewy
stench.

All she'd managed to do, though, was to make
the dress *and* herself smell like a moldy flower
garden.

For the tenth time in as many minutes, she
called herself all kinds of a fool. Why was she
doing this? She could be back in her own tent,
stretched out on her cot. Or she could have gone
into town with Cutter and Sean. Hell, she should
be doing *anything* rather than what she was doing.

Her gaze shifted to the backside of Travis's
tent. There were more tiny candlelights shining
through the canvas walls now. It looked like a
dozen or more. Dangerous with canvas walls,
she thought, and wondered why he hadn't just
lit a lamp or two.

A pine scented wind lifted up out of nowhere
and tugged at her hair, threatening to drag it free
of its clumsily arranged topknot. "Dammit," Al
muttered, and dipped her head into the breeze,
hoping to keep the damage to a minimum. When
the wind faded away as quickly as it had come,
she lifted her head again to look at Travis's tent.
Each step she took brought her closer. And each
step was a bit more difficult than the last.

Why was she doing this? she asked herself
again. Why was she putting herself through all
this? She shivered slightly and tried to decide if
the rippling sensation had been caused by excitement—or by a last minute warning from her
brain.

A little of both, no doubt.

But she would prefer to concentrate on the excitement.

Though she'd never really admitted it to anyone, the fact that she'd never been the object of any man's attentions had always been like a small wound that refused to heal. Not once over the years had some man invited her out for a stroll in the night air. Or asked her to dance. Or, she told herself with another glance at the candlelight gleaming through the tent walls, taken her to supper.

And *no one* had ever kissed her until her toes curled and her teeth ached.

Now, for some strange reason, her new partner had.

True, he wasn't the kind of man she would ordinarily have looked at twice. But there was something in his eyes. Something that told her there was more to him than just those awful clothes he wore and the persnickety way he talked.

There was something about Travis Deal that struck an answering chord deep inside Al. She *knew* when he was watching her. She *felt* his presence without having to see him. He made her nervous, too. Not scared, nervous. Just nervous. Edgy. Like the way the air felt in the summer, just before a big thunderstorm hit.

He must have heard her approach. The tent flap opened and Travis stepped outside. Al dropped the hem of her skirt, folded her hands at her waist and tried to look like the lady he thought she was.

"Alice," he smiled at her and took a step closer. "You look . . . lovely."

She had to admit, he *did* lie well.

"I'm glad you came," he said.

"Me too."

"Would you like to come inside?" Travis took a step back and grabbed the tent flap, holding it up and back.

The candlelit interior shone like a jewel in a sack full of rocks. Al swallowed hard past the knot in her throat and nodded abruptly. She'd come too far now to back off. Before she could think better of it, she ducked her head and slipped into his tent.

Cutter reached out, cupped his hands around the pile of chips in the center of the table, and drew them back toward him. One of the players pushed himself to his feet and announced, "That's enough for me, boys." He shook a small leather money pouch and listened to the faint tinkle of very few coins. "Got just enough left to buy me a woman for a hour or two."

"It was a pleasure, sir," Cutter told him, and offered his hand.

"Reckon so," the miner allowed with a wry grin as he clasped the gambler's hand briefly. "You got most of what I took out of the mountain this week."

Cutter waited, hoping the man was a good loser. It was always annoying to have to deal with a man's regrets.

"But you got it honest, I'll say that for ya," the man said, and Cutter relaxed a bit. "Come next week, though. You just see if I don't get some of it back."

Next week? Jesus, Cutter thought as he waved

one hand at the miner now moving off into the crowd, he hoped not. With a little luck, maybe he and Sean could be back home by the following week.

And speaking of luck, Thompson's seemed extremely bad tonight. He'd lost every hand. Hell, he'd folded on most of them without a fight.

Cutter frowned and reshuffled the deck. There wasn't a doubt in his mind that the man was up to something. He just hadn't quite figured out what, yet.

The table was certainly less crowded now. As often happened, miners came and went from a poker game as their fortunes allowed. But since Thompson had planted himself in the game, no one else seemed eager to join their little group.

Now that three of the men had gone, it was only Cutter, Sean, Thompson, and one other man left at the table.

"If he ain't playin'," Thompson spoke up suddenly, jerking his thumb at Sean, "why's he takin' up space at the game?"

"Don't mind me," the Irishman countered with a smile, "I enjoy watchin'."

"Poker ain't for watchin'," Thompson told him. "It's for playin'."

Sean shook his head and leaned back, his hands still out of sight beneath the table. "I've no talent for the game, I'm afraid," he said. "Now, if you'd like to see some jugglin'... or perhaps hear a fine Irish tune ..."

"I *do* enjoy a good juggler," the miner said on a wistful sigh.

Thompson scowled at him.

Cutter chuckled under his breath and spoke

up. "Sean's my good-luck charm, you might say. I always seem to play a bit better when he's around."

"I say he's more than that," Thompson put in, his voice low and deadly.

Cutter's hands stilled on the cards. He looked at the gunman cautiously. It was coming. He could feel it. Years of experience in towns just like this one had taught him to recognize a challenge when it was building up to blow.

Forcing himself to shuffle the cards in preparation to deal, he asked quietly, "Are you in or out?"

"I'm out," Thompson growled, and pushed his chair back from the table, its legs screeching a protest against the scarred plank floor.

"Sorry to hear that," Cutter said. "The night's young."

"Not for some, it ain't."

The miner at the table shot a worried look from Thompson to Cutter and back again. Then, carefully, he gathered his remaining chips, stood up, and disappeared into the milling crowd.

"Mister . . . Thompson, isn't it?" Cutter went on, "Either you're playing or you're leaving. Which is it to be?"

"Neither," he countered, and stood up, kicking his chair out of the way. "I ain't leavin' till I get my money back from you mister. And I want it now."

A few of the nearby miners overheard Thompson and began to move back, looking for safety. When bullets flew, it was generally the man standing idly by watching, who got himself shot. As they shifted, the crowd began to get restive, and whispers rushed from man to man, spreading news of the trouble brewing.

Cutter never took his gaze off the man looking down at him. He saw how the gunman held himself ready, his right hand just a touch away from the butt of his pistol. Keeping his own right hand cupped, facing away from the man, Cutter flexed a muscle in his forearm. Immediately, his twin-shot derringer leaped from its hidden sleeve rig and slid into his waiting palm.

"I don't give refunds," he said coolly. Outwardly, Cutter was the soul of calm. But inside, his thoughts were racing. Why? he wondered. Why was Thompson calling him a cheat? Trying to prod him into a gunfight? He'd been at the saloon every night for two weeks. Why hadn't the man tried something before tonight?

Maybe Al was right. Maybe Thompson had simply been waiting for someone else to give the order. Obviously, that person had. But was that someone Rafe Bennet as Al suspected? Or was there someone else they didn't even know about yet?

"I reckon you didn't hear me, gambler." Thompson lifted his head and looked down the length of his nose at Cutter. "I just said you cheated me."

The piano music stopped.

A low pitched, murmuring hush swept over the crowd and the only other sounds were those of boot heels scratching against the floorboards as men jockeyed for a better view of the goings on.

"I don't cheat, as anyone here can tell you."

"I say ya do," Thompson countered quickly.

"Now, the question is, what're you gonna do about it?"

"Why," Cutter shrugged negligently, "nothing."

Thompson frowned, glanced at the faces of the men surrounding him, then looked back at the gambler. "Nothing? You're gonna just sit there and let me shoot ya?"

"Well, he's a patient man, Cutter is," Sean spoke up into the sudden stillness. "And, heaven knows, he might very well be willin' to sit and listen to you blather on and on until you finally decide to pull that gun your fingers are teasin'."

Thompson's jaw tightened as his gaze slid to the Irishman.

"But as for me," Sean continued, "well, I've no patience a'tall."

"Now, Sean . . ."

"Cutter me lad, 'tis true and well ya know it." Sean cut him off with a smile. Then the smile disappeared as the look he shot Thompson narrowed. "'Tis a terrible failin' of mine, impatience. God knows, me own good wife, Frannie, is tryin' her best to correct that small flaw. But so far"—he shrugged his massive shoulders—"no luck."

"You stay outa this, Mick."

"The name's Sean. And I'll not stay outa this, boy-o." He shook his head and gave the other man a grim, determined smile. "Truth to tell, I couldn't, even if I wanted to. Which I don't. Cutter here, he's family. And I would be in that much trouble when I get home if I have to tell the women that I let the likes of you blow a hole in the man."

"Decent of you," Cutter muttered.

"Think nothin' of it," Sean assured him.

"Shut up, the pair of ya," Thompson snapped. "I say this man cheated me." His voice was loud enough now to carry over the hushed crowd. "And the Mick here helped him somehow. How about the rest of ya?"

Several long moments passed before Thompson accepted the fact that no one else was going to speak up.

"They don't matter," he told Cutter. "This is between you and me." His hand moved closer to the gun butt.

"Ya do keep forgettin' about me, boy'o," Sean said.

"I'll deal with you next."

"I think now would be a better time," Sean drawled. And in the instant of silence following his statement, the distinctive double click of two hammers being cocked sounded out.

Thompson froze, his hand just an inch from his gun.

"There now," Sean smiled. "Ya see, Cutter? I knew the man would listen to reason."

"You're a wise man, brother," Cutter told him.

"Even better," the Irishman said softly, "I'm a wise man with a double-barreled shotgun cocked and aimed at the big fella there's belly." He shot a quick look at his brother-in-law. "Do ya suppose the blast will go right through the tabletop?"

"Oh," Cutter said as he watched beads of perspiration form on the gunman's forehead, "I would think so."

"Then it would be best if you moved your

hands. I'd hate for ya to pick up a sliver or two from the flyin' bits of wood that will soon be imbedded in Mister Thompson, here."

Thompson paled slightly.

"Good idea," Cutter agreed, and lifted his hands free of the table, making sure that his opponent got a good look at the derringer clasped in his hand.

Thompson drew one long, uneasy breath.

"Now, if you would be so kind," Sean said to the fuming man, "you'd do us the pleasure of layin' your gun on the table . . . *carefully* . . . and then leavin'. Now."

A snicker or two rose up from the crowd, and Thompson's features darkened angrily.

"This ain't over, Mick."

"Ah," Sean told him, "sure it is. We're on to ya now, man. You won't get another chance at any of us."

"Including Al," Cutter tossed in meaningfully.

Slowly, Thompson lifted his pistol from its holster. With the tips of his fingers, he set the gun down on the table and backed away. His gaze still locked on the two men who'd bested him, he glared at them, hate shining in his eyes.

"There now," Sean said. "It's all over. Be on your way."

Cutter held his derringer on Thompson while Sean pulled the shotgun out from beneath the table.

"Like I said, Mick. This ain't over."

Sean slid his left hand along the cold steel of the gun and lifted it until the twin barrels were pointed at Thompson's pale features. The man stared down those black holes of oblivion for a moment, then tore his gaze away.

"It's over, Mister Thompson. For you. Here. It's over."

The man wanted to say more, Cutter saw it in him. But even a gunfighter doesn't want to take on a shotgun at close range. Oh, Thompson was clearly choking on his rage, but he wasn't a fool. He wasn't about to go up against a stacked deck.

Sean was wrong, though. It wasn't over. Cutter could see it in the man's eyes.

The man in the shadows rested his back against a pine tree and let himself slide slowly down to the ground. His gaze locked on the tent where Mary Alice and her partner were having supper, and he settled in to wait.

# Chapter 12

I t was the ugliest dress he'd ever seen.

How in the devil, Travis wondered, did she manage to look so beautiful in spite of it?

All through supper, he'd tried not to stare. But the dress fairly shouted for attention. The aged lace at her throat had scratched her flesh raw. There was a thin red line of irritated skin circling her neck that looked like a scar from a bungled hanging.

Most of her hair on one side of her head was doing its best to escape the lopsided topknot and now lay dipped over her right eye. Every few seconds, Alice reached up to push it away, but it fell back again instantly.

Travis wanted to kick himself. It was obvious that she'd gone to a lot of trouble trying to dress up for this little supper of his. And it was just as obvious that she was miserable.

She looked as uncomfortable as a fish would if taken out of the water and thrown onto land. And she'd put herself through all of that, he reminded himself, for Travis Deal. He couldn't help wondering if she would have bothered for Travis Delacort.

Ever since the truth had dawned on him, he'd fought against the absurd notion of actually being jealous of himself. But he couldn't help it. She'd gone out of her way to please the man she thought him to be. And though that knowledge should have delighted him, Travis realized it didn't.

He was no citified dandy.

He had no more in common with the man he was pretending to be than she did. What would she say when she found out the truth? Would she still care for him when he was wearing jeans and carrying his guns? Sooner or later he would have to find out, because not even for Alice could Travis stand to live the rest of his life looking like a damned fool.

Rest of his life?

Christ, where had *that* thought come from? It didn't matter a damn if she could feel something for the real Travis or not. He wasn't staying. That had never been a part of the plan.

Kevin was paying him to solve his daughter's problem—or at least to protect her. The man sure as hell didn't want a guilt ridden ex-Marshal as his daughter's lover—or husband. Shit. Husband? Travis pitied the woman saddled to a man like him.

However, a voice in the back of his mind whispered, Why worry about the future right now? Why not enjoy the moment for what it was and save those worries for another time?

He poured her another cup full of wine, but she shook her head. "No thanks, Travis." She gave him a half smile and shrugged one shoulder. "Supper was nice, but I think I'll get going now."

"Not yet."

"Why not?" She reached up to push that hair out of her eye again. "Dammit," she muttered when it fell back instantly.

"This was a mistake, Travis," she said. She pulled the last few remaining pins from her hair and let the heavy mass tumble down around her. "Even you can see that."

"You didn't enjoy supper?" He glanced over at their makeshift table and the remains of the meal he'd served her. But for the almost empty wine bottle, most of it was untouched. Neither of them had eaten much. But Travis knew it had nothing to do with the taste of the rabbit Chucker had prepared. Supper could have been two bowls of sawdust for all either of them had noticed.

"Supper?" she repeated blankly, then shook her head. "It was fine. Just wasn't hungry, I guess."

He hadn't been hungry either, at least, not for food.

But it was something else entirely that had ruined their appetites.

Something that had burst into flower the night before when he'd held her in his arms and pressed his mouth to hers. They were supposed to have talked over supper. But the memory of that kiss seemed to hover in the air between them, making conversation near to impossible. He didn't know about Alice, but for him, it was damned hard to keep his brain focused on the troubles at the mine when his body ached with the need to possess her.

Now, though, she was leaving, and he wasn't ready to watch her go just yet. So Travis started talking.

"I think I've come up with an idea."

That stopped her cold.

"About what?"

"The mine," he said, and knew by the sudden glint in her eyes that he had her attention. "I believe that if we were to pay the miners more money, they might be less inclined to sell out to Bennet—or whoever is behind this."

"It's Bennet," she assured him.

Travis pushed the edges of his coat back and jammed his hands into his pants pockets. At least they were talking.

"Whoever it is," he said, "is paying the miners to commit sabotage. If the men make more money doing a good job for us, they'll think twice about ruining the source of their pay."

Alice shook her head at him and her wild, glorious hair shifted and swayed around her shoulders like a fire with a life of its own. One stubborn lock of hair fell forward to lay along her cheek. She tucked it behind her ear and glared at him. "We're already paying the highest wages in Regret! The miners make three dollars and fifty cents a day for an eight hour shift!"

Travis didn't think that was nearly enough money for spending so many hours in the dark belly of the earth. Any man who spent his life giving up the chance to walk in sunlight deserved as much money as he could make to compensate him for the loss.

"The only place that pays higher," Alice went on, "is Virginia City and Gold Hill. The men get four dollars there, but it's only because the union forced the mine owners into it."

"So then I suggest we raise the pay to four dollars as well."

"That's a damn sight of money to be going out every month, Travis," she snapped.

He bent down, picked up both cups of wine, and handed one to her. After taking a sip, he pointed out, "It does seem high, I admit."

She sniffed, took a quick gulp of wine, and nodded abruptly.

"However," he added, "it is considerably cheaper than having to completely shut down the mine for days at a time whenever a disgruntled worker causes a cave-in."

"True, but . . ." Alice scratched her upper arm and shifted her shoulders uncomfortably.

"From what Sean says," Travis went on, "most of your miners—"

"*Our* miners," she corrected him.

He paused, shifted his gaze away from her, and nodded. "Our miners. Most of them are loyal enough."

"That's good to know," Al said grimly. "Though judging by today, I wouldn't have guessed it. I had to fire two more men."

"Why?" Travis wondered why the hell no one had bothered to tell him about his.

She shrugged and took another drink of wine. "We found 'em out by the powder shack."

The powder shack? Dammit! His insides went cold and still. Just thinking about what angry men and gunpowder could do to the inner workings of the mine—and the people in it, including Alice—was enough to give any man pause. And Travis was supposed to be protecting her!

Immediately, memories of the last woman he'd tried to protect rose up in his mind. He'd failed then. Horribly. But he refused to fail this time. Travis deliberately forced the mental images down into the black corner of his soul where they hid until they could pounce at him again.

He stared at her, amazed. Alice didn't seem in the least bothered by this latest threat of danger. He watched as she drained the last of her wine, then leaned to one side and set the empty cup down on the cloth-covered crate.

"You should have told me," he said softly.

She straightened up and gave him a quick look. "Sean was there. The two of us ran 'em off."

"They'll probably be back," Travis pointed out.

Alice laughed shortly, then caught herself and sobered. "I don't think so."

"You can't be sure."

"Travis," she sighed patiently and explained. "Between Sean's fists and my knife . . . I believe it's safe to say they're gone for good."

Her knife? What the hell had she done? And why hadn't it been *him* standing beside her? Dammit, that's why he was in Regret! To take care of her. Watch out for her. Travis fumed silently. It was his fault. He knew exactly why Alice hadn't told him about the confrontation. She was convinced that he was a useless dandy. If not for this stupid disguise, she might have called on him when she needed help.

As for Sean, Travis promised himself to have a long talk with the big Irishman.

Apparently, Alice noticed the barely controlled fury shaking through him. "Look, Travis," she said quietly, "I've been handling the mine on my own for a year and a half. I guess I'm just not used to reporting whatever happens to a partner yet."

He didn't say anything. Until the helpless anger churning in his gut settled down a bit, he didn't trust himself to talk.

Alice took a step closer to him. Her deep green eyes were . . . *kind*. Jesus, he felt like a stray puppy she'd just discovered on a roadside. And dammit, the one thing he wasn't interested in getting from her was kindness—or pity.

"All right, I'm sorry I didn't say anything about it earlier." She laid one hand on his forearm and looked directly up into his eyes. "I tell you, though, that idea of yours about the pay raise? It might work."

She was tossing him a bone.

He nodded, unappeased.

"Got any other ideas?" she asked.

She shouldn't have asked that, he told himself. Not when she was standing so close to him. Not when he could almost feel the rise and fall of her breasts. Not when he was staring down into her shining eyes.

His simmering anger was gone in an instant. Desire rippled through him and Travis concentrated on the feel of her hand on his arm. The tip of each of her fingers was like a brand, burning through the fabric of his jacket to his skin. Heat

speared through him and settled low in his belly.
He drew his left hand from his pocket and
covered hers.

"I *do* have a few other ideas," he said.

"Travis . . ." She swallowed and pulled her
hand from under his. "We better not."

"I told you," he said softly, and reached out
for the lock of hair she'd tucked behind her ear.
Freeing it, he smoothed down its length with his
thumb and forefinger. "Nothing will happen unless you want it to."

Candlelight reflected in her eyes and shimmered at him, compounding the uncertainty he
read in those green depths. He released the long,
wavy strand of hair to lay across her breast. As
her breathing quickened, he watched, fascinated,
as that curl clung to her, rising and falling with
each breath taken.

"Travis?"

"Yes?"

"What if I don't know?"

"Don't know what?" he asked, threading his
fingers through the mass of auburn waves rippling down her back.

"If I want anything to . . . happen or not."

"Then nothing will," he assured her, past the
knot of regret lodged in his throat. The ache in
his groin deepened as if his body was already
acknowledging that there would be no release.

He fought down the desperate urge to grab her
and pull her close. By God, he wanted her more
than he'd ever wanted anything or anyone in his
life. And at that moment, he didn't care who it
was she wanted touching her. Travis Deal or
Travis Delacort. As long as it was *him*.

Another eternity flew by in the space of a few seconds. When she inhaled sharply and opened her mouth to speak, Travis's insides went still.

"I've been thinkin'," she said.

"About what?" God, it was a battle just to keep his voice calm and even.

"About last night." She dragged another deep breath into her lungs, turned her head, and looked at him. "About, well. About you kissin' me."

His gaze locked on her lips. He could almost taste their sweetness. "I've been thinking about that, too."

"Ya have?"

"Yes."

"I didn't hurt ya too much, did I?" she asked. "I mean, well . . . Hell, Travis, you surprised the life outa me, kissin' me like that. And I guess I just reacted without thinkin' when you . . . you know."

Lord help him if she ever stopped to think before lashing out.

"It's all right," he said, and inhaled the odd, musty flower scent surrounding her. "I shouldn't have scared you."

"Oh no!" She pulled away a bit and faced him. "You didn't scare me," Alice told him firmly. "Hell, I've been kissed before, you know."

"Of course."

Her gaze narrowed. "You don't think so, though. Do you?"

"If you say so, I believe you."

"Hmmm . . ." Her fingers closed around his hand and squeezed. "Well, anyway, like I was sayin'. You didn't scare me any, you just kinda

caught me off my guard, so to speak, when you
. . . uh . . . well, touched me."

Travis glanced down at their joined hands. It
sounded to him as though she was willing to try
that kiss again, but just didn't know how to start
the ball rolling. He smiled inwardly. He'd be
happy to help.

"So, you're saying that if I told you that I was
planning on kissing you . . . *touching* you, it
would be all right. Because you'd be prepared."

She nodded, but despite her reassurances,
Travis thought he detected a small glimmer of
nervousness in her eyes. He drew her over to the
cot, pulled her down to sit beside him, and found
out how wrong he was.

She half turned to face him and slowly reached
up to lay her palm along his jawline. "If you
don't mind," she said, "I'd like to try it again."

"The kiss?" he asked, and heard the raw hunger in his voice. "Or the touch?"

"Both," she whispered, and leaned toward
him.

Travis covered her mouth with his. She was
ready for him; her lips parted slightly to give
him entry. He dipped inside her warmth with
delicate, tantalizing strokes. She imitated his
slow caresses, sending him deeper into a passion
that seemed unending. Her breath puffed against
his cheek and when she leaned into him, sliding
her hands up his arms to encircle his neck, Travis
groaned and pulled her tightly to him.

The ugly wool dress couldn't disguise her figure or the heat of her skin burning through the
fabric. His hands moved over her with a restless
need that he couldn't seem to fulfill fast enough.

Cradling her head in the crook of his arm, he swept one hand up to smooth across her breasts.

She moaned and twisted herself against his hand. Travis pulled his mouth free and began to lavish nibbling kisses along the length of her neck. While her fingers clutched at his shoulders, his hand slipped to the row of buttons marching down the strip of ancient lace along the front of her dress. In seconds, the buttons had been dealt with, leaving the bodice of her gown open before him.

Beneath the hideous, dark blue wool, only a thin, white cotton chemise separated Travis from the flesh he'd dreamed of caressing. He gently pushed her dress off her shoulders until the soft wool slipped down as far as her elbows and lay pooled around her waist.

Carefully, he pulled at the tiny blue ribbon, then tugged the edges of the delicate material apart. He cupped her breast tenderly and smiled at her surprised gasp of pleasure.

"Holy God, Travis," she whispered, and dug her fingers into his shoulders. Letting her head fall back on her neck, her hair streamed out behind her like a waterfall of color. The long, deep red strands felt like fine silk. Travis wanted to strip that hideous dress from her and see her lying on his cot with nothing more than her glorious auburn hair to cover her from his gaze.

That mental image brought a deep throated groan from him, and he bent over her to press his lips to the pulse beat at the base of her throat. Alice's breath caught, and she tipped her head to one side, silently offering him access.

Her skin was hot. Sweet. Everything he'd

imagined it would be. He nibbled at her flesh with a slow deliberation that tortured him as much as it did her. Her breath came in shallow pants, and when he pulled back from her, Travis would have sworn he heard a soft sigh of disappointment.

There was no need for that, though, he wasn't nearly finished. Not after waiting so long to touch her. He wanted to linger over her, introduce her to the pleasures her body was capable of, and watch her face as a shuddering release claimed her.

He only hoped it didn't kill him.

Swallowing back his hunger for her, Travis leisurely stroked his thumb across her already hardened nipple. Alice moaned quietly and moved against his hand. Her creamy skin seemed to glow in the flickering light of a dozen candles. A sunburst of golden freckles dusted her chest just above her breasts, and Travis suddenly wanted to kiss each one. He wanted to spend his life exploring every inch of her body until he was too old to move anymore. And still, he thought, that wouldn't be enough.

For now, though, he told himself, he would be satisfied with this moment. He dipped his head and took her nipple into his mouth. His lips closed around her sensitive flesh, and his tongue drew slow, damp circles around the rigid, rose-colored bud. When he began to suckle her gently, Alice gasped, reached up and cupped the back of his head, instinctively holding him to her.

"Travis," she said breathlessly. "What's happening?"

He smiled against her warmth and suckled even harder.

She groaned and shifted her hips on the cot, moving deeper into the circle of his embrace. As his arms closed around her, she whispered, "You should have told me it would feel like this."

Travis lifted his head briefly to look into her eyes.

She gave him a half smile and shrugged. "I might not have tried to break your foot for you."

"I heal quick," he said. "Besides, it was worth it."

"I don't know about that." Alice smiled and ran the tip of one finger along his jaw. "But this is surely worth it."

He caught her hand in his, then turned his head to plant a kiss in the palm. "It surely is."

Easing her back onto the cot, he followed her down and stretched out beside her on the narrow bed.

"Think the cot will hold?" she whispered.

"If it doesn't, I'll buy a new one."

She chuckled. "Folks are going to start talking about a man who goes through so many cots, Travis."

"People here are more interested in gold nuggets than in how many cots I manage to break."

Propping his head up on one hand, he smoothed his right palm over the tips of her breasts. She shuddered in response and Travis smiled.

"Comfortable?" he asked.

"Not one bit, Travis."

"No?"

"God no."

"Good. I'm glad I make you a little nervous," he murmured, and bent to briefly taste one of her breasts.

"More than a little," she said on a gasp of surprise.

He grinned and lazily slid his palm over her ribcage and across her stomach. Then he frowned slightly, lifted his head, and threw her a quick look.

"Alice," he whispered, and propped his head on one hand to look down at her. "What do you have on underneath this dress?"

"Huh?"

His hand moved against her abdomen. "I can feel something under this skirt . . . and it's no petticoat."

Her eyes widened then closed quickly. A rush of bright color flooded her cheeks.

"Dammit," she said on a groan, "if you'd have let me leave earlier, you wouldn't have found out."

"Found out what?" Completely confused now, Travis waited.

She inhaled sharply, deeply, then blew it out in a disgusted rush. "I didn't have a proper petticoat to wear under this blasted dress. So I wore my jeans and boots, because this damned wool from G. W.'s precious English King sheep itches to high heaven."

His eyebrows lifted quizzically. English King sheep? Oh, he told himself, that story was probably worth hearing. But now wasn't the time. Instead, he had to convince Alice that he didn't give a good damn *what* she was wearing. In fact, if Travis had his way, she wouldn't be wearing anything.

She was clearly uncomfortable, so even though it would kill him to stop touching her now, he heard himself asking, "Do you want me to take you home?"

Her gaze snapped up to meet his.

"Maybe you should," she said, and turned her face from him.

"Is that what you want?"

After a long moment, she shook her head. "No."

"I'm glad, Alice." He waited for her to look at him again before adding, "I don't want you to leave yet, either."

A hesitant, tremulous smile hovered briefly on her mouth.

Jesus, she was amazing, he told himself. A woman brave and fearless enough to face down armed men, yet shy and virginal enough to be embarrassed by her body's reactions to his touch. And the fact that she'd worn jeans beneath her dress ... But that piece of information didn't surprise Travis. In fact, it seemed to point out the kind of woman she was. Half female, longing for frills and finery—and half warrior, ready to defend what was hers.

The scent of her perfume drifted up to him, and he told himself that he was in serious trouble. She was becoming far too important to him.

He moved his palm across her abdomen and down to the spot where her thighs joined. As Travis's hand parted her legs and covered the very heart of her, Alice jumped in his arms.

"Holy Mother!" Her eyes flew open. "Maybe

you better just come on back up here, Travis," she said, and grabbed his hand to pull it back to her breasts.

"It's all right, Alice," he whispered, and tried to hold back the rush of his own desire enough to ease her fears. "Let me show you how good it can be. How good you can feel."

She looked up at him, and her hesitation and newborn desire shone in her green eyes. "I don't know, Travis. Maybe we shouldn't go any farther—"

"And maybe we should," he told her before slanting his mouth across hers. His tongue swept past her parted lips for another taste of the magic he'd found with her. It was there, waiting for him. And this time, Alice responded quickly. Her momentary doubts had dissolved as she answered his passion with untutored eagerness that was more exciting than the most well-practiced lover's could have been. Their tongues twisted and danced together, creating a rising swirl of passion that crashed down around them, thundering through their veins, demanding release.

Travis's right hand began to move over her center. He ignored the wool skirt and the heavy denim separating him from the warm heat of her. If she was ashamed to have him know she wore jeans beneath her dress, he wouldn't add to her embarrassment by moving the yards of material out of his way. But by heaven, he would touch her. Until she asked him to stop, he would stroke her and caress her until her body trembled with the kind of quivering, shaking delight he knew she was yearning for.

Dragging his mouth from hers, he bent to claim one of her nipples again. Over and over, he drew on it, his tongue tormenting her even as his fingers rubbed at the fabric covered spot between her legs that would bring her the most pleasure.

Alice parted her thighs for him and lifted her hips instinctively into the feel of him. A starburst of sensation coursed through her, and she held Travis's head to her breast with one hand, hoping to tell him without words just what he was doing to her.

His fingers rubbed at a spot that seemed to be on fire. Each time she lifted her hips, he moved his fingertips harder, faster. She didn't understand what was happening. She didn't know how they had come to be doing this at all.

The only thing she was certain of was that she didn't want him to stop. She wanted these indescribable feelings to roll on forever. The more he touched her, the more she wanted. It was as if her body was burning up from the inside and Travis, she knew, was the only one who could douse the flames.

A brief, humiliating thought raced through her mind, and she was glad he couldn't know that she heartily wished she hadn't worn those blasted jeans. Incredible though it was to admit, even to herself, Al knew that she wanted to feel his touch on her flesh. She wanted his touch . . . *there* . . . without yards of material to separate them.

He lifted his head when she groaned and she was immediately sorry for making any noise at all. Staring up into the icy blue of his eyes, she wondered why she had ever thought him to be useless. How could she have looked at this man and not known what he was? How could she have not seen past his outrageous clothing to the magic inside him?

And then the fire within her leaped out of control and she stopped thinking entirely. Her hips rocking wildly, she twisted her head from side to side as she desperately, frantically fought to hold onto the feelings rocketing through her.

But she couldn't. They were already spiraling out of her control, and all she could do was hold on to Travis and ride the tornado.

The starburst between her legs shattered suddenly and she tried to shout, only to find Travis's lips locked onto hers. He gave her his breath when hers was stolen from her, and he held her until the trembling in her limbs finally quieted.

# Chapter 13

The applause started with one man.

His palms smacked together in a steady, heartbeatlike rhythm. Slowly, one after another, dozens of people in the Hopeless Cause Saloon joined in until the sound made the already shaky wooden walls tremble.

Cutter swiveled in his chair at the poker table, turning his head this way and that, looking at the satisfied expressions on the miners' faces. He threw a quick look at Sean, who shrugged, grinned, and lifted his half-full beer mug in silent salute to the crowd.

As the wave of applause receded, someone slapped Cutter on the back. He turned to see who it was, but the man had already drifted into the milling mob.

Snatches of conversation rose up and settled over the miners, and Sean and Cutter had no trouble at all listening in.

"Best damn thing I seen in weeks," one man admitted.

"Hell," another countered. "I'd have paid

good money to watch Thompson get set down."

"Yeah," someone else interrupted. "But it's just like you to find a way to get it free."

Sean glanced at Cutter. "Well, now, it seems Mr. Thompson's fewer friends than we thought he had."

"Fear doesn't buy friends, Sean." Cutter lifted his whiskey glass and drained the remaining liquor.

"Here's another round for you boys." Sam, the bartender and proprietor of the Hopeless Cause, stepped up and set a small tray on their table. He unloaded a fresh beer for Sean and an unopened bottle of whiskey with two glasses. "On the house," he said, and tucked the empty tray under one beefy arm.

"God loves a generous soul," Sean told him, and reached for the beer.

"Thanks," Cutter said, and uncorked the bottle to pour himself another drink.

"No thanks needed," Sam said with a grin. "Everybody in here enjoyed that little performance." He waved one arm at the still smiling miners jostling around the crowded, smoky room. "Lord knows, they've usually little enough to smile about."

"If they all hate Thompson so much," Cutter asked, glancing at the bartender from the corner of his eye, "why is it no one wanted to talk to us about him?"

"It's not that they didn't want to talk," Sam argued. "They didn't want to get shot for it."

Sean's eyebrows lifted as he used his sleeve to wipe beer foam from his upper lip.

"Men have a way of . . . disappearing, when they get on Thompson's bad side."

"Then he has a *good* side?" Sean snorted.

"Not so's you'd notice," the bartender agreed.

"You haven't done much talking yourself, Sam." Cutter eyed the other man warily.

"I know what you're thinkin'," Sam said. "And I can't say as I blame ya. Why the hell would I be willin' to talk now, you're wondering."

"It *is* a good question." Sean nodded.

"With a good answer," Sam shot back.

"Which is?"

The bartender looked at Cutter.

"There ain't been a man willin' to back Thompson down since he hit town a few months back." He folded his arms over his dirty white apron and glanced from Cutter to Sean and back again. "And you two have been askin' plenty of questions the last couple of weeks, but you ain't done a damn thing to let folks know how you stand. Until tonight."

Reasonable, Cutter told himself. People living in fear of one man would naturally be wary of yet another newcomer or two.

Sam chuckled and his girth shifted and rolled. He reached up, scratched his salt and pepper whiskers, and grinned in memory. "But when you made Thompson back up and take cover . . . well, I figure if you're willin' to make him an enemy, then I reckon you deserve a few friends, too."

"Friends who are willin' to talk?" Sean wanted to know.

Sam eyed him carefully before giving him a

slow nod. "Might's well," he said. "If somethin'
don't happen soon, the only customers I'm
gonna have are Thompson and Bennet."

Cutter's gaze snapped to Sean. The two men
exchanged a long, thoughtful look before the big
Irishman asked quietly, "Bennet, ya say?"

"Hell yes, Bennet."

A few of the men closest to their table stopped
talking and stared at Sam as if he'd lost his mind.
The bartender sailed right on.

"You see this crowd, here?" Sam asked, waving one hand at the miners and whores behind
him. "A few months ago, I had twice as many
in here. Every night."

Sean frowned, and Cutter knew exactly what
his brother-in-law was thinking. The ramshackle
little place seemed full enough, with unwashed
miners snuggling up to tired looking, over-
worked "ladies." Too many more people thrown
into the place, and no one would be able to draw
a breath without begging someone's pardon.

A few more men sidled up behind Sam to listen as the bartender talked.

"It was good times," he sighed fondly. "Whiskey and gold flowin' like the River Jordan." The
big man frowned suddenly and his eyes narrowed. "Then Bennet showed up in town,
Thompson along with him."

"Sam..." a wary voice spoke up from the
crowd.

"Ah," the bartender shouted back, "the hell
with Thompson. *And* Bennet!" He reached for
the bottle and the extra glass he'd brought Cutter
and poured himself a drink. Tossing the whiskey
down his throat, he choked and gave the empty

glass a horrified glance, as if just realizing what
he'd drunk. He shuddered, then slammed the
glass down and went on. "If they want to kill
me, they can go on ahead. Hell, they've about
killed me already, drivin' off my business like
they done."

"What exactly," Sean asked quietly, "did they
do?"

"Hmmph! Bennet starts right in takin' over the
mines. Little ones at first. A couple of small
claims that didn't mean shit to anybody but
those who worked 'em."

"What about Thompson?" Cutter asked.

"Thompson does Bennet's dirty work," Sam
sneered. "If a man fights to hold on to his claim,
Thompson 'convinces' him to sell."

"It's true," a little man standing to one side
piped up. "Thompson pushed me off my claim.
Now I'm workin' day shift for somebody else instead of myself."

"And your mine?"

"Bennet's now," the man told Sean. "And may
he never have a minute's luck with it."

A rumble of agreement rose up from the
crowd, and Cutter noticed that the piano music
had stopped. It seemed that everyone in the
place was listening to their conversation. Idly, he
wondered just how many of Bennet's spies were
in the room. Then he told himself it was far too
late to be worrying about that.

"I hear tell Bennet's bought up the land on either side of the main road to Gold Mountain," a
voice from the back of the room shouted.

"Yeah," someone else cut him off. "Word is,

he's gonna be chargin' a toll to the ore wagons
headed off the mountain."

"The son-of-a-bitch."

"Greedy bastard," someone else muttered.

"Bennet's an odd one, if ya ask me," Sam said.
"Don't see him much. Stays in his rooms. Keeps
to himself."

"And Thompson?"

"Goes wherever he has a mind to," the bartender said quickly. "Oh, he takes Bennet's orders. As far as I know, he ain't killed anybody
yet, either. Leastways, not around here. But that
ain't to say he won't. You two best keep your
eyes open. He'll be lookin' for you—and not to
thank ya for takin' him down a peg or two in
front of this bunch."

Cutter glanced at Sean.

"I'm thinkin' we'd best go have a talk with Al
and Travis," the Irishman said.

Sam chuckled and bent forward, leaning one
palm on the tabletop. Keeping his voice low, he
looked from one to the other of them and said,
"I wouldn't go interruptin' that city man right
now, were I you."

"Why's that?" Cutter asked quietly.

"He come by earlier today. Bought some wine.
Some of my best. Paid dear for it, too." The bartender's bushy gray eyebrows wiggled and
danced over his eyes. "I'm figurin' he's got some
notions about Al." Straightening up, Sam shook
his head. "Looks like some man finally looked
past them buckskins of hers and noticed what
kind of woman she is. Funny. When first I saw
that dude, I didn't figure him for that much
brains." He sighed heavily. "Why if I was twenty

years younger, I might have tried for her myself."

Cutter grinned at Sean and the Irishman nodded, pushing himself to his feet.

Before Cutter could join him though, the floor
jolted beneath them. A low, deep mutter issued
up from the earth, and the floorboard shuddered
and groaned in response. The table shook and
the open bottle of whiskey toppled to one side
and rolled off the table, liquor pouring out the
uncorked top.

A woman screamed, someone shouted, and
then the groaning roar died as abruptly as it had
started. The floor steadied again and Sean
crossed himself.

"Holy Mother of God!" he looked around him
and noticed that most of the miners had gone on
about their business, paying no attention at all to
the momentary shifting of the earth.

"Earthquake," Sam shrugged. "Just a small
one." He bent down, picked up the whiskey bottle, and wiped the neck clean on his dirty shirt.

"First quake, Sean?" Cutter asked as he stood
up.

"Aye," the Irishman nodded. "And my last as
well. I hope."

The man seated in the shadows of the pine
came awake in a rush. Planting the palms of his
hands flat on the churning earth, he pressed his
back more firmly against the tree trunk and
waited for God to stop moving his furniture
around in Heaven.

One glance at the tent across the clearing from
him was all he spared. He knew he hadn't been

asleep long. The moon was still high in the sky, so Travis and Al were no doubt still in the tent.

Now, thanks to the earthquake, he'd be wide awake too and watching for them to leave.

Al rolled with the ground's motion, feeling the pitch and sway of the cot beneath her. One candlestick fell over, but before she could remark on it, Travis snatched it up and blew out the flame. She blinked, startled at his quickness. She'd hardly seen his hand move.

Then he laid that same hand on her bare waist to steady her as the quake grumbled on and she forgot about everything but the warmth of his flesh on hers.

Dear Lord, what he'd done to her. Somehow, she thought, it was fitting that even the very ground sat up and took notice of the change that had overtaken her that night. Here she lay, breasts bared to a man she hadn't even known existed a few weeks ago. And was she ashamed?

Hell no.

God help her, she wanted more. She wanted to feel that slow climb to pleasure again. She wanted to feel her knees turn to water and her insides explode into fire once more. She wanted Travis's chest bared to her touch. She wanted to know what it felt like to have a man's body pressed along hers. No, she corrected herself mentally. It wasn't just *any* man she wanted lying against her.

It was Travis.

The man who had looked at her and seen a woman. The man who had made her, for the first time in her life, *glad* that she was a woman.

The grumbling and groaning slowly died away, and the cot steadied itself like a ship sailing out of a storm.

"Not a very long one," Travis said.

"Hardly worth noticing," she agreed. "But most folks act a bit more surprised than you are right now."

He looked away from her briefly, then turned back and shrugged. "I've been in California before."

She nodded, but watched him thoughtfully as he eased himself off the cot and began to pick up the remains of their toppled dinner.

Even for a man who'd been through one before, he was damned calm. Especially for a man who'd nearly fainted clean away the first time he heard gunfire. If a gunshot had scared him so, an earthquake should have pushed him over the edge.

Hell, most people she knew were terrified by the earth's wild, sudden movements. Of course, around San Francisco, they had more reason than most to be frightened. What with all the wooden buildings that inevitably caught fire, burning down entire city blocks, and the brick buildings that exploded, raining heavy blocks down on crowds streaming into the streets. After a really bad shaker, people even refused to go back into their houses. Usually they slept outside, in as open an area as they could find.

But there was something about an earthquake that Al liked. Well, maybe not liked. Respected was probably closer to the truth. Only a fool didn't respect something he had no control over. And it was damned impressive to watch the raw fury and power of nature. Something inside Al responded to the untamed, unsettled feeling in the world directly after a quake. A time where everything was possible and nothing was certain.

Travis bent down and quickly blew out several of the still burning candles. The ground beneath his feet seemed to shiver as if relaxing again after the little shake-up.

Little shake-up. He glanced at the woman lying on his cot and felt his insides quake and roll with the same intensity as the earth had only moments before. Her soft green eyes held a glimmer of something that was as effective in cooling his desire as a bucket of ice water poured over his head.

He saw the glimmering shine of hope in her eyes. Dreams. Promises.

And he had to look away. For both their sakes.

Thank God for that quake, he thought. Who knew what might have happened between him and Alice if not for the very heavens reaching down to slap some sense into him.

He straightened up and deliberately turned his back on Alice, giving her time to cover herself again. Staring at the canvas wall opposite him, Travis called himself every foul name he could think of. For the life of him, he couldn't understand how he had so lost control of the situation. He knew damn well that he had nothing to offer her. Hell, he couldn't even stay in town!

There were obligations waiting for him. Other people with trouble who were looking to him for help. But besides all that, he wasn't sure if he could ever be the kind of man she wanted. Deserved. He'd failed before, what would keep him from failing Alice when she most needed him?

Behind him, he heard her shifting position on the cot and prayed that she was buttoning up her dress. Jesus, what had he been thinking of? Alice Donnelly was no fast and easy kind of woman. She wasn't the sort a man rolled around on a cot with for a few hours and then dismissed.

She was a good, honorable woman in her own right. And beyond that, she was the daughter of a friend. A friend who had trusted Travis to look out for her.

His teeth ground together. If he had caught some fella trying to do to Alice what *he'd* been doing ... Travis would have shot him where he stood. But suicide didn't seem like much of an answer. No, the only answer lay in getting her back to her own tent as quickly as he could.

"I'll walk you back to your tent," Travis said suddenly.

Al frowned and looked at him. She finished buttoning up that ugly dress again before saying, "You don't have to."

He shrugged deeper into his coat, and the yards of green fabric seemed to swallow him up. Before her eyes, he changed. The man who'd touched her, kissed her, and introduced her body to delights she'd never thought to experience was gone.

In an instant, he'd disappeared.

Well, dammit, she wanted him back.

Al swung her legs over the edge of the cot and stood up. Facing him, she planted her fists at her hips and shook her hair back out of her face.

"Who the hell are you?"

"What?"

"I said, who the hell are you?" Al looked him up and down, then continued. "You're sure not the man who was here a minute ago. That fella was all over me like beggars at a feast!"

His mouth quirked into a lopsided smile. "A lovely comparison."

"Don't sidestep this, Travis," Al warned him. "I want to know just what's goin' on in that head of yours. And I figure I got a right to know."

"Do you?"

"Yeah."

A long, silent minute passed, with each of them trying to outstare the other. One of the candles guttered, and the flame hissed and snapped before it died. Cold air slipped beneath the tent flap, whispered around the two of them, then settled itself into an icy chill.

"All right," he finally said, "maybe you do, at that."

The look on his face told Al that she wasn't going to like what he had to say, and just for a moment, she considered stopping him before he started. But that moment passed in a heartbeat. She'd never been one to hide from the truth, and she wasn't about to start now. Besides, you couldn't fight what you didn't know.

"The truth," Travis muttered more to himself than to her. Dammit, she did deserve to hear the truth. But which part of the truth? The reason he was there? Who he really was? Or the fact that touching her, stroking her skin, had brought him more peace than he'd ever thought to experience in his lifetime?

Looking at her now, with her eyes blazing, her head tilted at a belligerent angle and her feet planted wide apart in a fighting stance, he could almost believe that those few minutes together on his cot hadn't happened. But they had, and he would carry the memory forever. Her heat was still with him. Her scent clung to him, making every breath a sweet torture. And her sharp, direct gaze was locked with his, demanding answers.

What answers could he give her?

"The truth is," he said softly, deliberately avoiding looking at her, "that though this distraction was very pleasant, I believe that it behooves us both to prevent it from happening again."

"Behooves?"

"As partners," Travis went on, hating his own words as well as the sound of his voice, "we should strive to maintain a business relationship."

"Is that right?" She undid the top three buttons on her dress and scratched gently at the exposed vee of flesh.

His gaze slipped unerringly to follow her movements then shot back up to meet her eyes.

Alice smiled knowingly, then slowly nodded. "All right, Travis. We'll do as you say. We'll be partners. Nothin' else."

He watched as she shook her wild mane of hair back from her face and told himself again that he was doing the right thing. Then she pulled a deep breath into her lungs and Travis stared at the swell of her bosom.

"So *partner*," she went on, and waited until he was looking her in the eye again. "You goin' to walk me back to my tent? Or do partners not do that sort of thing?"

"Of course," he said, and headed gratefully for the tent flap and the cool, sharp night air.

Alice ducked under the flap, followed him outside, then stopped alongside him.

"You know something, Travis?"

"What?"

She linked her arm with his and started walking. "Maybe it's best we do like you want."

"I'm sure of it." The heat of her pressed along his side, and he was willing to bet that she was deliberately rubbing her breast against his arm.

"Why," Alice went on, "with my partner, I can be honest. Say things that I couldn't . . . or *shouldn't* say to a beau."

"Certainly," Travis whispered, concentrating on the dark, rocky ground.

"Well, then, partner," she said, "step quick and get me back to my tent."

"Why?" He looked at her warily, but in the moonlight, it was impossible to read her expression.

"Because this damn dress itches something fierce! I can't wait to yank it off!"

Travis bit back a groan at the thought, then stumbled slightly on an oversized stone in his path.

The watcher under the pines was still a little shaky from the earthquake, but he managed to keep Travis and Al in sight until she slipped into her tent. Frowning, the man turned and stared back the way he'd come, toward Travis Deal's tent.

Somebody ought to tell those two that candle-light can throw a mighty bright shadow on canvas walls. Idly, he wondered if anyone else in camp had noticed the two bosses wrapped up together, tighter than two beads on a string. And more, he wondered what he should do about it.

Lord knew, it was past time for Al to find herself a man who would appreciate her. The problem was, he wasn't at all sure that Travis *was* that man. Dammit, he was still willing to put cold money on the fact that he knew Travis Deal from somewheres else. As *someone* else.

Scratching at his sparsely whiskered jaw, the watcher shook his head and told himself sourly that maybe he should just keep his big old nose out of things. "Mayhap," he said aloud, "she knows what she's doin'." Then a moment later, he argued with himself. "Hell, ain't a man alive can hold his own with a woman when her mind's set."

"Amen, brother."

Chucker spun around, his breath caught in his throat, as his gaze swept over the surrounding shadows. A short, squat bush on his right rustled gently, and Chucker turned to face whoever was hiding there.

A hand came down on his shoulder, and the old man knew he'd been fooled by the oldest trick in the book. A rock tossed into a bush to create a diversion while giving a man time to sneak up behind his prey.

"What in hell are you doing, Chucker?"

The camp cook released his pent-up breath, stepped out from under the hand Travis still had clapped on his shoulder, and spun around.

"Keepin' an eye on you, that's what."

"Why?"

He snorted and looked Travis up and down slowly. "Mister, I don't know you from Adam's great aunt. But I know that girl, yonder. And her pa. I figure it's my business to see she's all right."

Travis raked one hand through his hair, glanced off in Alice's direction, then brought his gaze back to land on the old man in front of him. Short, stubborn, and old as the hills, Chucker obviously didn't think much of him. But on the other hand, Travis told himself, at least now he knew that there was someone else watching out for Alice.

Of course, if the camp cook was going to make a habit of trailing people through the trees, he'd better learn to be a damn sight more quiet. Hell, Chucker had done everything except wear a bell around his neck.

Travis had heard every step the old coot had made while trying to slip through the woods. He must have stepped on every twig and rubbed against every loose branch in his path. But it was more than the noise that had alerted Travis. It was the undeniable sense of feeling someone's eyes on him.

"How'd you sneak up on me like that?" Chucker demanded suddenly.

"You were so busy talking to yourself, you didn't hear me approach."

"Hmmm . . ." The old man cocked his head and stared hard at Travis. Rubbing his chin with one gnarled hand, he muttered, "I didn't hear ya, 'cause you didn't make a sound. Now I call that mighty odd for a city man."

Travis didn't say a word. Pushing the edges of his coat back, he jammed his hands into his pants pockets and planted his feet in a wide, easy stance.

Chucker's eyes widened and a slow smile crept up his weathered features. "I got it!" Shaking one finger at the other man, he added quietly, "*Now* I know where I seen you before."

Travis's lips tightened into a thin, grim line.

"It was down in Abilene," Chucker continued with a snort of laughter as his gaze swept over Travis. " 'Course, ya wasn't dressed like *that*."

"Chucker—"

"No, no," the old man interrupted. "This's been plaguin' me for days. Now it's come to me, I got to say it."

Travis closed his eyes briefly, tiredly, then opened them again to stare at the cook's expression of delight.

"You was a marshal, as I recall," he said, tapping his index finger against his stubbly chin. "You come into town to pick up some fella from jail, and a couple of his boys tried to throw down on ya."

Texas Jack Hyde, Travis remembered, was the prisoner in question. Wanted in Santa Fe for rape and murder. Memories rose up in his mind, and Travis saw again the wide, dusty street in front of the Abilene sheriff's office. He'd just stepped outside after presenting the warrant that would allow him to take Texas Jack to New Mexico for trial. The day was hot and dusty with the air so still it was hard to breathe. He stepped off the boardwalk into the dirt, and a couple of Jack's friends decided to complain about his arrest.

They'd faced him down, twenty feet separating them, apparently trying to ensure that even if Travis got one of them, the survivor would surely kill Travis. Cocky and sure of themselves, the two outlaws had laughed aloud at Travis's predicament. They joked with each other about how they'd managed to trap a U.S. marshal. Then they each took a moment to tell Travis exactly how he was going to die.

In memory, he felt the hot Texas sun beating down on the back of his neck. He saw the interested, but frightened faces of Abilene's citizens, peeking from behind the safety of curtains and windowpanes. He experienced again that feeling of helplessness against fate. There would be no talking those two out of the fight they'd come so far to find.

Then he saw the man on the left draw his pistol.

Travis threw himself to one side, dropped into a crouch and shot the first man through the middle button of his shirt. Then half turning, he shot the other man, aiming his bullet for the tag hanging from a tobacco packet stuffed into the man's shirt pocket.

In seconds, it was over. The afternoon was still hot and dusty. Faces were still pressed to window glass. And two men were dead.

"That was the best piece of shootin' I ever did see," Chucker told him. "Dropped 'em both without hardly blinkin'."

Travis sighed, returned from his memories and looked down at the much shorter man. "That was a long time ago."

"Not so long that I can't remember your right-

ful name. And it ain't *Deal*." Chucker folded his
spindly arms over his narrow chest. "It's Delacort. Travis Delacort."

Shit.

# Chapter 14

~~~~◯◯~~~~

**A**l stepped into her tent and kicked the first thing she saw. Her tin washbasin, thankfully empty, shot across the floor and clanked to a stop against a rear leg of her cot. She scowled furiously as she thought about that walk from Travis's tent to her own.

What an idiot she'd been!

Leaning into him . . . staring up into his eyes coyly—holding onto his arm, as if she *needed* a man's guiding hand over that rocky path.

Fool.

But when he'd closed himself off from her so soon after introducing her to those amazing sensations, she'd had the feeling that perhaps he was embarrassed somehow. Al was willing to bet that a city girl didn't go around letting a man who wasn't her husband touch her in places that a "good" woman didn't even think about! Al had told herself that being a dude and all, maybe she'd just overwhelmed him with her response to him.

But all of her silly female behavior hadn't

changed a thing. In fact, it had probably made things between them even worse. And she could only assume it was because she was so blasted terrible at being a woman.

Suddenly a wild, stray thought rose up.

Was that *kindness* she'd seen in his eyes?

She thought back to the moment he'd left her in front of her tent. He hadn't said anything. In fact, he hadn't spoken at all while walking her home. He'd simply let her prattle on and on, trying her best to do a reasonable job of being flirtatious. Then, when they'd reached her tent, he'd just stood there. A too-thin man in a too-big coat, moonlight spilling over his features, his downcast eyes lifting to meet hers.

Yes, Al told herself furiously. Kindness. And what was kindness but a bit more civilized version of pity? That's what he thought of her? That she was worthy of pity?

Is that what he'd been thinking when the two of them were stretched out together on that damned cot? Had he been doing her a favor? No sooner had *that* idea taken root than Al picked up the notion and ran with it. And the longer she thought about it, the wilder her imagination became, until she could almost hear what he'd told himself.

*Poor Alice. No man to show her what it is to be a woman. Well, the least I can do is give her a small taste of what she'll never know. After all, she's not exactly the kind of woman to inspire everlasting love. Like as not, this little bit of affection is all she'll ever have.*

The son-of-a-bitch!

All of the little niceties he'd performed for her

over the last couple of weeks took on a new meaning. He hadn't been treating her like a lady. He'd been feeling sorry for her.

Hell, he'd probably even been laughing at her!

Fuming now, she reminded herself of the way he'd hustled her out of his tent. Why, the minute she'd had her clothes straightened out, he was headed for the canvas flap and freedom. Al could have guessed why, too!

The damned fool man probably figured that now that she'd been initiated into his lovemaking abilities, he'd never have a minute's peace. Why, Al thought, he was probably convinced himself that she was going to insist he marry her or something. He was probably terrified that she would start spending her days trailing after him like some lovesick pup, hoping for a pat on the head!

The son-of-a-bitch!

Grumbling under her breath, Al stomped across the tent, yanking at the buttons on her dress as she went. Absently, she heard the tiny jet beads as they landed, but she was too angry to care that she'd just ruined a three dollar and fifty cent dress.

Besides, she never wanted to see it again.

She undressed quickly, quietly, in the darkness, then rummaged around for something to wear against the chilly night air. Grabbing up an old cotton workshirt, Al gratefully pulled it on and buttoned it haphazardly. The tails of the shirt hit her mid-thigh, so she hurriedly climbed under her blankets.

Stretching out on her cot, Al stared up at her canvas roof and tried to think calmly, rationally.

She folded her arms across her chest, pinning her blanket down along either side of her. Travis's image floated to the surface of her mind, and though she wanted to hurl mental rocks at it, she didn't.

Instead, she carefully thought out the whole situation, just as she'd done about every problem facing her throughout her life. And Travis Deal was certainly a problem.

Pity. She frowned and narrowed her gaze at the water-stained canvas above her. Had she seen even a trace of pity in his eyes while he was loving her? Touching her?

No.

She smiled softly into the darkness and let the memory of his hands on her body race through her again. Her breathing quickened. Her mouth went dry. She threaded her fingers together and squeezed tightly when a now familiar curl of desire began to throb deep in her center. Al took a long shuddering breath and told herself that there had been many things in his pale blue eyes, but pity wasn't one of them.

Her smile faded just a bit. Maybe it wasn't until *after* their time together that he'd begun to regret what he'd done. Maybe he didn't think of her as a lady anymore. Maybe her own passions had killed that notion of his.

She frowned.

But maybe not.

Hell, she was so bloody confused, she didn't know what to think. There should be rules to this kind of thing, she told herself. A body should know what to say and think and do. She shouldn't have to lay there alone in the dark, trying to second-guess everything he'd said and done!

Dammit! Al rolled to one side and punched her flattened pillow with her fist.

How in the devil was a person supposed to know these things?

And why didn't she have anyone to ask?

Oh, there were her sisters, of course. At least, Maggie and Frankie. But for that matter, Teresa probably knew more about this man/woman thing than Al. As pretty and lively as Teresa was, there were bound to be a few beaux hanging about. But her sisters were all too far away to do Al a damn bit of good, and this wasn't exactly something she could say in a telegram.

No, she'd just have to figure this out on her own. Like every other problem she'd ever faced. Did Travis care for her? Or not? Did he still think of her as a lady? Or had she ruined that for all time because of her moaning and groaning? She grimaced in embarrassment as she remembered how wantonly she'd behaved under his magical touch. Lord, how would she ever be able to look him in the eye again?

Hell. A person could go stark staring crazy trying to work this out. Deliberately, Al closed her eyes and tried to relax enough to sleep. All she could do was what she always did. She would be the only person she knew how to be. It had been good enough for him before. It should be good enough for him now.

"If not, then the hell with him," she muttered. But her heartbeat staggered slightly at the thought, and a strange, churning sensation started low in her stomach.

She squeezed her eyes shut even tighter and ordered herself to quit thinking and go to sleep.

It was a long time before her body obeyed, and when sleep did finally come, she found no peace. Images of Travis haunted her.

"Not a word," Travis told the cook. "You can't say a word about who I am to anyone."

"But Al—"

"Especially not Alice," he interrupted. Hell, he didn't even want to think about having to deal with her reaction to his masquerade right now.

"Why the hell not?" the old man shot back. "Heck, why not tell the whole damned town? You can sure as shit bet that if Thompson finds out who you really are, he'll lay off Al mighty damn quick."

"Maybe," Travis said. "And maybe it'd be enough to push him over the edge to doing something we'd regret." He'd already gone over all of the options, more times than he cared to count. And though the idea of meeting Thompson on equal ground was tempting, the thought of Alice getting caught up in the confrontation wasn't.

Travis dragged one hand across his eyes then let it slip down to rub the back of his neck. As complicated as this whole mess had been before, tonight it had taken a whole new turn.

There wasn't a chance in hell that he would ever be able to be objective about Alice. Granted, he hadn't been very objective even before he'd met her. But now, after holding her—however briefly—he felt as though the last threads of the professional detachment he used to pride himself on had unraveled like an old, neglected tapestry.

Travis tossed a quick glance at her tent. He thought about how Alice felt in his arms, curled into him, her eyes wide with surprised pleasure, her voice a hushed whisper. He tasted her kiss again and let himself remember the incredible sense of completeness that had stolen over him while holding her.

But he had no right to those feelings. He wouldn't be staying with Alice, no matter how much he might wish the truth were different. A woman like her should have a man to love her—and if he did anything to lessen her chances of finding that happiness with someone else, he'd never forgive himself. Even though the very thought of some other man being the one to introduce her to lovemaking stabbed at him like a knife through the heart.

His gaze narrowed, and he ground his teeth together in frustration. Travis only wished he'd met her before. Before he'd made a fatal error in judgment that had cost him everything.

Even his right to happiness.

He straightened up, fought back his personal regrets, and looked down into Chucker's animated features. Travis didn't have a future with Alice Donnelly. But he would make damn sure that *she* had a future. Even if he had no part in it. As long as there was a breath in his body, nothing was going to happen to her.

Nothing.

"Travis?"

He dropped and spun around in an instinctive half-crouch. When his gaze locked on Cutter and Sean, standing outside his tent, Travis relaxed and started walking toward them. Chucker followed along right behind him.

"There you are." Cutter turned at the sound of footsteps and grinned.

Sean glanced at the old man behind Travis and laughed. "Mary Alice, darlin'," he said to the cook. "How you've changed!"

Chucker grumbled something unintelligible.

Travis ignored them both. "What do you want, Cutter?"

"Thought we'd stop by and tell you and Al about our evening. Is she still here?"

"No." Frowning, Travis walked past Cutter, lifted the tent flap, and bent to go inside. The three other men followed him. "And how did you know she was here, anyway?"

"Sam told us," Sean offered, and his eyebrows wiggled. "He also told us about the wine . . ." His glance fell on the empty bottle. "Hmm . . ."

"Half of it spilled during the earthquake."

"Sure, sure it did."

"Maybe it's a good thing Al has left already."

Now *that* statement had more truth in it than the other man knew.

"Since her father's not here," Cutter tossed in as he seated himself on the edge of the cot, "it's up to me and Sean to ask you something, Travis."

He frowned, first at his old friend, then at the Irishman, who was helping himself to some leftover rabbit stew. A low, scratching sound slipped past Chucker's throat, and Travis had the uncomfortable notion that the old man was laughing. At him.

"Ask me what?"

"Just what are your intentions toward our Al?"

"Intentions?"

"Aye," Sean said around a mouthful of rabbit. "It's marriage or nothin', boy-o. There'll be no patty-fingers goin' on. Not while we're here to stop it."

Chucker garbled another laugh, and this time Travis threw him a glare guaranteed to stop a man dead in his tracks. Chucker ignored him.

"Now, now," Cutter interrupted, tipping his hat back further on his head. "A little patty-fingers is not a bad thing." He shot his brother-in-law a knowing look. "I would, however, advise you to stay out of confessionals."

Sean flushed, and Travis told himself to be sure and hear the rest of *that* story sometime.

"And," Cutter went on, snatching Travis's attention again, "I've no doubt that Al can put a stop to anything she's of a mind to stop."

"True enough," Chucker mumbled.

"Still, I'd like to hear what you're planning, Travis."

He looked at the gambler closely. Under the teasing note, Cutter was dead serious. Travis couldn't blame him. If the situation was different . . . if *he* was different, he'd be plenty damn serious himself. He'd ask Alice to marry him and keep at her until she agreed. Then he'd build them a house somewhere and help her make some babies.

But things weren't different.

And Travis couldn't be the man she deserved.

Dear God, just the thought of being responsible for anyone else besides himself again made his blood run cold. It had been hard enough accepting this job from Kevin. And it was only because the person in danger had been Alice that he'd taken it at all. But this job was temporary. He wouldn't be responsible for her for the rest of her life. As much as he might like the idea, it just wasn't possible.

If they were married and had kids, what then? What if he made another mistake? What if it was Alice who paid for it this time? Or their child?

No, he couldn't take that chance. And he wouldn't allow Alice to risk it either. But he would be damned if he was going to explain all that to Cutter.

"Stay out of this," he said quietly.

"Wish I could." Cutter shrugged. "She's family."

"That she is," Sean added.

"She may be family," Travis told them, "but she's long past needing a nanny." He planted his feet and bent his knees, preparing himself for a fight, should either Cutter or Sean decide they needed one. "And I don't recall asking for any advice from either of you."

Cutter stared at him thoughtfully for a long minute. Travis had no idea what the gambler was thinking. His features set in the studied blank expression that served him so well in a poker game, the man was unreadable.

"All right, Travis. We'll stay out of it. For now." Holding one hand up to silence his brother-in-law, Cutter stared hard into Travis's eyes and went on. "But if she's hurt . . . in any way . . . you and me are going to have to *talk* about it."

Slowly, Travis nodded. It was all he could expect and more than he'd hoped for. All he had to do now was finish his business in Regret and get the hell out of town.

"Well!" Cutter said and leaned forward, his elbows braced on his knees. "Now that that's settled, we wanted to talk to you about what we found out tonight." He slanted a questioning look at Chucker, then glanced back at Travis.

Travis shrugged, relaxed, and plopped down onto one of the nearby crates. "He knows who I am."

"Really?"

The old man nodded abruptly. "Saw him work once, in Abilene. How'd *you* know?"

"Saved my neck once." Cutter grinned. "In a card game."

"What did you want to tell me?" Travis asked loudly, hoping to hurry them up and chase them all out. He was in no mood for company.

Before Cutter could so much as open his mouth again, Sean started talking. He went on for several minutes, pausing only for an occasional interruption from Cutter, telling the entire story of what had happened at the Hopeless Cause.

As Travis listened, his thoughts raced. Alice had been right. It was Bennet behind everything. But knowing that didn't make anything easier. Even though every man in town would swear to it, they still had no proof. Nothing that would stand up in a real court. And the chances of getting Bennet before a miner's court were slimmer than Chucker's chances of being elected King of Nevada.

In fact, Bennet had the money and the men to escape any kind of court. He could either buy or fight his way out of trouble.

Cutter's, Sean's, and Chucker's voices faded into the background as Travis concentrated fully on the elusive Rafe Bennet. There had to be a way. Some way to get rid of the bastard without shooting him or endangering Alice or anyone else. All Travis would need is a little time to come up with something.

The explosion shattered the early morning quiet.

Al raced out of her tent, boots stuffed under her arm, still tying the laces on her buckskin pants. She started running toward the mouth of the mine where an all-too-familiar cloud of dust and smoke was rolling out into the predawn light.

Miners, still heavy lidded with sleep, surrounded her, grumbling, cursing and even praying, but she paid no attention. Balancing on first one foot, then the other, she tugged her boots on and started forward. A firm hand on her arm halted her abruptly.

She turned to see Travis frowning at her.

"Where do you think you're going?" he demanded over the rush of voices.

"Inside," she snapped, yanking her arm away. "Where else? Someone's got to check on the men."

His jaw tightened. "How many?"

"Two," she said. "The driller and the powder monkey." Al swallowed back a rising tide of fear and forced herself to speak calmly. "Today's

Thursday, so that means it's Mick and Deacon in there." Her gaze shifted to the gaping mouth of the mine. When she spoke again, it was more to herself than to Travis. "Mick's the best single jack driller in Regret—and Deacon—" A knot in her throat threatened to strangle her, and she clamped her lips tight together.

He nodded and took a step. "Stay here."

"The hell I will!"

"Here, Travis," Sean spoke up quietly, and handed him something as he passed.

"Jesus, Al." Cutter's tired voice came from right behind her. "Would it gall you that much to listen to someone else for a change?"

She glared at him, then started after Travis.

Cutter made a grab for her and missed.

Al stepped into the still-rising cloud of dirt and wrinkled her nose at the overpowering stench of burned gunpowder. She snatched at Travis's white shirt and tugged at it until he turned to look at her.

Strange, the night before she didn't think she'd ever be able to look at him without feeling a rush of embarrassment. But now, in the face of this latest disaster, everything paled beside her need to get into that mine. To see if there was anything she could do for Mick. For Deacon.

"This is *my* mine," she told Travis firmly. "And nobody tells me I can't go in."

His jaw still tight, she noticed a muscle twitch and figured that beneath his mustache, his lips were one grim line. But she didn't care if he was mad. The men who worked for her risked their lives daily and deserved more from her than standing outside in safety, wringing her hands while someone else went in to check the damage.

Long moments passed. She met his cool blue gaze evenly, refusing to back down. This was about more than what had happened between the two of them. This was about her. Who she was. Who she would always be.

Finally Travis sighed, waved his hand at the dirt and smoke, and jerked her a brief nod. "Fine. But stay behind me."

She would have argued further, but he was already moving. Besides, what difference did it really make if she was first or second into the mine? She'd made her point.

Darkness dropped down onto them with the finality of a shroud, and an eerie stillness echoed off the rock walls and far back into the tunnels.

Without realizing it, Al grabbed a fistful of Travis's shirttail and held on tight. She heard something scratch, and the noise was as loud as a gunshot. A whisper of light struggled against the blackness, and Al almost sagged with relief. Apparently, Sean had had the good sense to hand Travis matches and a candle before he entered the mine.

Thank heaven that they were close enough to the entrance that they didn't have to worry about flammable gases. Many times over the years, miners had survived cave-ins only to be done in by the gases themselves or another explosion and fire set off by an innocently struck match.

Al watched as the tentative, wavering light fell onto the piles of rock tumbled around what had been a ten-foot-wide clearing. She tilted her head back and looked straight up. From what she could see, the beams seemed to be holding. That was *something*, she told herself.

"Goddammit!"

Travis's voice was harsh and strained. As if the words had been squeezed past his throat. Her grip on his shirt tightened reflexively, and she leaned to one side to look around him.

Immediately, Travis spun around, using his free hand to hold her against his chest. For the first time, Al noticed that in his rush to the mine, he hadn't taken the time to button his shirt. Now, with her cheek pressed against his broad, bare chest, she heard his heart pounding in a frenzied rhythm. His grip on her tightened as if he was trying to pull her inside him somehow. Instinctively, Al released the hold she had on his shirt and moved both palms to his chest. His muscles tightened at her touch, but he made no move to let her go.

Whatever he'd seen had been bad enough that he was trying desperately to keep her from seeing it, too. It was then she knew for certain that the men who had worked for her were dead.

She leaned into Travis for a long moment, drawing strength from his silence, from the feel of his arms around her. Al listened intently to the sound of his heartbeat and tried to block out everything else around her.

Travis's hand slipped up to cradle the back of her head, and she thought she felt him brush the top of her head with his lips. But she couldn't be sure.

"Alice?" he whispered, and his voice rumbled through her.

She tilted her head back to look up at him. In

the candle's glow, she saw his grim features and
the ashen color staining his usually tanned skin.

"They're dead?" she asked unnecessarily.

"Yes." His jaw even tighter than before, he still
managed to say, "Go on outside. Tell Cutter and
Sean to send some men in. Help me..." His
words trailed off, but she understood.

The men had been killed in an explosion. In a
very small, enclosed space. There probably
wasn't much of them left to bury.

She swallowed heavily. Dead. Mick and his
good-natured bragging. And Deacon. Everyone
would miss the lanky, would-be preacher—
though probably not his impromptu Sunday
morning Bible readings. A single tear slipped
from the corner of her eye and rolled down her
cheek.

Briefly, Al's head dropped forward and she
rested her forehead on his chest. The reassuring
beat of his heart wasn't enough, though, to stop
the thoughts racing through her mind.

Vivid, mental images rose up one after another, depicting the carnage strewn about the
mine entrance. Despite her efforts to block them
out, they came and came again until she was
breathing in short, frantic gasps. Her stomach
churned and rolled violently. Bile climbed up her
throat and she had to battle it back down. For
the first time in her life, Al was glad to have a
man help her.

She lifted her head and looked up at Travis
again. At the moment, she didn't even care if it
made her a coward to admit that she couldn't
bear the thought of having to witness what had
happened to Mick and Deacon.

Still, after the impassioned speech she'd made to Travis not five minutes before, Al felt as though she should at least *offer* to stay.

Using her will to keep her boiling stomach under control, she said, "I'll help, Travis."

He looked down at her, and she saw his features soften briefly. Admiration flickered in his eyes, and he softly touched her cheek before shaking his head. "Not this time, Alice. Not now. Just this once, let me take care of things."

She turned her face into his touch. He brushed his thumb across her cheek, wiping away the stray tear. Then he bent low and slanted his lips across hers for an instant before straightening up again.

"Go on. Go tell Cutter."

Al nodded slowly, then turned her back on the darkness and walked steadily toward the light.

# Chapter 15

As services went, it hadn't been much.

A few snatches of half-forgotten Bible verses and an off-key chorus of "Amazing Grace."

But if sentiment carried any weight at all with the dearly departed, he supposed Mick and Deacon would have been pleased with their send-off.

Travis stared down into the two open graves and the raw pine coffins resting inside them. There actually hadn't been enough left of either of the miners to require a coffin—let alone two. But the very least those men had deserved was a decent burial.

He looked up and let his gaze slide over the somber crowd of miners gathered close around the graves. The Four Roses was closed for a day or two. Not only to clear out the rubble and shore up the supports again, but out of respect. Travis's gaze snapped to Alice, standing beside him. There weren't many mine owners, he knew, who would shut down operations even if their own mothers were dying. But in this, like in everything else—Alice was different.

Several of the men started to fill in the grave-site. With each shovel-full of dirt thrown onto the coffins, Travis felt, rather than saw, Alice flinch. Instinctively, he reached for one of her hands and folded his fingers around her smaller ones. She clasped his hand tightly, and the cold edges of anger wrapped around his heart began to thaw.

She was alive.

She was unhurt.

He closed his eyes briefly and sent a heartfelt "thank you" to Whomever was listening. Ever since entering the mine that morning and finding what was left of those men, Travis had been tortured with thoughts of what might have been.

What if Alice had risen early and gone in to help Mick and Deacon? She had before. What if it was *Alice* they were burying now under the afternoon sun? An ache began deep inside him, and he knew that if anything were to happen to her, that pain would grow and grow until it finally swallowed him.

Today they'd been lucky. A hideous thought, he knew, as they stood beside the graves of two good men. But the fact that he realized he shouldn't entertain such thoughts didn't stop them from presenting themselves.

Be it luck, or fate, or chance, Travis wasn't willing to risk Alice's life any longer. He had to find a way to stop Bennet. And he had to do it soon.

With low-pitched murmurs of discomfort, the miners began to shuffle away from the cemetery at the edge of Regret. Travis looked down and saw that the graves were filled. The service was over. He gave Alice's hand another squeeze, then spoke up quickly before the men could leave.

"If I could have your attention," he said in a voice meant to carry. "There's something Miss Donnelly and I want you all to know."

"Travis?"

He ignored her for the moment and studied the wary faces turning toward him. Under the pallor gained by working underground, the hard-working men in worn clothing bore the stamp of the mines on their features. Their skin was mottled and stained with dirt too ingrained to be scrubbed off and scarred from bits of flying rock. They'd just buried two of their number, and in each of their faces was the knowledge that at any moment the same end could come to them.

Most of them were honest, Travis thought. But in among that waiting crowd were perhaps two or three men who might be willing to sell their services to Bennet for a little extra money. Which is exactly why he wanted to let them all know about their increase in wages. The sooner he could head off any possible trouble, the safer Alice would be.

"We've decided to raise your daily pay from three dollars and fifty cents to four dollars."

A half-hearted smile or two appeared in the crowd, then disappeared again, just as quickly. One of the men closest to Travis spoke up.

"You figure more money makes it all right what happened to Mick and Deacon?"

Deep-throated whispers rushed through the

mob of men, and Travis had to wait a moment for the voices to subside before answering.

"Of course not," he told them. "But at the same time, I—*we* want you to know that we realize how dangerous your work is and how much we appreciate your efforts."

Someone in the back snorted a choked laugh. Travis let it go. He knew damn well what the men thought of him. A citified dandy, not worth the powder it would take to blow him to hell. And he couldn't blame them any, either.

Alice's voice cut into the momentary stillness. "You men know I wouldn't throw money into a grave to try to right things . . ." She paused and glanced down at the raw, mounded earth in front of her. "But we've been together a long time now. . . ."

A few men nodded and Travis squeezed her hand again, silently telling her to go on.

"The mine's doin' well. It's only fair you get a share in that, too."

Cutter and Sean stood off to one side. Travis glanced their way and caught the small, satisfied smile the gambler directed at him.

More rumbles of conversation rose up from the crowd, but this time there were more heads nodding. More smiles. It was going to be all right. The extra fifty cents a day would no doubt be enough to insure most everyone's loyalty. But for the benefit of the few who might still be tempted to sell out, Travis decided to make yet another announcement.

"At the end of every week," he called out, and the miners settled down immediately to listen, "we'll do a tally of the ore taken from the mine.

The man who's brought out the most will earn a twenty dollar bonus."

Stunned into speechlessness, the miners stared at him. From the corner of his eye, he noted that Alice's features were frozen into the same mask of surprise. A momentary doubt flickered through his brain, and he wondered if he'd gone too far.

Then a cheer broke out and some of the miners rushed forward to grab Travis's hand and shake it. He stood his ground while the men jostled around him, slapping him on the back and telling him what a fine fellow he was. But he didn't release the grip he had on Alice's hand, even when he felt her fingers go limp.

When she was pushed into Travis for the third time, Al glared up at her partner. What had he been thinking? He couldn't just offer a twenty dollar a week bonus to the miners without even *asking* her.

One of the men stomped on her foot and Al winced. She nodded at his mumbled apology, then took a half-minute to study his face. She couldn't recall his name. It would have been impossible to know personally every man who worked for her. There were just too many of them. But Al *had* seen him occasionally at the mine.

An older man, his features were drawn and lined. Scars pockmarked his cheeks and forehead, and his eyes were squinted and watery against the unfamiliar sunshine. But there was something else as well. A pleased smile deepened the lines in his face and softened the shadows in his eyes.

Al glanced up at Travis again. He'd created that smile. Oh, the daily wage hike was part of it. But that bonus he'd offered as a reward for their hard work had completely won the miners over. She was ashamed now that she'd begrudged them that extra prize, even for a minute. She was more ashamed that she'd never thought of the idea herself.

Twenty dollars a week was a lot of money, yes. But the mine *was* doing well. She could afford that bonus. And as she looked around at the men still clamoring to pump Travis's hand, Al realized that by paying twenty dollars extra each week, she would be receiving as much pleasure as she was giving.

Her lax fingers curled around Travis's hand again, holding on tight.

He felt the difference immediately. Travis had no idea what had been running through her mind, but whatever it was, he was glad she'd settled it. Absently, he went on shaking hands, smiling, nodding away bursts of gratitude, while his mind worked furiously.

Something about this whole situation was still bothering him. Whoever had caused that explosion obviously wasn't concerned about killing people. Why was it, then, that those men who'd attacked Alice a couple of weeks ago simply hadn't killed her on the spot? Why had they been so determined to kidnap her and carry her off?

It didn't make sense.

And until it did, Alice wouldn't be safe.

Travis needed answers and he needed them quickly. As soon as he got her back to camp safely, he'd leave Cutter or Sean to watch out for her and head into town.

It was past time for him to get in touch with a few people.

"Fool!"

Thompson shifted uncomfortably in his chair and kept his gaze locked on his employer's back. Rafe Bennet's spine was poker straight. His hands clasped tightly behind his back, the man rocked back and forth on his heels as if he couldn't bear to be still another minute.

"You said to shut down the mine," Thompson reminded him.

"I also said no killing." Bennet shot him one quick look, then turned back to stare out the window at the setting sun.

"Hell," Thompson said, cold anger rippling through him, replacing a momentary burst of unease. "How was I supposed to know that miners only drill out half a hole the night before and finish in the morning? I loaded the hole last night, figured the powder monkeys would put their own loads in come morning." He shrugged away any responsibility for the dead men. "No one should have been in the mine. They'd drilled the holes. All they had to do was load it, add a fuse, light it, and run for cover. Blast would have knocked down some rocks and a few timbers." Thompson grimaced tightly. "But no. Those idiots had to hammer at it again. Hell, one spark was prob'ly all it took." He rolled his shoulders nervously. "How the hell could I know they were gonna do that?"

"I pay you to know those things," Bennet answered finally, his voice clipped, harsh. He swiveled his head around to stare at Thompson, and the gunfighter fought against the rising tide of apprehension swelling in his chest.

What was it about the man that got to him so? Hell, Bennet didn't even go armed! If he wanted to, Thompson could shoot the bastard right here. Why he didn't was a mystery even to him.

"It's just a couple of miners," he said at last. "In a town like this, they'll never be missed."

Bennet shook his head.

"I told you. Killing complicates things."

"Don't see how. Seems to me it's the best way for straightening out a problem." Thompson smiled to himself as he contemplated shooting a certain gambler and his Mick friend. He still owed them for that night in the saloon. "It's easy enough done."

Slowly, the other man walked to his desk, his gaze never leaving the gunfighter's. As he sat down in the leather-tufted chair, he asked, "Don't you think the people at the Four Roses will be a bit more alert to trouble now that you've botched this?"

"They were waitin' on trouble anyway."

"They were getting complacent. Careless," Bennet shot back. "That is precisely why we've done nothing for two weeks. I wanted them to think the danger was past."

"You wanted the mine shut down, too. It is." Thompson reached up and pulled the brim of his hat down lower, shading his eyes somewhat from the cool stare directed at him.

"I wanted it to look like an accident. You might have sawn through a timber or two.

Started a landslide from above to block the entrance." Bennet drew a long breath, obviously hoping to calm himself. "But apparently your idea of an accident is to blow something up."

"It worked."

"That's hardly the point."

"What is?"

"How will you get Mary Alice Donnelly away from her mine now? She will undoubtedly have guards stationed everywhere."

Thompson shifted again, but started breathing a bit easier. Bennet still needed him. "When do you want me to snatch her?"

"The sooner the better."

"Tonight?"

"No," Bennet snapped, then paused again to collect himself. "Tomorrow night would be better. They'll be too worked up tonight."

"Consider it done." Thompson pushed himself up from his chair, rested his right hand on his gun butt, and nodded. "Tomorrow night, Al Donnelly will disappear."

"*Not* permanently," Bennet warned him, in a steely tone. "I want her out of the way for ten days. No more. No less."

"I remember." Thompson edged sideways and walked to the door, still managing to keep one eye on his boss. It paid to be careful.

"This time," Bennet told him as he opened the door, "see that you *do* remember."

Halfway to Travis's tent, Al told herself she was being foolish. That she ought to go back to her own place and try to sleep.

But she'd *been* trying for hours already, and

she was no closer to sleeping than she had been when she first lay down. Every time she closed her eyes, she relived the day's events. From the first sound of the explosion, to the cloud of dirt and smoke, to the short, stilted funeral. Over and over again, images crowded through her brain. And in all those flashes of memory, there was only one constant.

Travis.

Travis holding her in the mine, cradling her head against his chest so that she wouldn't see the devastation he'd witnessed. Travis wiping away her tear as tenderly as he would have a child's. Travis brushing his lips across hers in a gentle kiss. Travis entwining his fingers through hers at the funeral, silently offering her his strength.

Al wrapped her arms about her middle and squeezed. She shivered slightly in the night air and stared at the darkened tent not twenty feet from her. She hadn't stopped to think about the impulse that had brought her to him. She'd simply reacted.

She hadn't wanted to be alone anymore.

After staring death in the eye, she wanted to feel alive again. She wanted to hold and be held. She wanted to kiss and be kissed. She wanted—no—*needed* to feel that rush of expectancy. That thread of pleasure that curled throughout her body at his touch.

Clouds scuttled across the moon's face, closing off the light as effectively as a candle being snuffed. Al's gaze narrowed, adapted to the utter blackness, and remained fixed on the tent where she so wanted to be.

A swarm of butterflies flew about in her stomach, and an entirely different, but no less strong sensation settled a bit lower. She inhaled deeply, drawing the scent of the mountains inside her. Rubbing her hands briskly up and down her arms, Al told herself that it was up to her. Travis was inside, unaware of her presence. He wasn't going to step out of his tent and issue an invitation.

Glancing over her shoulder at the way she'd come, she thought briefly about going back to her own tent. It was the proper thing to do, she knew. But then, she thought as she slowly turned back around to look forward, when had she ever cared about what was proper?

She nodded to herself and started walking before she could talk herself out of it again. As if a blessing was being bestowed, the string of clouds went past the moon and a silvery glow shone down once more. Al hurriedly took the last few steps separating her from her goal, then paused again.

From inside, she heard Travis's voice, hushed, anguished. She couldn't quite make out what he was saying, but the torment in his tone was clear. Al reached for the tent flap just as he called out, "No!"

*He heard it. A quiet moan that lifted into a soul-chilling scream. The hairs on the back of his neck stood straight up. The wall of flame in front of him seemed to part for an instant, and Travis scooted across the hot floorboards, determined to reach her.*

He knew it was coming. He knew the nightmare was upon him again. He tried to wake up.

Fought against the terrible strength of the dream. But it was no use. He had to go on. There was no escape. Ever.

*Standing before him like a Biblical pillar of fire, she spun helplessly in a tight circle, unconsciously fanning the flames already engulfing her.*

Travis groaned and kicked at the blankets pinning him to the cot. Different. The dream was different this time. The same, but different. The woman's long skirt and frilly blouse had changed, shifted, become a pair of worn buckskins and a tired, oversized man's shirt.

*Without hesitation, Travis drew a deep breath, ignoring the burning pain lancing through his chest, held it and launched himself toward her. He saw the pain, the terror in her deep green eyes a split second before his momentum carried them both toward the window and through the glass. Together, they landed on the hard-packed dirt and he began to roll with her, trying to smother the flames between his own body and the earth.*

*Her screams filled him, and he brushed the palms of his hands across her tight-fitting clothes, desperately attacking the flames consuming her. He looked down into Alice's wounded, pain-wracked gaze and watched helplessly as the spark of life drained from them.*

"No!" Travis shouted and sat upright. He dragged one gasping breath after another into his heaving lungs and tried to rid his mind of the lingering images.

"Travis?"

His head snapped up and his gaze shot to the tent flap being lifted. Backlit by the soft glow of moonlight, Alice entered his tent, and instinctively he reached for her.

# Chapter 16

**S**he went to him without hesitation.

Crossing the tent floor in a few quick strides, Al seated herself gingerly on the edge of his cot and moved into the circle of his embrace.

As his arms closed around her, Travis sighed heavily and held her tightly to him. Al ran her hands up and down his naked back, caressing him gently, silently. Her fingertips smoothed across well-defined muscles and much broader shoulders than she'd expected him to have. She felt the frenzied pounding of his heart against hers and told herself absently that his chest was every bit as hard and muscular as his back. Vaguely, she remembered noting that very thing only that morning when he'd held her to him in a tight, protective gesture.

When his arms threatened to crush her in a hard, unyielding embrace, Al realized just how strong this partner of hers really was. Then he spoke and her thoughts shattered.

"You're alive."

Astonished bewilderment colored his voice,

and she drew her head back to look at him. But he'd buried his face in the curve of her neck and shoulder. Al reached up and slowly combed her fingers through his hair. Quietly, she tried to give him the comfort he'd given her in the mine earlier.

"I'm alive," she whispered. "That must have been one helluva dream."

"Jesus," he whispered, and she felt the heat of his breath against her neck. "It was so real."

Travis drew a long, shuddering breath and released her only to cup her face between his palms. She watched him as his gaze moved over her features hungrily, desperately. As if it had been years since he'd last seen her. He leaned closer and pressed his lips to hers in a hard, fast kiss that was more triumphant than romantic. When he pulled back again, she let him go, even though she wanted another kiss more than anything.

She missed the feel of his arms around her, but she sensed somehow that he needed a moment or two to compose himself and gather his wits. Al scooted a few inches away from him and watched as Travis raked one hand through his hair and forced several deep breaths into his lungs.

He drew one leg up, propped his left elbow on his knee, and leaned his head into his hand. Al's gaze, fully adjusted now to the darkness, swept over him unobserved.

Free of the pomade he usually wore, his hair looked soft and shiny as it tumbled across his forehead. His wide shoulders were hunched now as if carrying too much weight for him to bear.

A sprinkling of hair dusted his chest and trailed down his stomach to disappear beneath the blankets bunched just below his waist.

Al swallowed past the sudden knot in her throat and tried desperately to shift her gaze away from the bedclothes pooled around Travis's hips. A damp heat began to course through her, settling low in her belly, and she squirmed uncomfortably on the cot.

"Alice?"

"Yes," she answered quickly, and guiltily lifted her gaze to his shadowed face.

He choked out a half laugh. "I can hardly see you."

"I'll light the lamp."

"No!" Travis almost shouted the word, then another laugh shook through him. "Jesus, no flames. Not now, anyway."

Though surprised at his agitated reaction, Al knew she was probably better off without a lamp burning. At least in the dark, he couldn't see where her eyes were roving—or the resulting blush still staining her cheeks with heat and no doubt, brilliant color.

This visit with Travis wasn't going at all as she'd thought it would. But then, she hadn't really thought much beyond the need to be with him, either. Now that she was there, though, in his tent, in the dark, she felt awkward. Clumsy. And as the silence lengthened, that feeling only intensified. Finally Al spoke up, just to break that ominous quiet.

"Are you all right?" she asked, even knowing what a foolish question it was. Of course he wasn't all right. He still looked as though he'd stared directly through the gates of hell. "Can I get you something? Coffee? Water?"

"Whiskey would be good."

"I'll be right back."

"No!" he snapped, and reached for her. In the indistinct light, his hand brushed her breast just before his fingers closed around her upper arm. "Don't go."

She hadn't had a chance to move before he grabbed her, and now she wasn't sure her suddenly shaky legs would support an attempt to walk. So she settled herself more firmly onto the cot beside him.

He squeezed her upper arm again, more gently this time and let his thumb caress her slowly. "Just . . . don't go yet."

His voice sounded hollow, empty, and Al knew she wouldn't leave him. Not until whatever still held him in its grip had released him. She reached up and covered his hand with her own. "I'll stay," she whispered, and wished she knew what to do. What to say.

Travis released her arm and captured her comforting hand in his own.

Silent minutes crawled by. This time, though, the silence seemed more companionable to Al. As if she and Travis were facing down his demons together—as *real* partners. Only inches from him, Al could feel the tension in his body and wondered what kind of nightmares a man like Travis would have. Why had he been so surprised on waking, to find her still alive? What could be haunting him so that he would wake up in a cold sweat, shouting?

She frowned thoughtfully. She'd had nightmares. Hell, everyone had. But generally, the first thing Al wanted when she woke from a terrible dream was a light. *Any* light. What kind of images were they that made Travis prefer darkness to a match being struck?

"Why did you come to me tonight, Alice?" His hushed voice sounded unnaturally loud in the stillness and startled Al out of her reverie.

"I . . . couldn't sleep."

"And?" he prodded gently.

"*And*," Al repeated, stalling for time until she could come up with something brilliant to tell him. But her mind, unfortunately, was blank. Her insides quivered and the truth was on the tip of her tongue, but she couldn't quite bring herself to say, *I wanted you to make love to me.* Instead, she finished lamely, "I thought we could talk."

"Talk? Now? In the middle of the night?"

What in heaven was wrong with her? A bit late to be feeling bashful about why she'd come, wasn't it? Uncertainty ricocheted through her body like a bullet fired into a narrow cave. Apparently not, she thought dismally. It wasn't too late. Al inhaled sharply and reminded herself of her recent decision to be herself. To accept who and what she was.

She told herself that she had nothing to be ashamed of. Hadn't Travis himself taught her to want him? Hadn't he been the one to show her exactly what her body could feel?

Then, why, she asked herself, should he be surprised to find out that she wanted another lesson?

When she didn't speak again, Travis said, "I

don't think tonight's a good night for talking, Alice."

"Neither do I."

"What?"

"I mean," she said, thankful again for the shadowy darkness in the tent, "I don't want to talk. And that's not why I came here tonight."

"Why then?" His voice was strangled, as if something was choking him.

With her free hand, Al reached up and brushed his hair off his forehead. He flinched slightly when her fingers smoothed across his skin. She battled back a last minute surge of nerves and forced herself to admit, "I want you to touch me again, Travis. I want you to hold me."

"Alice," he groaned and squeezed her hand a bit tighter. "You don't know what you're asking."

"Yes, I do." Her fingers curled around his and returned the pressure of his grip.

Travis groaned inwardly and knew he was lost. He could no more send her away than he could stop his heart from beating. With his free hand, he cupped the back of her neck and drew her close. When he felt her breath brush against his face, he bent his head and pressed his lips to hers.

She tasted of salvation. Her mouth opened to him and his tongue swept past her defenses to claim her sweetness. He took her breath into him and felt the rush of hope and life fill him. A groan scraped from his throat as he pulled her tightly to him, and she wrapped her arms around him. He tore his lips from hers and began to trail hot, hungry kisses down the length of her throat. She tipped her head to one side, allowing him more of her flesh, and he took it as the gift it was.

His right hand smoothed up her body and cupped her breast. His thumb moved back and forth across her nipple until it hardened and peaked against the fabric restraining it.

He heard her breath catch and felt her short, sensible nails dig into his shoulders. His heart pounding in his chest, he held on to her tightly and stood up, dragging her with him.

"Travis?"

He speared his fingers through the hair at her temple and turned her face toward him. "It's all right, Alice. This will only take a minute."

She staggered slightly, and he tightened his grasp on her.

"What are you going to do?"

Travis yanked the blankets off his cot and threw them onto the ground. Then he reached behind him for the pillow and tossed it down as well.

"I'm going to make long, slow, sweet love to you, Alice," he promised, then dipped his head to taste her mouth again.

She felt him lift her braid. As she stood on very shaky legs, Travis untied the rawhide strand securing the single braid and slowly separated the ropes of her hair. When he was finished, his fingers raked through the long, wavy mass over and over, until her hair hung wild and free about her shoulders.

"Beautiful," he whispered.

And for the first time in her life, Al felt exactly that.

"Touch me, sweet Alice."

She didn't think twice. She planted her hands on his shoulders and let her palms slide down his chest. So warm. So strong. His breath caught as her fingertips glided over his flesh, exploring, caressing.

Then his hands were on her shirtfront and she felt him sliding buttons from their holes. She should have been nervous. But she wasn't. Not anymore. All Al could think of was that she wished he would hurry. She wanted to feel his chest against hers, skin to skin. Feel his warmth melding into her. Feel his heartbeat pound in time with her own.

In seconds he had her shirt unbuttoned and was sliding it down her arms. She dropped her hands to her sides and shrugged out of the suddenly confining material. Then he started on her chemise. She looked up into his shadowed features and wished briefly for more light. The hazy glow of moonlight shining through canvas made them both look like slightly paler shadows in the darkness, but it didn't allow her to read his expressions. Or see his eyes clearly.

He tugged at the soft cotton fabric, and as he did, Al reached up again to let her hands slide further down his chest. She felt his narrow waist and his flat, hard stomach. Her palms slipped to his hips and stopped.

Travis was as naked as the day he'd been born.

A curl of nervousness spiraled through her, but she battled it into submission with the strength of the desire blossoming inside her.

He pushed her chemise down to her elbows, then lifted her hands from his hips and pulled the material down off her arms.

Travis bent slightly and kissed her throat. She shivered and she felt him smile against her flesh. Slowly, leisurely, he began to work his way down her body. His lips, tongue and teeth forged a trail of heat. He cupped her breasts in his palms and teased first one, then the other rigid nipple with damp, warm kisses. Each in turn, he suckled at her breasts, using his tongue to draw and pull at her until Al felt her insides dissolving under the onslaught of sensation.

She braced her hands on his shoulders, loving the feel of his muscles bunching beneath her fingers.

Travis pressed his lips to the valley between her breasts, then moved lower, still tugging at her nipples with his fingertips.

Tremors of anticipation rumbled through her, and Al swayed unsteadily. She didn't want to speak. She didn't want to move. She wanted nothing to interrupt the spell of sensations he was weaving. Instead, she curled her fingers even tighter into the hard muscles of his shoulders.

His fingertips pulled a bit harder at her nipples, sending arrows of pleasure shooting right down to the soles of her feet. She groaned and arched into him as he let his hands drop to the front panel of her buckskin pants. His fingers plucked at the rawhide laces she'd tied so hastily just a short while ago.

"Travis . . ." Her hands tightened on his shoulders, clutching at his corded muscles reflexively.

As he pulled the laces free, exposing her flesh an inch at a time, Travis left soft, lingering kisses on her quivering abdomen. His tongue traced damp patterns over her skin, teasing her into near oblivion.

"Holy mother!" Al murmured and let her head fall back on her neck. She swayed again, but felt his hands—his incredible hands—hold her in place.

When the laces were undone, Travis pushed the worn buckskin down her long, shapely thighs. He brushed feather-light kisses over her creamy skin and slid his fingers through the triangle of dark red hair guarding her secrets.

"Dear God," she whispered, this time digging her short nails into his shoulders. She gasped and shuddered violently when he kissed the juncture of her thighs.

Gently, Travis guided her down to the rough wool blankets. She stared up at the pale canvas roof as he pulled off her boots and buckskins then tossed them aside. The wrinkled blankets beneath her covered pebble strewn ground, but she hardly noticed the tiny rocks pushing against the wool fabric into her back. Instead, she concentrated on the incredible feelings quaking inside her. Then Travis was back, looming over her and she didn't notice anything in the world but him.

Al ran her hand over his chest again. She couldn't seem to get enough of the way his flesh felt under hers. He stiffened slightly when her fingertips brushed across his flat, hardened nipple, and she smiled to know that he was as affected as she. An ages-old sensation of womanly power swept over her, and her thumbnail scraped delicately across his sensitive skin. Travis sucked in a gulp of air and he moved in even closer to her.

He held her face cupped between his palms and slowly lowered his head to claim a kiss. She met his tongue's caresses with her own and gave herself over to the incredible rightness of being in his arms.

And then he moved to cover her body with his own. In one fluid motion, he was lying on top of her, supporting most of his weight on his forearms. Al's breath escaped her in a wondrous sigh. She smiled and closed her eyes to better enjoy the extraordinary feel of flesh on flesh.

The solid, heavy weight of him, pressed tightly to her, felt glorious. A sense of belonging welled up within her, and she wrapped her arms about him tighter, holding him as close as she possibly could.

He dipped his head and brushed a kiss across her mouth, and Al smiled against his lips. Then Travis shifted slightly, rubbing his body over hers and she gasped aloud. His desire equaled hers. The hard, ready proof of it prodded her belly, sending liquid heat to her center. She shivered as she ran her palms over his back. She heard his breath quicken as her palms dipped lower. Smiling to herself, Al reached further back and caressed the smooth curve of his backside.

He growled, slid to one side of her and lowered his mouth to hers. Fiercely, he claimed her with his tongue, his breath, his lips. No gentle teasing this, he was a man staking his territory, marking her as his woman while at the same time showing her more tenderness than she'd ever known.

Encircling his neck with her arms, Al arched into him and gave him freely everything he was trying so hungrily to take.

Travis rolled onto his back, dragging Al on top of him. Her hair fell down to hang in a dark red curtain on either side of them. His hands roamed quickly up and down her back, exploring, discovering. He cupped her bottom and kneaded that tender flesh until Al groaned and writhed in his grasp.

Need spiraled up inside her, hotter, more desperate than before. She felt the tip of his hardened body pushing at her, and she tried to inch her way down, anxious to capture his length and hold him in her body. To hold him so deeply within her that the core of loneliness she'd carried for most of her life would melt away in the heat of him.

But his strong hands held her fast. He tore his mouth from hers and shook his head, smiling. "Not yet, sweet Alice. Not yet."

"Jesus, Travis." She planted her hands on either side of his head and pushed herself up slightly. Unbidden tears stung her eyes as she confessed, "I need you . . . so much it scares me."

"Don't be scared," he whispered and stroked her cheek with the tip of a finger. "I'm here."

She nodded and turned her face into his touch.

His free hand slid between their sweat-slicked bodies and found that same delicate spot he'd shown her the last time he'd touched her. Alice's legs parted to give him access. Straddling him, she shifted position until she was nearly sitting straight up on his stomach. Instinctively, she moved into his touch, helping him find that magical bud of sensation. Her knees flexed when his fingers stroked that tender spot, and her hips began to buck wildly with her escalating need.

Amazing, she told herself, and let her eyes slide shut on a wave of delight. Without her dress and a pair of jeans between her body and his fingers, she felt every little touch. Every little stroke of his fingertip. Every little spark of heat sent waves of fire rushing through her blood.

She groaned quietly as he dipped one finger into her warmth, then rubbed her own damp heat on that too sensitive bud. It was coming again. She felt it building deep within her. That starburst of gentle torture. That incredible shower of light and warmth and joy and pain all mingled into one inescapable rush of relief.

It was hovering just out of her reach, and Al rocked her hips against his hand in a desperate, instinctive quest to claim it. She forgot to breathe. She forgot the cold. She forgot the pebbly ground pressing into her knees.

*Nothing* was more important than finding that thunderstorm of sensation again.

"Sweet Alice," Travis whispered, and his hips lifted slightly beneath her. "*Now* you're ready."

Gently, he rolled her over onto her back. Kneeling between her parted thighs, Travis slid his hands under her bottom and lifted her just a bit to ease his entry.

His blood racing, his heartbeat thundering so loudly in his ears it sounded like a brass band, Travis inched his way into her heat. Her body

held him tightly, and he felt beads of sweat
breaking out on his forehead with his effort to
go slowly, to keep from hurting her with the
force of his own need.

He ground his teeth together in an agony of
frustration and claimed another few inches of her
body. Travis groaned at the wet, tight heat closing around him, welcoming him home. Alice
twisted her hips, determinedly impaling herself
on him, and Travis's grip on her backside tightened in an effort to hold her still.

"Christ, Alice" he whispered roughly. "Don't
move."

"I've got to, Travis," she answered, just as bro-
kenly. "I need to feel you inside me. I need to
feel all of you."

"We have to do this slow, Alice." His voice
scratched past the knot in his throat. "I'm doing
my damnedest not to hurt you."

"Travis," she said as she looked into his eyes,
"the only way you can hurt me now is if you
hold yourself back."

Dear God.

What was a man supposed to do with logic
like that?

She held her arms out to him and he forgot all
about self-control and leaned over her. Bracing
himself on his palms, Travis stared directly into
her eyes as he pushed his body completely into
hers. Alice's eyes widened briefly, and he held
perfectly still, allowing her time to adjust to his
body's presence. Then she lifted her legs, wrap-
ping them about his waist, and held him tightly,
deeply within her warmth.

An incredible sense of completeness settled

over him. As if he'd found the other half of himself after empty years of searching for her. He wanted nothing more in life than to bury himself so deep inside her that he would never be able to leave her. That even when they weren't together, they would still be a part of each other.

Smiling up at him, Alice whispered, "I can feel you touching my heart, Travis."

Something inside him splintered as he bent to claim a kiss. Then slowly, he began the ancient, rhythmic dance of passion. Alice moved with him, following his lead, matching his ardor with a wild, open desire he'd never experienced before. As they rocked together, taking each other higher than either of them had expected, Travis felt a soul-shattering release only moments away. And still he held on, watching her face, enjoying the wonder, the pleasure, streaking across her features.

Then her legs tightened convulsively around his waist, and she buried her face in his shoulder to muffle a cry that she couldn't contain. Shuddering ripples of satisfaction trembled through her. He felt her inner muscles clench around him, and then his own world splintered into tiny jagged pieces and the only stable thing left in Travis's world was the woman in his arms.

She woke in the soft, half-light of dawn, Travis's arm draped across her middle. She smiled, stroked her fingertips along his forearm, and paused for a moment to relish the delicious sense of contentment she felt. Though her body was sore from a long, full night of loving, her soul had never been more at peace.

But as much as Al would have liked lying there next to him all day and into the night, she still had a mine to run. Her muscles aching, she slipped out from underneath him and snatched up her clothes. As she dressed, she looked down at the man who'd changed her life so completely in a matter of weeks.

Sleeping soundly in a tangle of blankets, Travis looked as though he was going to sleep the day away. She smiled to herself as she tugged her boots on. The man had a right to be tired. Hell, by rights, *she* should be exhausted, too. But strangely enough, after a night of loving, Al was full of sass and ready to move. Why, she had so much energy, she felt as though she could go on down to the mine and clear out that rubble all by herself!

Lacing up the front panel of her buckskins, Al's stomach flip-flopped at the memory of Travis pulling those same laces free. She could almost feel the brush of his mustache against her belly's sensitive skin. She sighed at the memory and told herself to get moving. Grinning, she yanked her shirt on and quickly did up the buttons.

She'd let him sleep. No sense in him getting up early. The only work to be done that morning was the heavy stuff. Dragging out the rocks and timbers, then shoring up the support beams. Lord knew, there were plenty of men to do all of it.

Al looked down at him as she braided her hair tightly.

In the growing light, his bare chest looked broad, tanned, and strong. She frowned slightly and took a good, hard look at the man to whom she'd so gladly given her virtue.

Strange that she hadn't noticed his magnificent physique the night before, she thought. But then, she'd been too busy enjoying what he was doing to her to notice that he wasn't nearly as skinny as she'd thought. Or the fact that despite what it looked like when he was wearing those ugly coats of his, Travis's shoulders weren't narrow *or* hunched.

A hard knot of suspicion formed in her gut as she continued to stare at the man who was more of a stranger than she'd realized.

Why was he hiding his strong, muscular build under a set of oversized clothes? And if he was who he said he was, how did a city man come to be so damned tan?

He mumbled something in his sleep and rolled to one side. Al thought briefly about waking him up and demanding some answers but changed her mind. He'd wake up soon enough.

And when he did, he had a lot of explaining to do.

# Chapter 17

**T**ravis stood outside the telegraph office and glanced up at the second story of the narrow wooden building. Bennet had taken over the upstairs rooms for his own offices. No doubt, Travis told himself, because of the proximity to the telegraph. A man as committed to profit as Rafe Bennet, would want to be close to the wires that could connect him to opportunities across the country.

A slow smile crossed his face as he remembered the last of the telegrams he'd received in answer to the ones he'd sent. He still had a few friends in high places, and they'd been able to give him a bit more information on the man causing Alice so much trouble.

Alice.

Jesus, just the thought of her name was enough to set off a blaze of renewed desire. His body tight and hard, Travis told himself that he was as bad as some half-grown kid after his first woman. But it didn't seem to matter. At least, not to him. Alice, he wasn't so sure about.

She'd been gone when he woke up, and he'd left camp soon after to come to town, so he hadn't seen her yet. He could only hope that she hadn't sneaked off because she was regretting their night together.

Because he didn't. Not a minute of it.

Not even the paralyzing thought that she might have conceived a child was enough to make him repent. Although, when that idea had finally occurred to him just an hour or so before, it had almost been enough to stop his heart.

A child. Jesus! *There* was a sobering notion. He frowned thoughtfully and promised himself to stay in Regret until he knew if she was carrying or not. But if there really was a God—and He gave a damn about Alice—she wouldn't be pregnant with Travis's child.

No self-respecting God would do such a thing to an innocent woman and baby.

His gaze shifted and he stared at his own reflection in the dirty window. Soon he'd be able to drop the disguise and become himself again. He wouldn't miss the damned derby, that was for sure. Yet when the need for a disguise ended, so would his time in Regret. With Alice.

Travis shook himself and looked beyond his image at the telegrapher, a tall, thin man seated behind the counter. When their eyes met, the man quickly looked away. The fella worried Travis. He'd had to bribe the man into forgetting the name Delacort. Hopefully, the man's fear of him would outweigh his greed and keep him from going to Bennet.

He remembered the flash of unease in the thin man's eyes, and the sudden pallor in his cheeks when he'd seen the name Travis had signed to the telegrams he sent. The man's hands had trembled so badly that Travis had had real doubts about the fella's ability to handle the telegraph key.

Apparently, though, he'd done just fine, judging by the answering wires Travis had received. Mentally, he reviewed everything he'd discovered. It seemed as though Bennet was more than willing to steal whatever he could lay his hands on. Although, he was also smart enough to not leave a trail to incriminate himself.

There were no warrants out on Bennet, so even if there *had* been a sheriff in Regret, there was nothing he could have done. It seems that in his past, Bennet had escaped prosecution, but there were a helluvalot of places where the local law had made him uncomfortable enough to make him move on quietly.

Apparently, Rafe Bennet would rather set up business in a new town than fight to stay where folks were on to him.

Now all Travis had to do was accomplish the same thing in Regret.

He took the stairs quickly, quietly, and paused on the second-story landing. He adjusted the hang of his too-big yellow coat, then pulled his bowler off and held it in his left hand. Out of habit, he kept his right hand free, though he had no pistol to draw should he get into trouble. Old habits die hard, he told himself on a half smile, then reached up and knocked briskly on the door in front of him.

It swung open almost immediately.

Rafe Bennet was a tall man. Almost as tall as

Travis's own six feet two inches. But for the small scar over his right eye, he was what some would call a handsome, well-set man. His blond hair was combed straight back from a high forehead, and his dark brown gaze locked with Travis's in a silent, challenging stare.

"Mr. Deal," the man said, and took a step back, swinging his left arm wide, inviting Travis inside. "How good of you to call on me."

Remembering to keep his shoulders a bit hunched and his voice sounding a shade intimidated, Travis walked into his enemy's territory.

"I'm flattered, sir," he said, "that you know my name."

"I make it a point to know everyone of substance who lives in our little town." Bennet closed the door before crossing the room to sit behind his desk.

"Again, I'm flattered." Travis didn't sit. He preferred being on his feet. Able to move around. And Lord knew, he'd found out long ago that a moving target was much harder to hit.

Bennet hadn't been violent in his past. But people had been known to change.

"I understand there was some trouble at the Four Roses yesterday," Bennet said, and poured himself a brandy from the crystal decanter sitting on the edge of the desk.

Travis glanced at him, eyebrows arched high on his forehead. "I suppose you could call an explosion where two men were killed trouble."

"Yes," Bennet said, a properly horrified expression on his face, "a tragedy." Shaking his head solemnly, he filled another glass and held it out to Travis. "I hope Miss Donnelly is well?"

If she wasn't, Travis thought grimly, Bennet would right now be looking down the barrel of a cocked pistol. He was amazed by just how good that mental image felt.

"Oh my, yes," Travis took a sip of the rich, amber liquid and swallowed back his anger along with it. Now more than ever, he needed to remain calm. The excellent brandy smoothed down his throat. "Naturally, she was quite upset by the accident."

"Naturally. A woman's sensibilities, of course." Bennet leaned back in his chair, propped his elbows on the polished wooden arms, and held his glass between both hands. "A woman simply doesn't understand that these things happen. In life . . . and in business."

Now they were getting to it, Travis told himself and just managed to hide a small smile of satisfaction. If that wasn't an implied threat, he would eat that damned derby of his.

"Oh, I believe Miss Donnelly *understands* everything quite well." He took another small sip and went on, "As a matter of fact, it was *she* who explained the situation to me."

"Really?" Bennet reached up and stroked the scar over his eye slowly. "A curious woman."

"Not at all." Travis bent down and set his still half-full glass down on the desktop. "But she is a determined woman."

Bennet looked at him over the rim of his glass. The air in the office was hot and still. Every window was shut tight, preventing any breeze that might have swept through the pristine room, littering the place with dust . . . and life.

Staring at his adversary, Travis silently admired the man's obvious show of confidence as he relaxed behind his wide, uncluttered desk. As Bennet took another sip of brandy, though, Travis noted the man's grip on the fragile snifter.

His knuckles were white and the veins on the back of his hand were standing out like taut ropes.

Maybe, Travis thought, Rafe Bennet wasn't quite as in control as he would like others to think.

"You seem to be a reasonable man," Bennet commented.

"Some have said so," Travis allowed. Though silently he admitted that more people had said the opposite.

"If you'll forgive me for saying so," the other man continued, studying the liquid in his glass, "you also appear to be somewhat out of your element here in Regret."

In an effort to appear unconcerned, he took his time about answering.

Travis wandered over to the windows overlooking the main street and stared down at the bustling crowds. The sun had been shining for the last few days, and as a result, the muddy street had almost completely dried out. But typically, it wouldn't be that way for long. He glanced out at the ominous clouds staining the horizon and knew that the rain would return by nightfall. Maybe earlier. Like everything else in Regret—nothing, not even the weather, was certain.

Looking over his shoulder at Bennet, Travis asked, "What makes you say that? Why I feel quite at home here, actually."

Bennet's lips curved slightly, and Travis noted that the man's eyes didn't reflect his smile.

"Your clothing for one," Bennet pointed out. "And," he shrugged, "there are other things as well."

Straightening up slightly, Travis said quietly, "You, Mr. Bennet, are hardly the typical resident of a mining community yourself."

"True," Bennet nodded. "But I've made my home here. I have . . . *friends*. You, Mr. Deal, are quite alone, but for a young woman who is, I think, involved in something far beyond her abilities."

"These *friends* of yours," Travis countered through gritted teeth, "have a nasty habit of visiting the Four Roses uninvited."

"*Tsk, tsk, tsk.*" Bennet shook his head and his fingers tightened even further on the stem of his glass. "You disappoint me, Mr. Deal. Surely you don't think *I* am behind your difficulties?"

"I don't?" Whatever else he was, Travis thought, the man was a glib liar.

"Certainly not." Bennet crossed his right leg over his left and reached down to brush away the crease in his pant leg. "Should I have had any intention of causing harm to either you or Miss Donnelly, I'm sure you realize that I would have gone about it in a more thorough manner."

Maybe, Travis thought. And maybe Rafe Bennet wasn't as good as he thought he was. As he studied his opponent, Travis saw the other man's tight jawline, the rigid way he held his head, and the ever-tightening grip on his brandy snifter. Something inside Travis tightened as well. If the man wasn't in complete control of Thompson, there was no telling *what* might happen.

"As a matter of fact," Bennet said, "had you not visited me today, I would have sent for you. Soon."

"Why's that?"

Another meaningless smile curved the man's thin lips, and a spiral of foreboding began to worm its way through Travis's insides.

"I have a proposition for you."

"I'm listening."

"I'd like to buy out your share of the Four Roses Mine."

Travis inhaled slowly, deeply. For some reason, he hadn't expected the man to be so—forthright. Apparently, his foppish disguise had worked all too well. At least Bennet seemed to be convinced that Travis would be more than willing to sell out and leave Alice alone.

"I assure you," Bennet continued, "I shall make it more than worth your while."

"Why would I want to sell?"

Bennet's gaze dropped to the swirl of amber liquid in his glass. "It's unfortunate, Mr. Deal," he said softly, "but in a raw place like this, with the closest law a day's ride or more away, *accidents* happen."

"Like yesterday."

"Precisely." Bennet shook his head again, as if apologizing in advance for what he was planning. "Why, any number of things can happen to a man—or a woman—when they're not being . . . *careful*."

Fighting down the urge to leap across the room and curl his fingers around the other man's throat, Travis forced himself to stay still. What kind of man, he asked himself, can sit quietly and threaten a woman without turning a hair?

A man walking too near the edge of sanity.

Rafe Bennet, Travis told himself, was wound tighter than a fifty-cent watch. Oh, he played the gentleman well. He assumed the posture of a man unbothered by trivialities. But just beneath that cool, unruffled surface, Bennet was a dangerous man. By the looks of him, it wouldn't take much to make him fly apart.

And Travis didn't want Alice anywhere near the man when it happened. Just thinking about her made him want to hightail it back to camp. He wouldn't feel right about any of this until she was under his own watchful eye. Who the hell knew what else Bennet had planned? Immediately, though, he calmed himself with the knowledge that Cutter and Sean were with her. And, hell, if it came to trouble, there was Chucker, too, for a last line of defense.

"I thank you for your generous offer," Travis said, and started for the door. He needed some fresh air. He needed to think. "But for the time being, I believe I'll be staying on in Regret. As of now, I have no plans to sell my share in the mine." Especially since he didn't have a share to sell.

"I'm sorry to hear that."

As he walked across the room, Travis felt a crawling sensation along his spine. As if his body was preparing itself for a bullet's impact. When his fingers closed over the brass doorknob, Travis turned it, then glanced back over his shoulder at Bennet.

He stared into the other man's dark, unforgiving gaze and said, "I'll be sure to pass along your warning to my partner."

"You do that, Mr. Deal."

Al pushed her hair back from her face with one gloved hand and stared blankly at the activity swarming around her. Miners moved in a wordless dance, weaving in and out of each other's way as they trudged back and forth carrying fallen rocks to the ore cart. Each stone tumbled into the iron cart banged and rattled against the metal sides, and Al's already aching head began to pound with the rhythm of a single jack hammer.

She brushed her forearm across her brow, wiping away the sweat streaming into her eyes. With so many men clustered together in such a small, enclosed area, the temperature in the mine was unbearably hot. Though not as hot as the deeper, inner chambers of the earth. Al knew from experience that the further you went into the mine, the more you felt as though you were knocking on the very gates of hell.

"Lovely weather we're havin', eh?"

She threw a quick glance at Sean and frowned. It seemed that every time she looked up, she was staring into the Irishman's laughing blue eyes. How the hell did Frankie stand having someone that bloody cheerful around all the time?

"Don't you have something to do somewhere else?" she snapped.

Sean's black eyebrows lifted high on his forehead. "A bit churlish this morning, aren't we?"

One of the miners stepped up to Al's cart, dumped another huge rock inside it, then stared at Al and Sean.

"I'm not payin' you four dollars a day to stand there lookin' at me!" she said.

The miner grumbled, gave her a dark look from dirt-ringed eyes, and went back to work.

"Ah well, that's grand."

"What's grand?" she asked.

"It's not just me you're slicin' to ribbons with that harpy's tongue of yours." Sean shrugged and had the nerve to grin. " 'Tis everyone's lucky day."

Al bit back another, sharper retort and forced herself to take a deep, calming breath. Crossing her forearms on the cart's warm, steel rail, she looked up at him from the corner of her eye. He was right. She had been on the prod since the moment she'd walked into the mine prepared to work.

Hell, she'd *needed* to work. To sweat and strain and keep so busy she didn't have time to think about Travis. It hadn't worked. Oh, she'd worked her tail off and, no doubt, managed to offend every miner working for her in the process. But still, her thoughts were full of the man she'd left sleeping a couple of hours ago.

And the more she thought about him, the more sure she was that everything he'd told her about himself had been a lie. Once again, her mind filled with the dawn-lit image of him, bare-chested. No city man had a muscular, tanned chest like Travis Deal. No man who labored at a desk all day could become as work-hardened and strong as Travis.

He'd lied. There was no other explanation. And if he'd lied about who he was . . . what else had he lied about?

Damn the man! She'd half convinced herself she was in love with him! Imagine, Mary Alice Donnelly in love with a dandy. Hah! The very idea of Mary Alice in love *at all* was enough to bring a chuckle or two. So, she asked herself, why was it she didn't feel like laughing? Her head dropped to her chest, and she reached up to rub her tired eyes.

"Al darlin'," Sean asked quietly "are ya all right?"

She straightened up slowly to face him. "Yeah. I'm all right." He didn't look convinced, though, and truth to tell, she hadn't expected him to be. Frankie's husband didn't appear to be a stupid man. "Just thinking."

"Ah . . . and I'll wager I know who it is occupyin' your thoughts so."

"Sean . . ." She paused as another miner came forward and dropped a massive stone into the ore cart. "It's not what you think."

"Of course not."

"I mean it."

"Sure ya do, darlin'." His eyebrows wiggled, and one corner of his mouth tilted in a quick grin.

Brother-in-law or not, Sean was too sure of himself by far. "If you're waiting on me to marry my new partner, you've a long wait coming."

He slapped one big hand to his broad chest and his eyes widened innocently.

"Who said anything about marriage, lass?"

"Just because my sisters married their partners doesn't mean that I'll follow right along."

"Surely not!" He looked offended.

"The name of this mine is the Four Roses," Al

said tightly. "And it won't be changing anytime soon."

"And why should ya change it? 'Tis a lovely name."

"The hotel and the saloon had the same lovely name, if you'll recall."

He grinned again and rubbed his chin with one hand. "Now, there ya have me! But no one's tellin' ya to change anything, darlin'. What reason would ya have?"

Al wasn't fooled by his artless protests. She knew bloody well what he was thinking. What they were *all* probably thinking! "The same reason my sisters changed the names of *their* places."

He didn't say a word, just kept that silly smile directed at her.

"I'm telling you now, Sean, and you can tell Cutter. There'll be no changes around here!"

Her fingers tightened around the metal bar. When Maggie had changed the Four Roses Saloon to the Four Golden Roses, it had almost made sense. After all, she had merged her saloon with Cutter's, the Golden Garter.

But when Frankie had changed the Four Roses Hotel to the Four *Irish* Roses, Al sensed a pattern was forming. Well, she wouldn't be changing the name of her mine to the Four *Dandy* Roses anytime soon.

"Ya never know, Al darlin'." Sean leaned in close to her and winked. "Life is full of surprises."

Exasperated, Al snapped, "When are you and Cutter goin' home?"

A shout of pain interrupted their conversation.

They followed the commotion to the pile of rubble, and Al saw immediately who had cried out. One miner was lying flat on his back, his left hand clutching his right arm, just above the elbow. Blood oozed out from between his fingers.

"Pick got him," someone offered as Al stepped up close to the fallen man.

"He walked right in front of me," one of the men whined in self-defense.

She ignored the crowd of onlookers and carefully pried the man's fingers away from the wound. The arm didn't appear to be broken, but the gash needed binding to stop the blood.

"Yank your shirttail out, Sean," she ordered, and while he did, she bent down and pulled a knife from her boot.

"Jesus!" Sean's eyes widened as he looked at the long, thin razor-sharp blade. "You always carry that bloody thing with ya?"

"You never know when you might need it," she told him, and sliced into the tail of his shirt. As she ripped a long strip of fabric off over his loud protest, she echoed the words he'd said earlier. "Life is full of surprises, Sean."

Travis waited while the bartender jammed his thumb and forefinger into a customer's gold pouch and pulled out a pinch of dust. The miner frowned at the amount Sam managed to grab hold of between his meaty fingers, but wisely, he said nothing.

For small purchases, it was customary for the seller to help himself to a pinch of dust from the buyer's poke. For the larger orders, a bartender, like every other merchant in town, would use a balance scale. However, there was still plenty of grumbling about thick-fingered men helping themselves to more than they were entitled to. But until a better system arrived, it was all they had.

After Sam finished brushing his gold dust into a small jar behind the bar, he turned to Travis.

"Mr. Deal," he smiled. "What can I get ya?"

"Another bottle of wine, please."

"Ah, your evenin' with Al went well, then?"

"Well enough," he said shortly, and watched the other man move off toward the storeroom. Travis had no intention of standing about a bar discussing Alice with a nosey bartender.

Especially since he wasn't sure what was happening himself. Images of the night before raced across his mind and Travis's body tightened in response. He was going to have to stop thinking about her in public. It was damned embarrassing to have his groin leap to attention every time he heard her name.

But Lord, last night with her had been more than he'd ever dreamed possible. Becoming a part of her had touched a chord in him that he hadn't known existed. And later, holding her in his arms, he'd actually slept the entire night through. For the first time in he couldn't remember how long, there'd been no nightmares. No memories of past failures haunting him. Just the quiet haven of her arms, and the soft blessing of her breath brushing his chest.

He ran one hand across his face. Travis had never expected to feel such a rush of tenderness ... such ... what?

Love?

Yes, God help him. Love.

For all the good it did him.

If Alice had any feelings for him at all, they weren't for Travis Delacort, ex-marshal and sometime gunslinger. Her feelings were centered on a town dandy. A man who didn't exist.

And maybe that was for the best, he told himself. Once she found out who he really was, she'd want nothing to do with him. Hell, he'd be lucky if she didn't shoot him. Luckier if she did. At least, then, he wouldn't have to live the rest of his life missing her.

Maybe, he thought, he should tell her now. Today. That way, she wouldn't start building up any long-term dreams or plans for the two of them. It would hurt her, he knew. But better she be hurt now than disappointed later. They had no future together, and it was best if she found that out right away. Travis nodded, despite the pain beginning to build up in his chest. She'd be so furious with him and so anxious for him to leave, that it would be easier to go when the time came.

Easy. Nothing about Alice had come easy—and leaving her would be the hardest thing he'd ever done.

"It'll be just a minute," Sam shouted, and his voice was muffled. "Got a bunch of boxes and such piled up in front of the wine bottles."

Wine. Travis frowned. If he was going to tell Alice the truth, he didn't need wine. What was he really hoping for? One more night of lovemaking? One more risk of making a child? One more night to take advantage of her affection for another man?

But it wasn't another man she cared for. It was him. Just a different him.

"Dammit!"

How the hell could he be jealous of himself? And how could he not be?

"You seen Dickie Meyer?" Someone further down the bar asked.

"Nope," another miner answered. "Not in about three days now."

"Shit," the first man muttered.

"Yeah. Don't figure ol' Dickie will be back for another seven days or so."

"Just long enough."

"Damn Bennet's eyes."

Travis frowned thoughtfully and half turned to the first man. Glad to be focusing his thoughts on something besides his own misery, he asked, "What's going on?"

"Who're you?"

"Ah, he's all right," the second man offered. "He's Al Donnelly's partner."

"What were you saying about this—Dickie?"

"Dickie Meyer," the second man said with a nod that sent his limp black hair swinging about his long, narrow face. "Went missin' three days ago. Ought to be back in a week or so, though."

"How do you know that, if he's missing?"

"'Cause when mine owners go missin'," the other man piped up, "they're always gone ten days."

A thread of suspicion started low in Travis's belly and quickly spread. "Why is that?"

"That's all Bennet needs. That's why."

"Needs?" Travis prodded, suddenly impatient

for the man to finish what he was saying. "Needs for what?"

The narrow-faced man spoke up again. "If a mine owner don't show up at his diggin's for ten straight days, anybody who wants it can lay claim to the mine."

Travis's heart stopped, staggered, and slowly began beating again. He'd never known much about mining law. Hell, the only reason he'd known about a miner's court was because as a marshal, he'd had to deal with them on occasion. But this. This was something new.

Missing. Mine owner. Ten days. Kidnapping.

Goddammit, that's what Bennet was up to. That's why no one had tried to kill Alice outright. Why the hell should they when all they had to do was hide her somewhere for ten days and claim her mine?

His insides seething, Travis fought hard to maintain a calm demeanor. "And you say that this happens quite a bit?"

"Only a couple of times." The first man snorted. "Didn't happen hardly a'tall though, till a few months ago. Then Bennet showed up. Kinda makes a man think, don't it?"

"Yes," Travis muttered thickly, turning away from the bar, his wine forgotten. "Yes it does."

"Hey, mister," the narrow-faced man shouted, and Travis looked back over his shoulder at him. "Some of your boys was in here last night, after the funeral?"

"Yes?" Travis snapped.

"Is it true, you're payin' your miners four dollars a day?"

"It's true."

"And a twenty dollar bonus to the man who brings out the most ore each week?"

Travis nodded, anxious to be on his way.

The man looked disgusted. "I got to say, I didn't believe it when I heard it. Bennet's only payin' three fifty, and he wouldn't know a miner's bonus if it jumped up and bit him on the ass." He brightened a bit and asked, "How about a job, mister?"

Now was not the time to be hiring more men, Travis thought, and said, "Not now, I'm afraid. But why not ask Bennet for a raise in pay?"

"Fat chance of that," the other man snorted.

"Nah," his friend put in, "there's nothin' we can do to make ol' Bennet pay better."

An idea came to him in an instant. It might work. In fact, it might just be the thing they needed to drive Bennet out of Regret. If they made things uncomfortable for him in Regret, the man would move on to easier pickings. He'd done it before.

Despite his need to hurry back to the mine, Travis told the men, "Sure there's something you can do. Without you men, Bennet can't work his mine. Simply refuse to go down until you get better wages."

One of the men straightened up from the bar and looked at Travis through thunderstruck eyes. "Ya mean ... strike?"

"Like them fellas in Virginia City done a few years back?"

"Why not?" Then he turned and hurried to the door. He didn't hear Sam yelling after him that he'd forgotten his wine.

# Chapter 18

*Four Roses Ranch*

**T**eresa signed the delivery slip and gave the boy a smile. "Just take the wagon out to the barn, Davey. Some of the men will help you unload it."

"Yes, ma'am," the boy said, nodding his shaggy head like a duck in a pond. "I mean, miss. I mean . . ."

Teresa, still smiling, at last managed to close the door despite Davey's drooling admiration. Once it was firmly shut on the local mercantile's heir apparent, Teresa leaned back against the door and stared up at the ceiling.

Day after day, week after week, nothing changed. The ranch rolled right along, the same problems being solved the same way, month after month.

All right, she told herself with a grin. One thing had changed. Davey Tuttle had discovered that he was desperately in love with her. She turned her head slightly and looked through the sheer white curtains covering the glass panes set in the top half of the door.

Davey, all five feet six of him, was backing off the porch, his gaze locked firmly on the closed door. At sixteen, he was all bones and promises. In a few years, he'd probably fill out and steal the heart of every girl for miles around. But for now, he was just another reason that Teresa wanted to leave.

Even with the ranch being four miles from the town of Pine Hill, it seemed that young Davey found an excuse to come to the Donnelly ranch nearly every day. She could hardly walk without tripping on him.

As she watched, Davey reached the steps and, still in the throes of love, didn't notice. He tumbled down the short flight of stairs to the dirt below, but was back on his feet in an instant. Brushing himself off, he glanced around the ranch yard frantically, obviously hoping that no one had seen his fall.

Shaking her head, Teresa walked through the polished, sun-splashed oak entryway and down the hall to the ranch office. She strolled to her desk, plopped down onto the chair, and stared thoughtfully at the painting on the opposite wall.

Her father had commissioned it a few years before. Four sisters, staring blankly ahead, smiling. Teresa's gaze moved over each of the women in the portrait.

Maggie, the oldest, proud and confident, even then. Frankie, the second in line, shy, pretty, a demon for propriety—until recently. And Al, Teresa laughed gently. Even for a formal portrait, Al had insisted on wearing her blasted buckskins—as proof, she supposed, of Al's desire to do just what she damned well pleased.

And finally, there was herself, Teresa. The last Donnelly and the one who looked like no one else in the family. Oh, she'd heard the stories about how she was the very image of her mother. She'd even seen the daguerrotype of the woman who'd died giving birth to her.

Teresa'd inherited her black hair and blue eyes—even her name—from her mother. And each of her sisters took their coloring from their da, Kevin.

Even at birth, she thought suddenly, she'd been stamped as different. But it was more than just looks. It went far deeper. The others were content with the family businesses they'd been given to run. But Teresa wanted more than the ranch. She wanted a life beyond cows and fences and range wars. And she certainly didn't want to end up tied for life to a man selected for her by her father!

Jumping to her feet, Teresa glared at her sisters' faces for a moment longer, then rushed out of the room. It was already early summer. If she was going to do something, she didn't have any time to lose.

"Kidnapping?"

"It makes sense, in a twisted sort of way."

Cutter shook his head and frowned at Travis. "He couldn't get away with it. Bennet has to know that we'd come looking for Al."

That had already occurred to Travis, and he had an answer ready. "Sure he does. But he must have a safe spot to stash whoever he takes. Some place too hard to find."

"Why the devil has no one said anything about this?" Sean wanted to know. "We've been here weeks now. And not so much as a whisper have I heard about kidnappings."

"I don't know," Travis shot back, raking one hand through his thickly pomaded hair, then grimacing at the grease on his hand. He reached for his handkerchief and wiped the mess from his palm. Squinting against the early afternoon sun, he said, "Maybe the men he kidnapped left town right after. They had no reason to stay, with their mines being taken over."

"And no sheriff to complain to," Cutter threw in.

"Exactly."

"Ya think some of our boys is helpin' that bastard any?" Chucker's voice wheezed into the conversation and Travis looked at him. Worry deepened every crease in the old man's features.

"I don't know. Maybe." Then he shook his head. "Maybe not, though. The men seem happier than before. They sure as hell have been treating *me* better since yesterday."

Better? Hell, they were treating him like a damn king. Smiles of greeting, tipped hats, and best of all, the muffled laughter whenever he walked by had stopped.

"Aye"—Sean nodded, a half smile on his lips—"money has a way of changin' things."

"That's what I'm worried about," Chucker said sharply. "If Bennet's willin' to pay good money, what's to stop our boys from takin' him up on it?"

"Us."

All three men turned to look at Travis.

"We'll stop them."

Grimly, the others nodded.

"We'd better tell Al," Cutter said softly.

"No." Travis had thought the whole thing through on his walk back from town. Knowing Alice, if she were to find out about this kidnapping threat, she'd march straight into town, face Bennet in his office, and force his hand. Who knew what would happen then?

Alice's accusations might be just enough to push Bennet over the edge of that fine line he was straddling.

"I hope you know what you're doing." Cutter shook his head. "When she finally does find out about this—and she will, I guarantee it—she's going to have your head on a stick."

Travis gave him a tight smile. What Cutter didn't know was that Alice was very probably going to have his head no matter what happened with the kidnapping thing. The minute she found out about all the lies he'd told her, he was finished. He knew it. And he'd accepted it.

As long as she was safe and healthy enough to attack him, Travis would be almost glad for it.

Sean, though, shuddered. "When she comes at ya, mind that right boot of hers, man."

"What?"

Cutter chuckled. "Never mind. Just hope you don't have to find out what he means."

Shaking his head, Travis brushed Sean's mysterious comment aside for the moment. He stood up, then waited while the others did, too. "It's settled then? Chucker and Sean will watch her this afternoon. Cutter and I will take turns standing guard over her tonight."

"Aye, it's settled." Sean turned, patted the old man's shoulder, and jerked his head toward the cook-fire. "C'mon then, you. I'll have a snack before me supper. If I'm to be a bloody guard, I'll need me strength!"

"By rights," Chucker grumbled, "you should already be the strongest man in the world. I never seen a body eat as much as you do!"

Cutter waited until the others were out of earshot before turning to Travis. "You want me to take first watch or the second tonight?"

"First." Travis's gaze shifted to the cluster of miners a hundred or so feet away. He carefully swept the crowd until he spotted Alice. "Wake me at midnight, I'll take over."

"Midnight till dawn?" Cutter mused. "That's a long watch."

"If I get tired, I'll wake you."

"Uh-huh." Cutter stepped in front of Travis, cutting off his view of the camp. "Any reason why you want that shift in particular?"

Travis's gaze narrowed. "What's that supposed to mean?"

"Only that nighttime is a bit more . . . romantic than afternoons."

Romantic! Travis scowled at his friend, took a step to one side and looked at Alice again. Since coming back from town, he hadn't been able to get *near* her. It had taken nearly two hours to get Cutter, Sean, and Chucker together in one place long enough to have a meeting. And during that time, he'd tried occasionally to talk to Alice. But

everytime she saw him approaching, she found
someone else to talk to, or something else to do.
He'd never seen anyone so busy at doing nothing in particular.

Was she regretting her time with him so much
so that she couldn't bear the sight of him to remind her of her mistake? Was she embarrassed?
Ashamed?

Why the hell wouldn't she talk to him?

He inhaled sharply, shoved his hands into his
pants pockets, and kept his gaze locked on her.
Partly because simply looking at her was enough
to fill his soul. And partly because Cutter was a
man who didn't miss much, and Travis didn't
want the gambler reading the expression in his
eyes.

"Just wake me at midnight, Cutter. All right?"

"Sure, Travis." He shook his head and started
toward the cook-tent. "Anything you say."

Alone, Travis watched the others. He heard
snatches of conversation blown to him on the
cool, pine scented breeze. Occasionally, a burst
of laughter reached him. From the mine came the
muted, solid *chunk* of a hammer and drill at work
on stone.

Chucker bent to stir his pot of chili and the
rich, spicy aroma swirled in the soft wind. Men
lined up, each clutching a tin plate and cup. Apparently, Sean wasn't the only man wanting a
snack.

Alice laughed suddenly, and her voice carried
to him, reminding him of the soft whispers and
sweet moans they'd shared the night before. A
sharp pain lanced through Travis's chest, and he
recognized it immediately.

Loneliness.

From his vantage point on the rocky slope, Travis watched them all and once again became what he had always been.

A man on the outside of life, closed off from everything and everyone he wanted most.

She shouldn't have avoided Travis all day, she told herself. Mary Alice sat up and swung both feet to the ground. Obviously, she thought, she wasn't going to be getting any sleep. It had to be past midnight, and she was no more sleepy than when she'd first lain down.

Her father had always said that Mary Alice could fall asleep standing up on a picket fence. But that was before Travis Deal had entered her life and confused her so that she hardly knew her own name anymore. Snatching up her boots, she yanked them on, one after the other, then propped her elbows on her thighs.

Travis. Lately, everything going on in her life seemed to come back to him.

By refusing to talk to him, all she'd done was bank her anger. It was a terrible, blazing fire, searing her insides. She couldn't sleep, think, eat. She'd barely tasted Chucker's chili—another thing to be mad about. She loved that old man's chili.

She rubbed one hand tiredly across her features and realized that her face actually *hurt* from the forced smile she'd kept slapped on her lips all day. But, she supposed it had been worth it. Al simply hadn't wanted Travis to know that she was thinking about him. At least, not until she was ready to talk to him.

Pushing herself to her feet, Mary Alice walked across the tent and pulled the edge of the flap back a bit to look around camp. A splash of moonlight lay across the canvas tents, giving them a soft, silvery look that faded under the harsher sun. Everything was still, quiet. Not a soul was stirring in camp, but, Al told herself, that didn't mean a blasted thing. No doubt someone was out there, just waiting for her to show herself so they could sidle up to her and make pests of themselves.

Maybe she wouldn't have been all worked up into such a lather if she'd been able to find a moment's peace all day. Just a short time to be alone. A minute or two to gather her thoughts. To remember what she'd felt in Travis's arms and try to figure out if he'd really experienced the same thing. Mary Alice scowled, disgusted with herself. There was no question in her mind about what they'd felt and shared. The questions all lay in the fact that she didn't know who in the hell it really was she'd given herself to.

Was he no more than he appeared? Or was he another man entirely, hiding behind a dude's clothing for his own purposes?

"Dammit!" she muttered, and her own voice sounded unreasonably loud in the quiet.

She wanted to be able to think calmly, rationally, about how badly she wanted to take a horsewhip to Travis Deal until he started telling her the truth.

But no. All afternoon, whenever she turned around, either Sean or Chucker were right there beside her. She'd hardly been able to take a step in any direction without bumping into one or the other of them.

Then, just a couple of hours ago, when the entire camp should have been sound asleep, Al had decided to go for a walk. To clear her head. Naturally, she'd run smack into Cutter. Trying to explain her sleeplessness to him had not been something she'd wanted to do, so she'd ended up back in her tent—a tent that seemed to be getting smaller every minute.

It was as if the canvas walls were shrinking, folding in on themselves and burying her alive. She needed to be outside, where she could stare up at the wide sky and lose herself for a little while in the vast silences of the countryside. She needed to get away from all of the people who suddenly seemed thicker than flies around her.

And she needed to talk to Travis. To somehow *make* him tell her the truth about himself and what he was doing in Regret.

Mostly, though, she wanted to know exactly what, if anything, he felt for her. Alice's eyes filled unexpectedly, and she angrily blinked back the unshed tears. "No man is worth cryin' over," she mumbled. "Especially not one who's making you so blasted mad!"

Lord, Travis did have the ability to make her angrier than anyone else she'd ever known, before or since meeting him. Of course, it was his *other* abilities that had brought her to such a fix. The way he spoke to her—looked at her—treated her. She'd never before felt as . . . special as she did when she was with Travis. And if she was to admit the whole truth, she'd have to say she even enjoyed arguing with him.

Hell, Al thought grimly, the real problem here was, she'd gone and done the dumbest thing she possibly could have. She'd fallen in love with the miserable, sweet-talking, good-looking, lying son-of-a-bitch. A slow grin curved her lips, and briefly she enjoyed the knowledge that love had finally happened to her. Unfortunately, the man she loved had more secrets than a fifty-cent whore had customers. It was time, though, she told herself firmly, for those secrets to end. Now, she needed to know if she was all alone in this love thing—or if he felt the same.

She jerked herself a nod. That's just what she was going to do. Now. Find Travis and demand some answers. Something cold and hard settled in her belly. Be it determination or just plain cussed stubbornness, she didn't know and didn't care. Either way, it would be enough to see her through the coming confrontation.

Decision made, Al started to lift the tent flap, then stopped. The way her day had been going, there'd be a damn marching band passing her tent the moment she set foot outside. Grumbling under her breath, she turned and went to the back of her tent. She grabbed one end of her cot, shoved it aside and dropped to her knees. Digging her fingers into the dirt beneath the canvas, Al lifted the tent wall just high enough to slip under it.

"A fine thing," she muttered, "having to slip out of my own place just to avoid runnin' into folks who've got nothing better to do than bother me." Brushing her palms against her jeans, Al took a step and stopped.

"Alice?"

"Goddammit!"

Her stomach lurched and her heart shot up into her throat. Ridiculous, since she'd half expected to find *someone* hanging around. But her mind just wasn't working properly at the moment.

And it was all his fault.

She whirled about and frowned at the man walking up to her. Lowering her voice to an outraged whisper, she said, "Jesus, Travis, you shouldn't sneak up on me like that!"

"Where are you going?"

"To see you." Mary Alice cocked her head and narrowed her gaze suspiciously as she stared at him. "What are *you* doin' here in the middle of the night?"

"Taking a walk."

"Huh!" She lifted her arms high, then let them drop to her sides. "All of a sudden, everybody and their uncle is taking walks outside my tent. Why is that, do you suppose, Travis?"

He stopped when he was no more than half an arm's reach from her and asked quietly, "What did you want to see me about?"

Al studied him for a heartbeat or two. Just long enough, in fact, to notice what she should have noticed about Travis three or four weeks ago.

In the hushed, moonlit quiet, he stood tall and easy. He didn't seem the least bit out of his element. Rather, he appeared to be quite at home, wandering around a campsite in the middle of the night. And *that's* what she should have noticed about him right off.

*He* wasn't out of place in Regret.

His *clothes* were.

Hell, she had noticed something amiss early on. Hadn't she caught herself, at different times, thinking that he was stronger than he looked? Faster? More sure of himself?

Had she been blinded to the man by the outrageous clothing he wore? And was that exactly what he'd intended all along?

A soft wind picked up out of nowhere and brought the sharp, clean scent of his shaving soap to her. Butterflies swarmed up in her stomach, and Al fought that swirling, teasing sensation with all her strength. She couldn't afford to let her judgment go astray now. Even though the temptation to throw herself into his arms and have him hold her until her doubts passed was incredibly compelling.

Giving in to her feelings and not listening to her mind was what had brought her to this in the first place.

The moonlight wasn't strong enough to allow her to read the expression in his eyes. And she needed to. She needed to see him—watch his reaction when she called him on his lies.

"Come inside," she said quietly. "We can talk in my tent."

He shook his head. "Not tonight."

Somehow she hadn't expected him to refuse. Hell, she'd been dodging him half the day. Now that she wanted to talk, he said *"no"*?

"Why the hell not?"

"Tomorrow," he told her, neatly avoiding her question. "Go back to sleep."

She took a step toward him, reacting purely

on instinct. "Go *back* to sleep? I haven't *been* to sleep yet, damn you!"

"Alice—"

"No. Don't start in sweet-talking me again. I won't stand for it. You owe me some answers, Travis. And by God, I want them *now*."

"I can't. Not yet."

"I want this settled between us, Travis."

"Alice," he sighed. "You don't understand."

"It's *Al*," she shot back, and scowled at the break in her voice. "Until you can tell me why you've been lying to me—why you used me—you can call me Al. Just like everybody else."

"I didn't *use* you," he snapped, and she heard the growl of anger in his voice.

Well good, she thought. Maybe a good, loud fight is just what they needed.

"What would you call it?"

"I'd call it making love."

"Love?" Her hands fisted and flew to her hips. Leaning toward him, she challenged, "You're sayin' you love me?"

"I don't have the right to say that."

"Well, goddammit," she said, and her voice was a vicious whisper, "just what *do* you have the right to? My bed and then a quick good-bye?"

"Christ, you've got a tongue on you that could slice through steel."

"That's not what you said last night."

He groaned softly, but she heard him.

"Alice, there are things going on you don't understand."

"I know I don't understand! That's the whole

point here, Travis. I need to know what's goin' on."

"And you will," he promised her. "Soon."

"Not good enough." Last night he couldn't keep his hands off her, she thought wildly. Tonight, he wouldn't step into her tent. "Why don't you just explain everything to me, huh?"

"Not tonight, Alice." He backed up a step as if that would help keep him from accepting her invitation. "I can't."

"Why?"

"He's standing guard, Al." A new voice ended their argument. Low and dangerous, the voice came again. "He's out here to protect you. From me."

Mary Alice's head swiveled around and she watched Mike Thompson step out of the shadows, his gun drawn and pointed at her. In the utter stillness, she heard him pull the hammer back, cocking the gun into readiness.

"You make one sound, fancy man," Thompson told Travis, "I'll kill her."

"No you won't," Travis returned quietly. "You can't shoot without rousing the whole camp."

"Try me." Thompson stepped up behind Al and motioned for her to turn around again. "She'll be dead before she hits the dirt." He gave Travis a small, deadly smile. "And I might even have time to take care of you, too, before I disappear."

Al stood her ground, refusing to turn her back on the gunman. Maybe it was because of the day she'd had. Maybe it was facing down Travis and getting no answers to the doubts and questions plaguing her. But whatever the reason, she'd been pushed too far and refused to go another step.

Crossing her arms over her chest, she said, "Thompson, you worthless piece of trash—you're not going to shoot a woman. You wouldn't be safe anywhere if you do."

"You're no woman," Thompson sneered. "So don't tempt me. That mouth of yours has been itchin' to get closed for months." He glanced at Travis. "You! Over here."

When his eyes shifted momentarily from her, Al took her chance. Fisting her right hand, she drew her arm back and swung at him.

He ducked her punch easily, then clipped her across the chin with a hard left fist. Al's head snapped back, her eyes rolled up, and she dropped soundlessly to the dirt.

Travis watched her fall and something cold and deadly formed in his gut. Looking away from Alice's limp form, he stared evenly into the barrel of Mike Thompson's pistol.

With the gun aimed at his chest, Travis didn't stand a chance in hell of reaching the weapon he'd brought with him for his shift at guarding Alice. The pistol was stuck into the waistband of his pants. Cold steel pressed into his back, tempting him to reach for it and take his chances at beating the gunman.

But if he tried and failed, Alice would be on her own with Thompson. And that, Travis wasn't willing to risk.

"Get over here and pick her up," Thompson said, and waved his gun at Travis. "Was only s'posed to cart her off, but I might's well take you while I'm at it. Who knows? Might be worth a bonus. Besides, this way *you* can carry her."

Travis did as he was told. He couldn't risk Alice being hurt. As much as it pained him to take orders from Thompson, he was willing to do whatever he had to do to keep her safe.

"Hold it," the other man said suddenly. "You don't look like much, but I'm a careful man. Lift up that coat of yours and turn in a circle. Slow."

Dammit. Travis clenched his jaw tight to keep from shouting his rage, waking the camp, and maybe pushing Thompson into shooting Alice. Grimly, he turned around and stood stock still as Thompson yanked the pistol from his waistband and tossed it aside. Travis heard his gun hit the ground, and with it went his hopes of somehow overpowering Thompson. All he could do now was keep Alice safe and wait for another chance.

"Pick her up." Thompson took one step back and watched quietly. "You carry the bitch."

Travis flinched.

"Mister," Thompson said softly, "I just saw something flare up in your eyes that I don't much like. I saw a damn stupid idea. You can't beat me. You can't stop me from killin' her if I want to." His voice dropped even lower as he finished. "But you *could* stay alive. Both of you. If you do like you're told."

Travis ground his teeth together and dug his short fingernails into the scarred palms of his hands.

"If you don't," Thompson vowed, "I'll kill ya both. Her first, so's you can watch." After a long moment, he asked, "Do you understand me, mister?"

Travis nodded stiffly, then bent down beside Alice. He lifted her easily and cradled her close to his chest. Her limp form, draped across his arms, fueled the anger burning inside him until it was a churning, raging beast with a life all its own.

Not five minutes ago, she'd faced him down, gloriously fuming, demanding that he talk to her. Now, she lay unconscious in his arms, and her very life depended on the whims of one man.

Well, Travis promised himself, Alice Donnelly was *not* going to die. No matter what it took, he would wait for his chance and take it. If it meant his own worthless hide, so be it.

Alice would live.

# Chapter 19

‹‹‹ ✦ ›››

"**T**hey're gone," Cutter said flatly, and raked one hand through his sleep-ruffled hair. "Both of them."

"*Both* of 'em?" Chucker demanded. "Why in hell would he take Travis, too?"

"Perhaps because he's a partner," Sean muttered.

"It doesn't matter *why*," Cutter snapped, and held out the pistol he'd found in the brush behind Al's tent. "All that matters is that Travis and Al are gone. And we've got to find them. Fast."

Cutter couldn't believe it. He hadn't thought it possible for someone to get the best of Travis Delacort. Shit, he would have *bet* on it.

Something must have happened to prevent Travis from fighting. At that thought, a knot of fear lodged in Cutter's throat, threatening to close off his air. If Travis didn't fight, he had a damned good reason. And that reason *had* to be Al.

Why else would a man like Travis go anywhere quietly—*unarmed*.

"At least we know they won't be harmed," Sean said. "None of the others were."

"We can't count on that." Cutter squinted into the distance and absently noted that the sun was already climbing the sky. Time was passing too quickly. They'd already been gone several hours. And who knew in what direction? "Gather the men together," he told Sean. "We're going to need help."

"Aye," the Irishman agreed and took off like a shot down the path toward camp.

"What if we can't find her?" Chucker asked, unwittingly voicing the same worry tapping at the edge of Cutter's own brain.

"We'll find her," the gambler said. Then, in a poor attempt to ease the older man's worries, he added, "If we don't, Al just might kill the poor fool who carried her off."

"That bastard!" Al lay curled up on her side, her face in the dirt, several long strands of her hair lying across her eyes. She reached up with her bound hands and brushed that hair back off her face. "Tie me up and toss me down like a sack of rocks, will he?"

Travis grinned despite the situation. After long hours of waiting for her to regain consciousness, listening to her rant and rage was a pleasure. He rolled onto his side so that he could see her and told himself that even tied up, furious, bedraggled, and dirty, she was the most beautiful woman he'd ever known.

"I'm glad you think this is so blasted funny,"

she snapped, and clumsily pushed herself up to a sitting position. "I hurt all over and these damned ropes are so tight, they're biting into my wrists."

"I'm afraid that's my fault"

"What?"

"Thompson held his gun on me while I tied you up."

"Did ya have to make them so blasted tight?"

"Yes." Travis shifted position slightly and groaned when a sharp spear of pain stabbed through the back of his head. As that misery ebbed and became a dull, throbbing ache, he continued. "If I hadn't done a good job, he would have done it himself. And as you can see, he would have tied your hands behind your back." Travis lifted one shoulder to indicate his own uncomfortable position. "Take my word for it, Mister Thompson's methods are a good bit more disagreeable."

She fumed silently for a long minute, then said, "When you were finished tying me up, why didn't you try to jump him?"

Travis lifted his head slightly and immediately laid it down again in response to the pain. "As a matter of fact, I did try. He hit me over the head. With his pistol, I think." That son-of-a-bitch had a lot to answer for, Travis told himself. Scowling with disgust, he added, "I woke up to find myself like this."

"Oh." Alice winced, moved her jaw carefully from side to side, and muttered, "Wait until I get my hands on that bastard. Imagine him punching me in the face like that! It's a wonder he didn't break my jaw!"

"You were going to do the same to him," Travis pointed out.

"That was different." She turned her head slowly to look at her surroundings. "Where the hell are we, anyway?"

"I don't know." Travis let his eyes slide shut so he wouldn't have to look her in the eye while he told her the rest. Jesus, it was humiliating. "He forced me to tie a blindfold around my eyes while we rode here. We could be in Canada for all I know."

High rock walls climbed all around them to meet in a ceiling of rock at least ten feet high. In one corner, there were blankets and what looked to be a small pile of food supplies. In the center of the chamber, on the floor between them, a single lamp burned feebly. Travis still wasn't sure why Thompson hadn't blown it out. Maybe he'd forgotten all about it in his haste to leave. Or perhaps he enjoyed the idea of Travis lying awake all night staring at his stone prison.

That explanation was probably closest to the truth.

A long moment of silence passed before Alice said, "Then I guess we'd better find out where we are."

"And how do you propose we do that?" Damn stubborn woman anyway. Couldn't she see that they were in no position to find out anything? And if they did know where they were, what the hell good would it do them? He might have been blindfolded, but Travis knew they'd ridden quite a ways. They were probably miles away from Regret and help.

Besides, the first order of business was to try

and set each other free from their bonds. At the moment, neither one of them was in a position to do much of anything.

"I propose," Alice said, and drew her bound feet closer, "to take a look outside."

"Are you planning to roll your way to the mouth of the cave?"

"Nope," she flicked him a quick look, then began to fumble with her bound hands at her boot top. "I figured to walk."

Before he could ask how, Travis watched her slide a knife from her right boot. She held it up briefly and the long, gleaming narrow silver blade caught the lamplight and glittered menacingly.

Her right boot. Travis smiled and shook his head, remembering Sean's warning. Never again in this lifetime, he thought, would he ever doubt Mary Alice Donnelly. No matter what, she always seemed to have one more surprise in store for him. Feeling better already, Travis braced his forehead against the dirt and somehow managed to get his knees under him. Hell, he told himself, just sitting up was an improvement.

That Arkansas toothpick of hers had to be razor sharp. In seconds she'd sliced through the bonds around her ankles, then began to saw awkwardly through the ropes at her wrists.

He grinned when the last rope fell to the dirt and she pushed herself to her feet. She swayed unsteadily, then lifted one hand to her forehead. "Lord, my head's pounding like a blacksmith's hammer on a busy Saturday. Must've hit my head when I fell last night."

One more thing to settle up with Thompson

about, Travis thought, and added Alice's headache to the list of complaints he planned to take out of the gunman's hide.

"I hurt all over," she whispered, and slowly rotated her shoulders, letting her head fall forward.

"Alice," he reminded her, anxious to be free of the ropes and out of that cave, "how about cutting me loose?"

"Oh," she said softly as she met his gaze with hers. "I will. Soon."

"What?" His eyes narrowed and he watched her as a slow, wicked smile flashed briefly across her features. Something told him he wasn't going to like what she was about to say. "What do you mean *soon*?"

"First I want to take a look outside."

"I should go with you. There could be a guard out there."

"I don't think so," she shook her head gingerly. "A guard would have been back here by now to check on us." She started walking toward the dark tunnel leading out of the rock chamber.

"Alice . . ."

"Keep your pants on, Travis," she called out in a muffled tone from deep within the tunnel. "I'll be back."

"Goddammit!" His shout echoed out around him and Travis groaned. His head felt as though it was about to burst.

By late afternoon, it was clear to everyone that Travis and Al had disappeared off the face of the earth. No one had seen or heard anything. And despite the fact that every miner working for the

Four Roses was out scouring the countryside, Cutter didn't think the search would be successful.

Bennet had done this before and gotten away with it. That meant that no one had yet found his hiding place.

Cutter inhaled sharply, poured himself a cup of coffee, and drank it—hot, black and strong. It burned his throat, but he almost welcomed the distraction of pain. Glancing into the late-afternoon sky, he saw that it was only a couple hours until sunset. He'd give it until dark. If Travis and Al hadn't been found by then, he and Sean would go pay a little visit to Mister Rafe Bennet.

Bennet threw his brandy snifter across the room and didn't even flinch when it hit the row of precisely aligned glassware. Fine crystal exploded on impact and sent splinters of glass raining down to the floor.

As the last of the fragile crash died away into silence, Rafe Bennet dragged a long, deep breath into his lungs. Then he gathered the tattered ends of his calm around him like an old blanket.

"Ain't no call for that, Mr. Bennet."

He turned his head slightly to stare at the man standing beside the closed office door. Tall and thin with a shock of hair that looked as though it had been combed with a plough, the telegrapher's eyes were round with surprise.

Bennet's gaze shifted away again, disgusted. What did that fool know about his business? How could he possibly imagine what was "called for" or not?

Slowly, Rafe walked to the window and looked down on the familiar street scene. Regret. Who would have thought that the name would be so prophetic? For he certainly did regret ever setting foot in this damnable town.

It should have been so easy. Take over a few small mines and then, eventually, the big ones. Take as much ore as he could in as short a time as possible, then move on to the next town. Easy. He'd successfully accomplished the same thing in countless mining towns over the years.

But he'd been successful because he'd always known when to quit and move on to the next town. Now it was time again. Though he'd planned on being in Regret at least until Fall, things had changed.

Only that morning he'd been served notice that the workers in his mines had called a strike. His right hand clenched into a tight fist before relaxing again. A *strike!* Did those fools really believe that *he*, Rafe Bennet, could be coerced into paying them more money? Where would the profit be in that?

No. He would take the money he'd made in the last few months and move on to fresh territory. Although it was a shame to have his plans altered so unexpectedly.

When had he begun to lose control? he wondered. It was important to know these things so the mistake wasn't repeated in the future.

A small frown marred his studiously blank features. Thompson. His mistake had been in hiring a man unable to curb his own baser urges. Thompson's temper and too-ready-for-battle attitude had caused more problems than they'd solved.

Rafe nodded to himself. Very well, he would be more careful in the next town. He glanced at the afternoon sky and was pleased to note that he still had a few hours of daylight left.

"You're sure," Bennet said casually, "he said his name was Delacort?"

"Ain't likely to forget *that* name," the telegrapher assured him.

"No, I suppose not." Bennet dug into his pants pocket and pulled out three gold coins. Then he walked to his desk and set them down in a short pile on the edge.

"The fella sent out lots of wires askin' about you." The man bobbed his head and his untamed hair flew about his gaunt face. "Figured you'd wanta know what's goin' on, Mister Bennet."

"Of course you did." He forced himself to nod benignly at the toadying coward. No doubt, the telegrapher had come out of respect—not for the money stacked and waiting on the desk.

Even as that thought flew through his brain, the tall thin man stepped forward, scooped up the twenty dollar gold eagles, and pocketed them as if afraid they'd be taken from him.

"And did your Mister Delacort receive any answering wires?" His gaze locked with the other man's, Bennet nearly smiled when he saw the flash of unease in the telegrapher's eyes.

"Uh . . ." The man reached up and ran one finger around the suddenly too tight collar of his dirty white shirt. "I, uh, don't rightly recall."

"Good." Bennet looked away, effectively dismissing the man, and pulled open his top desk drawer. "See that you don't."

"Yes sir."

"Get out."

The moment the other man left, Bennet dismissed him from his mind. Carefully, he pulled out the money box he always kept handy in case of emergency. He snapped the lid open, ran his fingertips through the bills and coins quickly, counted out two hundred dollars, then shut the box again. From the bottom drawer, Bennet withdrew a pair of saddlebags and began to stuff each deep pocket with what he would need to start over.

Again. Ah well, he told himself. On to bigger things. The few mines he'd taken over in Regret weren't worth the bother of breaking a strike. And he certainly didn't want the Four Roses badly enough to go up against a man like Travis Delacort. Rafe shuddered slightly. The stories he'd heard over the years about the former marshal were more than enough to convince him to leave Regret without regret.

"Hmmph!" He snorted a muffled laugh at his own witticism and continued his packing.

A knock sounded out loudly and was immediately followed by the office door swinging open.

Rafe looked up, nodded at the man entering, then continued his task.

Thompson strolled across the floor, stopping on the opposite side of the desk. "Where are you goin'?"

"Virginia City, I think," Bennet said without bothering to look up.

"When?"

"Obviously," he waved one hand at the over-stuffed saddlebags, "now."

"What?" Thompson planted both hands on the desk and leaned in toward him, silently demanding his employer's attention.

Bennet sighed and looked up. "My business here is finished."

"Just like that?"

"Precisely." He glared at the gunman until Thompson pushed himself upright and backed up a step.

"What about the Donnelly bitch and her partner?"

"Let her go." Bennet shrugged and locked the strap and buckle on one of the bags. "She's nothing to me now." Then his hands stilled and he glanced up warily. "You say you have her partner, too?"

"Just like that, huh?" Thompson reached up and pulled the brim of his hat down lower over his pale gray eyes. "I took her and her partner. Figured he'd be worth a bonus to ya."

"A bonus?" Bennet laughed then, a deep, hearty laugh that shook him from his head to his toes. It was the first time he'd felt like smiling since that blasted telegrapher had arrived with his information. In fact, he was so pleased with himself, he didn't notice the gunfighter stiffen. Shaking his head, he looked into Thompson's narrowed gaze and said, "You'll get no bonus from me. Perhaps, if you're most unfortunate, the man himself will give you that prize."

"What are you talkin' about?"

Bennet locked down the second flap on his

saddlebags, then lifted the pair to drape across his shoulder. "You had better let them go. Quickly. For your own safety."

Thompson dropped one hand onto his holstered gun and said, "*My* safety?"

"Have you ever heard of Travis Delacort?"

Thompson went completely still. His right hand curled around the stock of his pistol. "Delacort? *Him?*"

"Good-bye, Mister Thompson. Your fee is on my desk." He started walking, but the gunfighter's quiet voice stopped him.

"You ain't goin' anywhere, mister."

Bennet paused, then went on again, more slowly toward the door. A small thread of worry snaked its way down his spine. Thompson had never used that particular tone of voice with him before. The man had always been . . . cautious. And Bennet was a man so used to being obeyed, it had never occurred to him that Thompson might turn on him.

Until now.

When it was too late.

He heard the whisper of sound when the other man pulled his pistol free of its leather holster. He heard the distinctive click of a hammer being drawn back. Bennet stopped cold. Beads of sweat dotted his forehead. The flesh between his shoulder blades itched and crawled as he waited for the impact of a bullet. Had all of his grand plans and hard work really come down to this? Being gunned down in his own office by a disgruntled worker?

He glanced at the door, still three feet away. He would never be able to reach it and make his escape before Thompson shot him. For the first time in years, he wished heartily—and futilely—for a weapon of some kind.

Slowly, he turned around to face the empty black hole of a pistol's barrel. Then he lifted his gaze to Thompson's eyes and saw the same emptiness.

Bennet's soul cried out for help. But no one would come to his aid.

"You promised me lots of money, Bennet."

Money. Here then, was a chance. Perhaps if he gave the man all the money he had with him, Bennet would yet live to see the promise of a new town. Though it galled him to give away money that he'd earned, at least he would be alive. And there was more money tucked away in various banks. Hesitantly, Bennet lifted his saddlebags and held it out toward the gunman.

Thompson smiled as he pulled the trigger.

Bennet dropped the bag.

A flash of light. A thunderous noise. And white hot pain assaulted Bennet as he fell to the floor.

Moments later, Thompson snatched the twin stacks of gold coins off the desktop and stuffed them into his pockets. Then he marched across the room, grabbed up Bennet's satchels and tucked them under his left arm.

Bennet lay flat on his back, his head lifted off the floor so that he could stare in astonishment at the spreading stain on his shirtfront.

Glancing down into the fallen man's eyes, Thompson smiled. "Delacort, huh? I'll give him your best, *boss*."

He left the room quickly, his mind racing. He

should have guessed the truth, Thompson told himself. Little things had been wrong about that man ever since he hit town. A real city dude, terrified of guns, would have been more scared when facing a gunfighter. He thought back to that day in the Mercantile, when he and Delacort had taken each other's measure. He'd thought at the time that he'd spotted a spark of gumption in the other man's eyes.

And last night, when Al's partner had tried to rescue her . . . he'd had a gun with him, surprising the hell out of Thompson. What was more, though, the man had been more than ready to use it.

He'd only stopped when Thompson threatened Al's life. The gunman stared blankly at the wall opposite as a new, even more interesting idea occurred to him. Could it be possible, he wondered, that Travis Delacort actually *cared* about the Donnelly bitch?

A wave of anger slapped against Thompson's soul, rocking him back with the sheer force of its rage. Delacort had been playing him for a fool for weeks. Laughing at him. Toying with him. Pretending to be afraid when all the time, he'd thought he was better than Thompson.

Well maybe, the gunman thought as he started for the door. Maybe it was time to find out just who was the better gunhand.

And once Travis Delacort was dead, Thompson could take his time killing Al Donnelly.

Bennet wasn't giving the orders anymore. He was free to do whatever he wanted.

Finally.

\* \* \*

Travis pulled and strained against the ropes binding his wrists. For his efforts, the knots became tighter and the stiff fibers of hemp dug into his flesh, scraping it raw. His shoulders aching from the pressure of his arms being dragged tight behind his back, he watched the mouth of the tunnel in grim silence.

Waiting.

She'd been gone long enough. Too long.

Or maybe time seemed to be flying past because he was so damned mad and feeling so blasted helpless. What the hell kind of good was he as a bodyguard? He'd allowed himself to be captured so that he could remain with Alice, protect her.

Now he was tied up in knots and she had cut herself free and was off exploring. Some bodyguard. Christ, he was going to have to change his name for real when he left Regret. If anyone ever found out about this, Travis Delacort would be a laughing stock.

Although, there was some consolation, however it pained him to admit it. Apparently, Alice Donnelly didn't need his help.

She was fine on her own.

And why didn't *that* realization make him feel any better?

Footsteps sounded out in the distance, and through his anger Travis noted that her steps were slow, leisurely. As if she was taking a Sunday stroll. He ground his teeth together in frustration and glared at the spot where she would appear.

Alice stepped into the dim light and had the bald-assed nerve to smile at him! Travis choked down his rage and forced his voice into steadiness.

"Now that you've finished your tour," he said. "Perhaps you wouldn't mind cutting these ropes off me?"

"Uncomfortable, are they?"

He kept his gaze locked on her as she crossed the cave floor toward him. "As a matter of fact, yes. They are."

"As uncomfortable as finding out you've been made a fool of?"

"What?"

Alice dropped gracefully to the dirt. Folding her legs up under her, she sat directly opposite him. Her sharp, green gaze swept over him slowly.

"Where *did* you find these clothes, Travis?" she asked. "If that is your name."

"What are you talking about?" He was stalling, and he felt the first stirrings of worry begin to uncurl in his belly. The expression on her face told him she was a woman on a mission.

And that mission, apparently, was unmasking him.

"I'm talking about you. And the lies you've been telling me since the day you got here."

Something cold and dark settled inside him. Travis's carefully constructed web of lies began to unravel around him, and he found himself wishing that it hadn't had to come to this. Even though he had known that none of this would last. That he shouldn't let himself care. That he would be leaving.

In a small corner of his heart he must have hoped otherwise. Because the shattering of that last hope was painful. And hearing her call him a liar cut at him deeper and sharper than even that knife of hers could have.

He owed her the truth. Jesus, Travis told himself, that was the least of what he owed her. But not now. Later, when she was safe and had all the time in the world to call him every sort of bastard. Now they had to get out of that damned cave and back to town.

To people. To her family.

"Alice," he said calmly. "Cut me loose. We can talk about all of this later."

"Nope." She reached down, pulled her knife from her boot and stabbed it into the dirt beside her, like a knight in ancient England issuing a challenge. "We'll talk now. *If* you want out of those ropes, you'll tell me the truth. Because we're not going anywhere, Travis, until you do."

"Dammit, Alice!" He scooted closer and winced at the throbbing in his shoulders. "We have to get out of here. Get back to town. Thompson might come back, and I don't want you here if he does."

She reached up and pushed her hair back from her dirty face. "This might surprise you, Travis. But I don't much care *what* you want at the moment."

He groaned. Mary Alice Donnelly was the most stubborn, infuriating woman he'd ever encountered. And while he admired her almost as much as he loved her, now was not the best possible time for her to dig in her heels.

"You might as well start talking. You're not getting out of those ropes until you tell me what's going on."

"Fine." He flicked a quick, uneasy glance at the mouth of the tunnel, half expecting to see Thompson looming up from the shadows. If only the truth, now, would get her moving, then the truth she would have. Even if it meant she would hate him for the rest of her life. "Where do you want me to start? And make it fast," he added.

She blinked, obviously startled that he'd given in. "Your name," she said softly. "What's your real name?"

"Travis Delacort."

She nodded stiffly. "Why'd you change it when you came here?"

It was Travis's turn to be surprised. Somehow, he'd thought that she would know his name. But then again, he told himself, there was no reason why she should. She wasn't a part of the circle of people who knew the name Delacort. She wasn't a fugitive. Or a gunfighter. Or a lawman.

"I used to be a marshal," he sighed. "I didn't want anyone recognizing my name and disappearing before we had your troubles worked out."

"Used to be?" She pounced on the phrase. "What are you now?"

"Nothing."

"Everyone is something, Travis."

He met her gaze and ignored the warmth he saw in her eyes. No doubt, it was only the banked fires of anger.

"I'm a hired gun, mostly."

"Huh!" She looked him over slowly. "I never would have guessed it by those clothes."

"That was the idea," he said, insulted despite

the fact that he hated his clothing every bit as much as she did.

"I thought something was wrong about you," Alice said, and unfolded her legs to draw her knees up to her chest.

"Really."

"Oh, you don't believe me, but it's true." She waved one hand at him. "You're too strong and too tanned to be a city man. And those hands of yours have seen more work than shuffling papers around a desk."

"If you knew I was a fake," he grumbled, "why are you so blasted mad about the lies?"

"It's the other lies that bother me, Travis," she told him, and leaned in close enough that he could feel her breath on his face. Lamplight touched her skin gently, making it glow like polished old ivory. She took his breath away even when she was mad enough to shoot him.

He knew what lies she meant. She was thinking about their night together. The night when he'd held her, touched her, and drove himself wild wishing for something that couldn't be. And he'd be double damned in hell before he'd let her think their loving had meant nothing to him.

"That night wasn't a lie."

"Hah!" She threw herself backward and landed in the dirt on her backside. "Oh, I *believe* you, Travis."

She didn't. The pain and misery in her eyes was clear enough for a blind man to see. An answering pain started low in Travis's gut, slowly climbed into his chest, and threatened to strangle his heart. "Alice—"

"Don't." Changing the subject abruptly, she asked, "How did you happen to become my partner?"

Travis hitched his shoulders a bit and nodded at her, silently agreeing to talk about something else. For now. But before he left Regret—and her—he promised himself that he would find a way to convince her that the night spent in her arms was the one *honest* thing he'd done since meeting her.

"I did your father a favor some years back. He came to see me in Denver."

She cocked her head and watched him carefully before saying, "Gunfighting must pay well for you to be able to buy a share in the mine."

"I didn't."

"What?"

He winced at her outraged shriek.

"I said, I'm not your partner."

"Well who the hell are ya, then?"

Travis groaned inwardly. There was no way to avoid her finding out. "Your father asked me to come out here and look into things for him. He's paying me to pose as your partner and clear up your troubles."

"Da!" She scrambled to her feet and began to pace in quick, hurried strides. As she moved, her boots kicked up loose dirt and pebbles, sending them skittering into the shadows beyond the dim light. "Of all the dirty, underhanded, treacherous tricks!"

"He wanted to make sure you were all right. He was worried."

"Aye, well." Alice jerked him a nod and shook one finger at him. "He'd do better to be worried *now*. When I get my hands on that wily old devil, I'll string him up with his own blarney spouting tongue!"

Jesus! She was magnificent! In her rage, he noted, her speech began to ring with the Irish accent she'd been raised hearing. The musical lilt made every word stand out and be noticed on its own, and made her outrage seem more passionate.

Travis watched fire shoot from her eyes and, for just a moment, experienced a pang of sympathy for Kevin Donnelly. In the next instant, though, that emotion was drowned in a churning sea of fury.

"Paid you to watch over me, did he?" she snarled and leaned over him. "And just how much did he pay ya to bed his poor, homely daughter?"

# Chapter 20

**C**utter dropped to one knee beside Bennet. The man's eyes were closed, and his pristine white shirt was stained by a brilliant splash of scarlet across his chest.

"Bennet?"

His eyelashes fluttered, then he slowly opened his eyes and stared up into Cutter's gaze.

The gambler swallowed heavily. The man was dying. His eyes were already losing the spark of life.

"What happened?" he asked.

"Thompson," Bennet whispered, then with a considerable effort, licked his dry lips.

"Is he dead?" Sean whispered as he came into the room

"Not yet," Cutter said. "But close."

Sean nodded stiffly. "I'll go for help."

Cutter listened to the big man's hurried footsteps on the stairs, and when all was silent again, he looked down at the man stretched out on the floor. "Your tame gunfighter finally turned on you, didn't he?"

339

Astonishment shimmered briefly in those darkening eyes. "Yes."

"You really should have left town, Bennet," Cutter said softly.

A long, rattling sigh was his only answer.

Pushing himself to his feet, Cutter stared down at the dead man and told himself that Bennet had probably only gotten exactly what he'd deserved.

Besides, all that mattered now was two things.

Where was Al?

And where was Thompson?

Travis looked up at Al, completely astonished. "Are you out of your mind?"

"Maybe," she shot back, and dropped to one knee in front of him. Alice felt the heat of blood rushing to her cheeks and knew they were stained a bright scarlet. In her heart of hearts, she didn't believe what she was accusing him of. But dammit, she'd listened to him, calmly explaining his pack of lies until she was ready to scream.

Anger still pumped through her blood. Her father tricked her, though she could understand his reasons. Travis however, was a different matter. He'd spent weeks at her side, making her believe he cared . . . making her care for him.

Was it all a lie?

Could he pretend feelings for her as easily as he'd pretended to be someone he was not? No, she told herself, he couldn't.

It was the distant tone in Travis's voice that bothered Alice so. As if he'd already left her in spirit. She told herself that if she could only break through that calm control of his, perhaps he might start telling her what he really wanted. What he really felt.

And, maybe, he would see that they belonged together.

Her voice broke with the threat of tears she wouldn't allow as she continued, "Perhaps I am crazy, but I'm sane enough to know that until you showed up, with your silly clothes and your idiotic way of treatin' me like I was some fine lady—" her breath caught and she had to gulp frantically for another. "Not one single man had ever gone out of his way to give me a moment's notice!"

Travis strained uselessly against the rope trapping him, keeping him from going to her. She watched him fight to get free and was thankful that he couldn't. Alice dragged another breath into her lungs and told herself that she had to know. She had to know and be sure of what he felt. What he thought of her.

Even more importantly, she had to make *him* realize that what they had together was too important to walk away from.

"I swear to God, Alice, if you don't cut these damned ropes off me, I'll break my own arm to get free."

He looked as though he would, too. Well, she'd done what she'd had to. She'd had her say and forced a few answers from him. If he left now without answering the rest, perhaps that would be answer enough.

Nodding, Alice walked to where the knife still stood straight up from the dirt floor and yanked it free. Stepping behind Travis, she sliced through the ropes at his hands and feet, then stepped back.

He groaned and rubbed at his wrists and ankles. After a moment or two, Travis pushed himself to his feet and faced her. He swayed unsteadily as blood rushed to his long deprived legs.

"All right," he admitted. "I lied. I lied about who I was and I lied about the partnership. But you should know I didn't lie about you. About what was between us."

"How should I know?"

His dark blond hair tumbled onto his forehead, and his pale blue eyes looked wild, desperate. Good, she told herself.

"How can you not?" he shouted suddenly.

"You, the liar, can ask me that?"

"I've admitted I lied, dammit! But a man can't lie about some things. At least . . . I can't."

"And I'm to believe that, I suppose." She pushed at him relentlessly, challenging him to confront the love that waited for him, if only he would wake up in time to see it.

Travis moved so quickly, she didn't have time to elude him. Grabbing her upper arms, he dragged her to him. He cupped the back of her head in the palm of his hand, and with the other, pulled her hips to his.

"Do you feel that, Mary Alice Donnelly?"

She did indeed. The hard strength of him pressed into her and brought a damp heat to her own body in response.

"Aye," she said. "I do. But lust and love are two different things, are they not?"

"They are," he whispered, and let his gaze

move over her face like a lover's touch. "But I do love you. I want you to at least believe that much."

"I want to," she told him, and saw him wince as if from a physical blow. "But how can I know for sure?"

"Because I'll be leaving Regret as soon as I've settled with Thompson."

She pushed away from him and took an extra step back for good measure. Damn his eyes. Would he leave her anyway, despite loving her? "You're leavin'? Just like that?"

"Alice—"

"And I'm to know you love me because you're leavin' me?" She shook her head and glared at him. "Make sense, man."

"It is sense. I love you enough to let you find someone better than me."

The bloody damned fool looked as if he believed the story he was giving her. Well, he might, but she didn't. "That's an excuse and you know it. Or better yet, another lie. Who are you to be deciding who I should love or not?"

"The man who loves you."

"Oh *that* makes sense!"

Travis inhaled sharply, then blew the air out of his lungs in a rush. Letting his head fall back on his neck, he stared straight up as he said, "There are reasons."

"Let's hear them."

He snorted a laugh and shook his head. "Jesus, you're stubborn."

"I've heard that before."

Travis straightened up and looked at her, a half smile on his features. "I can't stay, Alice.

There are people waiting on me. People who are depending on me to help them."

"And you're the only man capable of such help, are ya?"

"No, but I'm the one they're expecting."

"Send someone else."

"Even if I did, I still couldn't stay."

"Why?"

"I'm no good at it. I'd end up failing you somehow, and I don't want to do that."

"What do you call this?" she asked quietly, and moved closer to him.

"I call this protecting you."

"From you," she said, and shook her head. "Don't ya see, Travis? Ya can't protect me from hurt by hurtin' me!"

"I'm a gunfighter, Alice. It's all I know how to be." He tore his dirt-splotched yellow coat off and tossed it aside. Raking one hand through his hair, he shot her a hard look from the corner of his eye. "Oh, I'm more particular than most about which jobs I take, who I'll work for, but the job is still the same. Killing."

"That's not who you are, though," she said firmly, determined to reach him.

"It's what I do," he snapped. "And that's enough."

"You don't have to go on like that Travis," she insisted. "You can stay here. With me. Be my partner. Help me run the damn mine." He was closing himself off from her. She sensed it in the way he held himself, saw it in the sad shine in his eyes. Desperately, she tried again. "Hell, you've had good ideas. You know how to talk to the men. We could be good together."

"I won't do it again," he said softly, and she knew he wasn't talking to her anymore, but to himself.

"Do what?"

"Be responsible for someone else." His jaw clenched and his eyes narrowed as if he was staring off at an image only he could see.

Alice frowned, and for some reason, the memory of Travis, caught in a nightmare, rushed into her mind. She remembered the look in his eyes when he woke to see her, and the hushed wonder in his voice when he had whispered, "You're alive."

Alice pushed the memory aside quickly and looked at him. Every inch of him was hard, stiff. As if it was an effort to hold himself together. Instinctively, she knew that the nightmare was the source of the turmoil inside him. And to have a future with the man, she would somehow have to do battle with his past.

She stepped up close to him and laid one hand on his arm. The muscles beneath his shirt flinched at her touch.

"Christ, Alice," he ground out. "Don't."

"Don't what?" she demanded, tugging at his arm until he looked at her. "Don't love you? It's too late for that, Travis darlin'. I do."

His body jerked as if he'd been shot.

"And you love me," she insisted in a voice strained with the effort to reach him.

Travis turned his head to look at her, then his gaze dropped to her hand on his arm. "I've already admitted to that."

"Prove it to me then. Stay."

He whirled around and grabbed her so

quickly, her breath caught. His fingers dug into her upper arms, and she felt the tightly reined strength in his hands. Looking up into his eyes, Alice saw how close he was to the edge of his self-control.

Deliberately, she met his gaze squarely and pushed him the rest of the way over. "What happened? What is it you dream of?"

Something flickered in his eyes and his grip on her arms tightened even further.

"Failure," he snapped, and gave her a shake. "*My* failure. And her death."

"Her?" She was instantly ashamed of the jealousy that reared up in her breast. "Who was she?"

"Someone I was supposed to protect." He bent his head until his forehead rested against hers. His breath staggered, and she could feel the pain as it rose up inside him. "She died—burned to death because I failed." He released her abruptly and stared down at the old scars on his palms.

Alice clasped his hands in both of hers and squeezed. She had to make him feel her. Know she was there. That the past was gone and all that mattered now was the future.

Their future.

"I don't know what happened then," she said in a quiet, yet firm tone. "And God help me, I don't care. But I won't let you ride out of my life in some insane quest to protect me from you."

He said nothing, so she went on hurriedly.

"I swear to ya, Travis. If you leave, I'll chase you down. I won't give you a moment's peace. I'll—"

"Don't you understand?" he shouted at her,

and anguish colored his voice. "I couldn't stand it if something happened to you!"

He yanked her to him and kissed her long and hard. His tongue invaded her mouth, demanding entry. Shocked, Alice held on to him and felt his hard strength surround her. There was no gentleness as before. This was a desperate need to feed an even more desperate hunger.

His hands flew over her body, eager and strong. Alice was caught up in his wildness and gave herself over to the fierce need of his loving. In seconds their clothes lay scattered on the cave floor and he was leaning over her, dragging his mouth down her throat and lower to her breast.

He feasted on her as if the taste of her was all that was keeping him alive. Alice's back arched and she raked her short nails over his shoulders and down his muscled back. She moaned heavily and lifted her hips to press against his ready body.

Travis moved down her body, his mouth, lips, and tongue devouring every inch of her flesh. He felt her nails scraping against his shoulders and then along his arms as he slipped lower still in his effort to possess all of her.

When he lowered his mouth to her hot, wet center, she arched and choked a broken cry. The delicious feel of his tongue stroking her flesh swept through her, carrying her to a spot higher than she'd ever been before, and when her body shuddered, she reached for him, instinctively.

Before the last ripple of pleasure had subsided, he was covering her with his body and sliding his hard strength into her warmth. Again and again, their bodies slammed together and Alice lifted her hips to accommodate more of him, to take him deeper within her.

Travis plunged into her heat as deeply as he could and still it wasn't enough. He wanted more. He needed more. And he always would. Staring down into her face, he watched as a second climax claimed her. Her meadow green eyes clouded, hazy with wonder. Her fingers tightened on his hips, holding him to her and with one last thrust, he groaned and followed her into peace.

"Where the hell do ya suppose he went?"

Cutter shook his head. Bennet was dead. And Thompson hadn't been seen for a couple of hours. It didn't look good.

"Dammit!"

Sean frowned thoughtfully and glanced at the ever-darkening sky. " 'Twill be night soon. We'll never find Al and Travis in the dark."

"I know." Cutter shot a quick look at his brother-in-law and saw his own concerns staring back at him. "Let's get back to camp. Get some rest. We'll start again at dawn."

He could only hope that when they finally found the missing couple, that they would still be alive.

"You're a crazy woman," Travis muttered, and paused while buttoning up his shirt to examine a long tear in the fabric.

"Then we'll make a fine pair," she told him, and bent over to snatch up her boots.

He gave her behind a playful smack and wondered how in the hell it had happened. How had he gone from despair to hope in a matter of hours?

"Here now"—she stood up and fixed him with a firm stare—"mind your hands."

His eyebrows lifted.

"Until we're home," she amended.

He nodded. Home. Strange that a canvas tent now seemed like all the home he could ever want. Strange that in trying to convince her that he was all wrong for her, he'd succeeded in convincing himself just the opposite.

Travis looked at her through suddenly suspicious eyes. She'd played him like an old piano. Getting him to shout and rage until he'd admitted his love for her and confessed his fears—then not letting go until he realized that nothing meant a damn thing without her.

He wasn't sure if it was her persuasive arguments or her promise to follow after him or the wild, passion of her loving that had finally convinced him. And truthfully, it didn't matter. All that mattered now was that he was going to take the risk of loving her.

He had to. His only other choice was to leave her.

And that would kill him.

"You're a sneaky woman, Alice Donnelly."

She flashed him a wicked grin, and he wasn't even surprised that she knew exactly what he was talking about.

"Aye," she said, and stepped up close to him. "And you'd best remember that in future."

Future.

Travis had never really noticed what a lovely sound that word carried. She reached up and drew his head down to hers for a long, lingering kiss. She tasted of hope, of sunshine and promises.

"Well, now, I wouldn't have believed it if I didn't see it for myself," a voice spoke up in the quiet.

Travis went utterly still for a heartbeat or two, then slowly he lifted his head and pushed Alice to one side of him. "Stay there," he whispered.

"So you're Delacort, huh?" Mike Thompson stepped into the faint circle of light and looked Travis up and down dismissively.

"That's right."

"Reckon you figure it's been real funny, treatin' me like a fool."

"Haven't given you much thought at all." Travis's gaze swept the inside of the cave, futilely searching for a weapon.

"Guess you've been too busy with your little whore, here."

Travis refused to rise to the bait.

Thompson was playing a game. A game of nerves, hoping to push his opponent beyond the point of rational thought. And also, Thompson was the kind of man who enjoyed telling his quarry exactly what he planned to do.

He was probably used to his victims standing still to listen—anything to drag out those last few minutes of life.

So when Travis crouched and rushed him, he was unprepared.

Alice shouted his name, but he concentrated on his opponent. Travis's shoulder caught the gunman in his middle, and he heard Thompson's air rush from his lungs. They collapsed together onto the hard-packed dirt, and Travis swung his right arm back to bring his fist crashing down into Thompson's jaw. He shook it off and threw his own punch into Travis's face. Ears ringing, Travis snapped his head forward, slamming his forehead into the gunman's. The man snarled, groaned, and bucked Travis off, then scrambled to his feet.

Rolling to one side, Travis, too, regained his feet and started for the man again. Thompson reached for his still holstered pistol. Before he could think about getting out of a bullet's way, Travis heard the other man's scream as a knife whistled through the air and suddenly speared through his upper arm.

Travis spared Alice one wild, grateful look, then attacked. Stepping in close to Thompson, he delivered blow after blow to the man's midsection until the only thing holding the gunman upright was the strength in Travis's fists.

Thompson staggered heavily and slumped to the floor, Al's knife hilt still protruding from his upper arm. Travis reached down, dragged the man up by his shirtfront, and smashed one last blow against Thompson's chin. The man's head snapped back, his eyes rolled, and his body fell bonelessly to the dirt.

Exhausted and sore, Travis turned toward Alice and saw her smile. He tried a smile in return and felt a sharp pain from his split lip. Determined to reach her, he took one staggering step forward and then she was there, holding him, pressing herself to him so tightly, he could feel her heart beating against his chest.

And he knew he was alive again.

"Thanks," he said at last, and looked down at her. "You and that knife came in pretty handy."

"That's what I tried to tell you, Travis." Alice frowned as she gingerly touched one fingertip to his cut lip. He winced and she smiled at him. "We make a helluva good team, you and me."

"I suppose we do, at that." He leaned his head down and rested his cheek on her hair.

"Come on, then," she told him, and wrapped one arm around his waist for support. "We'll tie him up, then we can use Thompson's horse to get us back to camp."

Travis stopped and stared down at her. "We still don't know where we are."

"Oh, sure we do." She grinned at him. "When I went out to look around, I realized exactly where we are. China Joe's diggings."

He pulled his head back, looked at her, and waited.

"It's an old mine, mostly forgotten. The outside's grown over with bushes and whatnot." She shrugged. "Most folks have probably forgotten all about it by now. Hasn't been worked in years." Alice helped him to sit down, bracing his back against the wall. Then as she snatched up what was left of the ropes and dropped to the ground beside Thompson, she continued. "I only found it myself a year or so back, when I was wandering the hills."

"Uh-huh," he managed, and rested his head against the cold rock wall. "So how far are we from Regret?"

"About an hour." She smiled at him again. "We'll be home in time for a late supper."

"Alice Donnelly," he sighed, weariness stealing over him, "you are an amazing woman."

"That's something else for you to keep in mind in the years to come," she told him softly, then added, "but don't you worry Travis darlin'. I'll keep remindin' ya."

He looked into her eyes and lost himself in the promise of her smile.

ALICE AND THE GUNFIGHTER    353
ing over him, "you are an amazing woman."
    "That's something else for you to keep in mind
in the years to come." She smiled softly, then
added, "Don't ever forget it, Travis darling. I'll
keep reminding you."
    He looked into her eyes and lost himself in the
promise of her smile.

# Epilogue

*Two weeks later*

**A**s usual, Al was late to the family meeting.
      She hurried into the dining room above
the Four Golden Roses Saloon and took her seat
at the end of the shining walnut table. Sparing a
quick smile for her family, she glanced at the
empty doorway and shouted, "Hurry up,
Travis!"

A moment later Travis Delacort stepped into
the room, and Alice grinned at her new husband.
Dressed in worn Levis, a faded blue workshirt,
scuffed boots, and dust-colored hat, he was even
more handsome than ever. And though she
much preferred how he looked in his western
wear, she had saved two of the gaudy vests he
used to wear. Just to remember her city man.

"Well," Maggie said, nodding at the two new-
comers, "how are things at the Four Dandy
Roses?"

Travis rolled his eyes at the mention of the
new name Alice had insisted on christening the

mine. But when his wife laid her hand over his and squeezed gently, he smiled at her. A month or two ago, he never would have believed that he would be married to Alice Donnelly and a full partner in the Donnelly family mine.

Of course, he'd tried to refuse the partnership Alice had insisted on as a wedding present. But she was a hard woman to refuse anything. Especially, he thought with an inward smile, when she fought dirty. In fact, even remembering the night she'd convinced him to become a partner was enough to make his body hard and ready for her. Idly, he wondered if the need for her would ever lessen.

He didn't think so.

And every day, he thanked God for it.

Amazing how quickly life had become good. With Bennet gone and Thompson languishing in jail, everything in Regret had settled down nicely.

Glancing around at the people gathered together, Travis felt a now familiar tug of family. Belonging. And he couldn't imagine living without it.

"Is there another wire from Da, Maggie?" Frankie asked, her fingers entwined with Sean's. "Is it about Teresa?"

"Where the hell *is* Terry Ann?" Al demanded, and looked around the room as if half-expecting her youngest sister to come leaping out from behind a piece of furniture.

"I don't know," Maggie said.

"What do you mean?" Frankie leaned forward, concern stamped on her delicate, pretty features.

"Just what she says," Cutter spoke up, interrupting his wife. "No one knows where she is."

"She's not on the ranch?"

Travis heard the underlying thread of worry in his wife's voice and reached out one hand to clasp hers tightly.

"No." Maggie shook her head and jumped to her feet. Walking to the window, she pulled the drapes back, stared out at the sunshine spilling into the room, and said "Read them the letter, Cutter."

Maggie's husband nodded, picked up a sheet of paper and began to read.

*Dear Everyone,*

*I'm leaving for a while. I don't know where I'm going or when I'll be back. I'm sorry I didn't tell you this at Al's wedding, but I simply couldn't take the chance that you all would try to talk me out of it. I can't sit around and wait for Da to send me a husband, too. I don't want to be married. And I'm tired of being on that ranch.*

*Don't try to find me. I have enough money to see me for quite awhile, and I will be fine. I'll write when I'm settled somewhere.*

*For heaven's sake, don't worry. I'm a Donnelly. I can take care of myself. I love you all.*

*Teresa*

Stunned silence settled over the room for several long minutes after Cutter finished the letter.

Rose Ryan hustled into the room carrying a coffee pot in one hand and holding a crumpled handkerchief to her teary eyes with the other.

She sniffed audibly as she poured steaming hot coffee into the waiting cups.

"Come sit down, Maggie," Cutter ordered gently.

The oldest Donnelly left the window and took her seat at the table. Her green eyes watery behind a sheen of unshed tears, she blinked frantically, trying to clear her vision.

"I don't know what's the matter with me," she said. "I should be furious at her and instead, I'm tearing up like Rose."

Cutter set a cup of coffee down in front of his wife. "Have a sip or two, it'll make you feel better."

Maggie nodded, lifted the cup to her mouth, and stopped. Her face paled instantly. As the rich aroma of chicory drifted up to her, Maggie's eyes widened and her lips grew as white as her cheeks.

Clamping one hand across her mouth, she set the cup down hurriedly and leaped from her chair. Racing out the door, she didn't even appear to hear Cutter only a step or two behind her.

"What's wrong with her?" Alice wondered out loud.

In answer, Rose lifted the hem of her apron and covered her face completely. Her plump shoulders shook until Frankie went to her, draping a comforting arm around her.

"There, there, Rose. I'm sure Maggie will be fine. It's just the upset with Terry Ann is all."

"The brat," Alice fumed. "When she gets back—"

"It's not Teresa," Rose wailed, and dropped

the apron to reveal a wide grin on her face.

Everyone stared at her in astonishment.

"We must find Teresa and bring her home in time for the baby!" the housekeeper insisted.

"Baby?" Sean asked no one in particular. "What baby?"

"Ooooh," Rose wailed in ecstasy again. "My darlin' Maggie's goin' to have a baby!"

Speechless, Frankie dropped into a chair opposite Alice. The two sisters stared at each other before sharing a soft smile.